John Saxon had been on his own since he was sixteen. He'd built a cabin and a barn, had a start on a herd, and was planning to marry Mary Wilson, the prettiest girl in town. Then Bob Witherell decided he had to have Mary, no matter what.

Witherell set out to destroy everything Saxon had worked for. Rebuilding his ranch would only mean hard work for John Saxon, but he also had to rebuild his pride—and the only way he could do that was by killing Witherell, a man who had the whole town on his side.

Warner Books

By Max Brand

MAX BRAND

The Rancher's Revenge

WARNER BOOKS

A Warner Communications Company

CHAPTER I

SOMETIMES when a limb is slashed off a young tree, half the strong juice of its life seems to flow away through the wound, and instead of growing, it shrinks, withers, hardens, and so endures for a long time, looking in the forest like one of those stunted trees which grow against the arctic winds of timberline. Daniel Finlay was like that. He was not much past forty, but he looked sapless, dry, hard of rind, like a man of sixty. His right arm had been cut off at the wrist, and with the loss of that hand went his possibilities of leading a happy life. He had to withdraw from physical action; there was left him only his mind and even of that he made a left-handed use. He was a trouble maker.

He had a law office in the town of Bluewater, but his real business was conducted in other places. In a courtroom the handless gestures of his right arm often had a terrible effect on a jury and convinced it of the honesty of his passion; at those times his restrained voice and his quiet words gave a sense of a life so tragic that deception was now too small and mean to enter it, and that was why he was a better liar than most men and a more efficient trouble maker. On this bright Sunday he began the work which was his masterpiece both for the nature of the mischief that he led toward and for the number of lives that were involved.

He hated the peace of this day. Not long before, Bluewater had been just a shade noisier and more dangerous on Sunday than on week days, but since the Reverend Joseph Hunter built the white church on the hill at the end of the street, law and order had begun to organize in the town. The saloons closed on Sunday. Quiet fell over the street, and Finlay hated that quiet. During the week, when all men were busy, laboring, sweating, scheming, conspiring to make their way in the world, Finlay was only unhappy in the evening when other citizens returned to their homes without fear of the long and lonely night; but on Sundays of quiet, all the bitter hours of sunshine told Finlay that he was alone in this world.

5

And on this Sunday, as he walked slowly down the street, he detested everything, from the empty, dusty ruts to the bald faces of the frame shacks and stores, and so up to the shaggy sides of the mountains and their saw-toothed edges against the sky. As his eye could travel outward through the thin blue of space, so it could turn inward without finding peace; and always he was hearing the hurrying, confused, disputing voices of Bluewater Creek as it rushed on about a business that was never completed.

Here and there he passed householders sitting in their shirt sleeves on front porches. If there was a woman present, he took off his hat, first making a gesture up with his right arm and then seeming to realize that the hand was lacking and hurriedly snatching off his hat with the left. The women never got tired of seeing that mixed gesture because women are never tired of things that make their hearts ache just a little.

Because we pity the sufferers and the maimed, we feel that their hearts must be good. The pride of Finlay was like that of the damned, but it was written down as decent dignity. Malice hardened his face and wrinkled his eyes, but his expression was attributed to pain of body and mind. He knew exactly what people thought about him, and therefore, no matter how grim his bearing might be most of the time, he performed every year two or three small and secret acts of charity because he knew that secret charities are always published abroad in convinced whispers. There were people in Bluewater ready to swear that Finlay was one of the best men in the world.

On this morning, he was debating in his mind what he would do about the church. He so loathed the mild eye and the open face of the good minister that even to contemplate sitting with the congregation was a torment to him, but when he saw the number of people who were turning out in their best clothes to hurry up the hill, he realized that he would have to do something about a social fact that had grown to such importance. Even big Hank Walters, with two dead men in his past, was striding up the walk with his wife and three children, and looking perfectly happy and contented!

Daniel Finlay decided that he would go once a year

6

to the church. He would enter it for the Christmas service. He would come in late and last. He would sit quietly in one of the rear seats. Best of all if he found the church filled and had to stand in the back, listening, grave. After a time, people would know that he was there. They would turn covert heads. A whisper would run about the church even in the midst of the service. The startled eyes of the minister would find him and dwell on him. When the plate was passed, he would slip a hundred dollars into it, folding the bill very small. Afterward the size of the donation would be noticed, and everybody would know about it, and, when he passed, the women and the children would open their eyes at him.

He saw that by this act he would gain more respect and wonder and admiration and sympathy than by praying on his knees in public every Sunday of the year. And just as much as he despised and loathed and envied all strong and happy people, so he yearned to have their sympathy.

On this day, when he came to the general-merchandise store, he found it closed and felt that this was a personal affront. But on the wide veranda, their chairs tilted back against the wall, were Bob Witherell and several of his men. They were tools fit for mischief, and therefore they pleased his eye. Only six months before he had defended Bob Witherell on the charge of robbing the stagecoach to Warrenton. He had said to Witherell: "You're as guilty as anything, but I'll take your case. You're young enough to know better."

He always covered up his dishonorable action with a wise or a noble maxim. When Witherell asked him, after acquittal had been brought about by one of those handless orations to a jury, what the fee was, he had told Bob, sternly, that he had not done this thing for money. He refused to name a price. And that was why Bob Witherell, with a sense of shame, stuffed five hundred dollars into an envelope and left it on his desk. He accepted the money with the careless gesture of one who was above considering such a thing.

Bob Witherell was vastly impressed. He felt that he had been delivered from danger by a man who believed in him in spite of the fact that that same man was aware

7

of his guilt. When Finlay came by, now, Bob jumped up from his chair and shook hands eagerly, respectfully. He was so big and gay, his eyes were so black and restless, there was so much red life gleaming through his cheeks that Finlay inwardly felt poisoned by the sight of a creature to whom the merest existence was sure to be a happiness. He loathed Bob Witherell because he knew that Bob was graced by the advantage of a vast physical content. He endured Bob Witherell because Bob was an instrument which might one day be used in giving pain to others.

Witherell introduced the lawyer to the others. They were unlike their big companion in many ways, but in all of their eyes appeared a certain bright restlessness. Finlay gave them his left hand, gravely, one by one; he knew that every one of them ought to be in jail or perhaps be hanging at the end of a rope. But he allowed a certain kindliness to appear through his austerity.

"Look across the street, Mr. Finlay," said Bob Witherell. "What's the name of that gal over there? Gosh, she's a beauty."

She was not a beauty, exactly. That is to say, when youth was subtracted, she would remain merely pretty. She was dressed up in a fluffy white dress that the wind fluttered, and through the wide, translucent brim of her hat the sun strained a golden light over her face. Goodness and gentleness shone from her, and she kept smiling as girls will when they are very young and very happy. Or youth alone and that mysterious knowledge which only the young possess will make them smile, and that hearkening to all that is obscured in our older ears. The house was a plain little white-painted shack like most of the others in the street, but it was distinguished from the rest by having a patch of garden behind its picket fence. And the girl was moving in the narrow garden walks, touching the flowers, leaning over them, smiling and even laughing at them.

"That's Mary Wilson, and she's not for you," said Finlay.

"Oh, isn't she?" asked Witherell. "Who's got her staked out and a claim filed?"

"Young fellow over yonder in the mountains," said

Finlay. "He's got a cabin over in a corner of the Bentley place."

"A dog-gone squatter, eh?" asked Witherell, frowning, staring at the girl.

"Don't call him that," answered Finlay. "Young fellow, hard-working. Been on his own since he was sixteen, and always working at that bit of land. Built a cabin and a barn. Raises some hay. Has a nice start on a herd. No nonsense about him, Witherell. A young fellow to be respected and envied. Very much so!"

Now, painting this picture of an honest man, and a good citizen, Finlay watched with a side glance the effect of his description on Witherell, and his heart bounded as he saw his poison take effect.

"A man that wanted to, I bet he could take the gal away from this hombre you talk about," said Witherell.

"Take her away?" said Finlay. "Not from John Saxon! There's a real man, Bob. As strong a fellow with his hands as any in the mountains around here, I suppose. No, no, whatever you do, don't have any trouble with John Saxon!"

He shook his head in agreement with himself, as he said this, and pretended not to notice the flush of anger in the face of Witherell, nor the quick glance of the highwayman at his own big hands. Finlay was so pleased with himself that his eyes shone. He knew, with a profound understanding, that he had made trouble for John Saxon.

He had no particular reason for hating Saxon, except that the fellow was a perfect type of the honest citizen, the man who never even looks askance at temptations, the man who labors straightforward all his days and wins a widening respect from his fellows, establishes a family in comfort, loves his wife and his children, and is surrounded by a profound affection to the end of his life. Such men troubled Finlay more than any other fact in his knowledge. They prove that to be honest and industrious is to win, in the end, the greatest happiness. They seem to deny by example that happiness can be gained by schemes, conniving, keen and treacherous wits. They accept the social harness with willing hearts and gladden themselves by the commonness of their lots. So Finlay hated John Saxon and wished him evil at the hands of Witherell.

"He's big, is he? He's strong, is he?" said Witherell. "All right, and maybe he is."

"He'll be along here, soon," said Finlay, "and take his girl—she's the prettiest thing in town, I suppose—and he'll take her up the hill to the church, and you'll see her smiling all the way, the happiest girl in Bluewater, and she has reason to be.

"Ah," added Finlay, shaking his head and looking firmly at Witherell in reproof, "you fellows who drift here and there, you rolling stones—what do you come to? What do you gain, compared with the gains of John Saxon? You ought to consider him, Bob. You know that I have your welfare at heart. You know that I'd like to see you change some of your ways. That's why I ask you to consider John Saxon. Put your mind on him, Bob. Honesty is the best policy, my lad."

He laid a hand kindly on the shoulder of Bob, after murmuring these last words, and went slowly up the street again, past the group of fine, hot-blooded horses which were tethered to the hitch rack. They were too beautiful to belong to any except rich men—and Witherell and his companions were not rich. They were only rich in mischief, and Finlay knew, with a profound satisfaction, that he had started that mischief, and that it would soon be eagerly under way.

CHAPTER II

WITHERELL, left alone with his fellows, stared straight before him through some moments.

"The lawyer socked you pretty hard, Bob," said one of his friends.

Witherell said nothing. He was thinking things over. It was true that he had not made a great success. He was stronger in his hands than most men. He rode a horse better. He was more handsome. He was quicker and straighter with a gun—this above all. He was enough of a leader to have gathered about him a formidable little group of reckless spirits. But he was not a great success. He had not startled the mind and filled the imagination of the world as his brother, The Solitaire, had done.

The Solitaire was a national figure. His list of dead men was long and crowded with important names. He had a Federal marshal on that list. Every man of sound information was able to name off most of the list of The Solitaire's twenty-two victims. Women smiled at him because he was notorious. Success was his middle name. And Bob knew that he had fallen far short and would always fall far short of his brother's greatness.

The sense of failure oppressed him, because he knew that he was not of a caliber to imitate his brother's achievements. He felt that these men who were beside him were cheap and small, also; unworthy tools for any great purpose!

And just as his teeth were on edge, he saw John Saxon come up the street, driving a pair of mules to a rattling old buckboard. He was a big young man, happy, brown-faced, cheerful. From a distance he stood up and waved his whip and shouted, and Mary Wilson ran out from the garden and fairly danced on the board walk, waving her hands back to him.

The mules broke into a hobbling canter.

"Hell," said Bob Witherell. "And that's Saxon, is it?"

"He's big enough," remarked "Boots" Russell.

"He looks like a big ham, to me," said Witherell. "But maybe he ain't too big to dance, eh?"

The thought struck him with a thrill of pleasure. The numb ache of delight came between his eyes, when he thought of making Saxon caper on the sidewalk, in the very presence of the pretty girl.

Saxon had dismounted with a leap, throwing the reins, and the mules stopped and dropped their heads in repose, instantly. There was a dust coat over the clothes of Saxon. He threw it off. He was revealed in a decent suit of dark gray. He wore a broad gray Stetson. He carried his bigness with the lithe ease of a man in perfect condition and very young. And Bob Witherell hated all of these details. Finlay had made them rivals.

Above all, Witherell hated the blond head which appeared when Saxon jerked off his hat and embraced the

11

girl. Afterward she got away from him, pulling at her dress, straightening it, laughing at Saxon, and protesting.

Witherell sneered. "Lookit," he said, barely aloud. "A fool. Got no manners. Mauling a girl around like that! Why, he's no kind of a man at all."

"He looks plenty man," said Boots, chuckling a little.

Boots was not "plenty man." He was little and narrow, and his soul was too small for even that shrunken body; but Boots was wonderfully master of the only art he knew, which was that of using a .45 Colt.

"He looks plenty man to you, does he?" said Witherell.

"Yeah, he looks big to me. Maybe he's bigger than you think," said Boots.

Witherell started to make a sneering rejoinder, but he forgot all about words, as he stared across the street. The hatred which he felt was so extremely violent and profound that he was amazed by his own emotion.

He looked suddenly away, and far off, down the street, he saw Finlay sauntering toward him slowly. The anger of Witherell increased. He stood up and shouted suddenly:

"Hey, Saxon!"

John Saxon turned from the girl and waved his hand. "Hello?" he called.

"Come here a minute, will you?" asked Witherell.

Saxon hesitated. But his good humor kept him smiling, and he nodded presently. "Sure," he said, and started across the street.

The smile dimmed. He frowned a little, with a curious wonder as he examined the strangers on the veranda. As he came up, he said:

"Sorry. Do I know you fellows?"

"I dunno," answered Witherell. "Maybe you'll get to know us better. Reason I called you over was that I seen your long legs."

Boots laughed. The others laughed, too, and the face of Saxon hardened. It was a good face, and handsome, with all the lines of strength well modeled. The sun had burned the eyebrows pale at the tips but left a darker shadow under. Hard work had kept the flesh lean, the eyes clear. The eyes were gray, with a tint of hazel in them that was beginning to brighten dangerously now.

"I don't know you," said Saxon. "I don't know what my legs have to do with you. And I don't give a damn."

"He don't give a damn," said Witherell, sneering.

"No, he don't give a damn," said Boots, chuckling again with infinite pleasure. "He's too big to give a damn."

"Maybe he could be cut down smaller," said Witherell. "Saxon, can you dance?"

Saxon looked them over calmly.

"You fellows want trouble. But I'm busy," he said, and started to turn away.

The flash of a gun halted him suddenly. Amazement stopped him more than fear.

"Dance, you!" shouted Witherell, and put a bullet right through the boards of the sidewalk, at Saxon's feet. The slug of lead peeled off a long splinter and slapped it up against his leg. He jumped into the air with an unconscious contraction of his muscles.

"You fool!" he shouted. "What're you trying to do?"

"Dance!" yelled Witherell, and fired again.

And again Saxon jumped, instinctively, from the danger.

A smooth stream of lead poured out of the gun of Witherell, five shots in rapid succession, and then he dropped a fresh Colt into his right hand and continued the rain of bullets. Across the street, the girl was screaming with terror. She started to run across toward Saxon, and Saxon, turning, panic-stricken, went back toward the girl as fast as he could leg it.

At every step he took, bullets smashed through the dust about his feet. And he bounded like a deer. One would have thought that the street was white-hot, and that Saxon was running over the flames in his bare feet. And as he ran, he shouted with his fear.

When he came to the girl, he caught her up in his arms and sprinting through the open gate of the garden, dashed up the walk and disappeared into the little white house, still carrying her.

Witherell was so delighted that laughter almost shook him to pieces.

People were pouring out into the street. Men were hurrying toward the sound of the shooting and the outcries.

13

"Come on, boys," said Witherell. "I'm tired of this dead town anyway. We won't see anything better than that dance, I guess."

They went out and mounted their horses as Daniel Finlay came up. He shook a forefinger at Witherell.

"Ah, Bob," he said, "I'm afraid that you're incorrigible. An incorrigible boy, Bob Witherell. Good advice is thrown away on you, lad! Now run away and try to make better habits!"

Bob Witherell rode away, but he was pleased, his heart was eased. He had shamed John Saxon before Saxon's girl, and so long as the handsome blond fellow lived, he would never be able to forget that shame, Witherell decided. As long as Saxon lived, he would shudder a little when he heard the name of Bob Witherell. And perhaps the girl, too, would have her eyes opened. She would come to understand that there are other sorts of men in this world than the plain and honest pluggers. A flash of a new idea might illumine her. Perhaps, now and again, she might sigh as she remembered.

That was the humor of Witherell as he led the riders up through the mountains, but it was really chance that took him by the south trail and onto the wide, sweeping hills of the old Bentley range.

"Hey!" called Boots. "That's the shack of the squatter. That's where Saxon hangs out. Let's go look-see."

They went into the shack. It was one room, complete, and one room incomplete, with a foundation dug and some squared logs of good size lying curing in the weather against the day when they would be laid up to make the walls. Before the marriage, no doubt, that room would have to be finished. Inside, there was exactly what one would expect to find in the cabin of a young settler who was just starting to build up his herd. From the walls hung a jumble of old clothes, harness, saddles, bridles, guns, gear of all sorts. There was no ceiling. Gaunt, crooked rafters stretched across from wall to wall, and on a platform above them appeared a stack of newly cured pelts. There was nothing about the place extraordinary in any way, except for a small shelf of books. Witherell curled his lip when he saw the books.

"Blame college man, likely," said Bob Witherell.

He lighted a cigarette and threw the match on the floor.

"What you fellows think of this sort of a place to live in?" asked Witherell. "Hell of a layout, ain't it?"

"You know," answered Boots, "you gotta have all kinds in the world. You gotta have the suckers for the sake of the gents with brains enough to trim 'em!"

"Look out!" warned another. "That match has set fire to the shavings, there. Stamp on it, boys."

Witherell looked down and saw the small smoke rising, and the little, weak-headed flame. Some shavings left by a carpenter's plane lay in a corner, together with some bits of paper.

"If he ain't got sense enough to sweep his floor, what should we care about it?" asked Witherell. "Leave it be."

Then he added: "There's not enough strength to that, to set the house on fire. And what if it did? He made me sick, the big yellow-belly! Hear how he hollered out? He made me sick at the stomach to listen to him. Leave the fire go!"

He led the way outside.

His companions, rather guiltily, followed him. But they would have been both afraid and ashamed to protest. The magnificently casual air of Bob Witherell seemed exactly that which most became a man of spirit.

"Lookit," said Witherell. "Why, he ain't a man. He's a squaw with a vegetable patch. Look at how he's tied up the tomatoes on sticks, too. And he's got onions and potatoes. Look yonder, at the little smokehouse. He kills his own pork and he cures his own bacon. Why, the devil with a miserly hound like that. He ain't no good. He never makes a dollar roll. Why, the devil with that kind of a thing. You can't call it a man."

"Hey, wait a minute, Bob," said Boots. "Look back there! The house is catchin' on fire, all right."

Witherell turned with a jerk of his body. The wood had been drier than he had expected it to be. After all, the pile of shavings had been fairly large, and perhaps there was a draft blowing across the floor, fanning the flames, which were now crackling and fluttering.

"Hey, wait a minute," muttered Witherell, and he hurried back to the threshold of the house. There he paused.

15

The whole floor was alive with red snakes of fire, and more flames were crawling up the wall. Already everything in the room was ruined. Already enough had been done to send them all to jail.

And then, with a savage reaction, he stepped back into the open and slammed the door behind him.

"Let it burn," he said. "What would we care about it, anyway? What kind of a man is this here Saxon? I wouldn't give a nickel for a dozen like him!"

He swung into the saddle. Inside the house, the fire was beginning to roar ominously. Smoke spurted out at a thousand cracks.

"Built like a cracker box—just as flimsy," declared Witherell. "He don't even know how to build a house. D'you see that?"

Suddenly, inside the cabin, a gun exploded. And the group of riders started and looked at one another.

"His ghost is in there shooting," said Boots, with a laugh.

"That's the only thing that would have the nerve to pull a gun," said Witherell. "Not handsome John. He wouldn't have the nerve at all. He'd rather run and yell like a dog."

"He's raised some good fat cows, up here," commented Boots.

"Sure," said Witherell. The delight of evil sent a keen tremor through him. "Sure, he raises beef for us to eat. Round 'em up, boys. I know where we can sell that stuff fifty miles from here—and a hundred head of beef like that is worth a price. I knew we wouldn't be wastin' our time when I started things with Saxon."

CHAPTER III

JOHN SAXON came up through the hills with only a rather dim anger remaining in his breast, the after-effect of the way he had danced across the street at the bidding and before the bullets of Bob Witherell. He had calmed his own shaken nerves and the hysteria of Mary Wilson and he had gone straight on to the church. He had felt that a church was a good place to be in after an experience such as he had been through. For his own part, he had never used a rifle for anything except to shoot venison. As for a revolver, he literally never had pulled the trigger of one, to say nothing of fanning the hammer of such an inaccurate weapon. To him, bullets meant less sport than hunting. Bullets brought meat and had to be safeguarded and spent with the greatest caution. He never practiced except at real game.

So he had little shame about his flight before Bob Witherell. On the way to the church he noticed that people looked at him, laughing. He simply did not understand what he had done that might amuse others. It was only on the way home that Mary Wilson said to him:

"They're hateful! People that laugh because you ran away!"

"Ran away?" he repeated. "Of course I ran away from a crazy man with a gun. I'd run away from a forest fire, the same way."

"Of course you would," said the girl.

But she lifted her eyes and looked rather unhappily away toward the blue of the sky. It was not that she really doubted, but that she was thinking a bit.

Afterward, at dinner, Mary's father mentioned the thing. First of all, he condemned savagely blackguards of the type of Bob Witherell. Such fellows, he declared, ought to be hanged at once, out of hand. He went on into a happier vein and told John Saxon with a whimsical humor that he had heard that John was a wonderful dancer and that he had done some of the best high jumping in the world, this day. Mr. Wilson laughed a good deal at his own humor, and his wife added her own chuckle, and, what Saxon noticed most of all, Mary flushed.

Whatever Witherell had done, it was plain that he had amused a large section of the town of Bluewater.

After dinner, Saxon found a chance to talk alone for a moment with Wilson. He said bluntly: "You think that I ought to have stood up to Witherell?"

"Stood up to him? No one but a drunkard or a fool

17

would have done that," declared Wilson. "No, my boy. It was a great deal better to turn and run—and besides, that gave people a chance to see some of the best dancing in the world."

Mr. Wilson laughed again, very heartily, but Saxon was not at all amused. He brooded a good deal about the adventure of the day. There was a great deal of simplicity in Saxon. He had taken a lot of things for granted ever since he was a boy, and, among others, he never had thought about courage at all. Now and then, as a youngster, he had had fist fights, and he had always won them because he was naturally stronger and quicker than other boys of his size and height. Back in his memory was lodged the recollection of a day when he had been matched against a boy who was distinctly *more* than his own height, weight, and age. It had been a long and desperate battle, waged against superior skill, wisdom, strength, and craft. But in the end, Saxon was able to draw upon a greater power, a well of which was always rising in his heart.

He had thought that that greater power was his superior fortitude. He had thought, always, that fortitude was the same thing as courage. He had thought that when he went out into the face of a winter hurricane to look after the welfare of his cattle, he was showing courage. And the day he had ventured down the face of a cliff to save the sheep that was caught there between rock and bush— well, that he had thought to be courage. He had distinctly thought so.

It seemed that there was another way of looking at things. According to this, the only way a man could demonstrate courage was by standing unarmed up to an assassin armed with a revolver in the use of which he was professionally accurate.

The injustice of this conception troubled the usually serene mind of Saxon. When he said good-by to Mary, later that day, he thought that her brow was clouded. And he questioned her directly.

"You wish that I'd taken that gun away from Witherell and thrashed him. That's what you wish, isn't it?" said Saxon.

"Do I wish it?" said Mary dreamily. "I don't know

18

what I wish. I only know I'm glad you're safe, and I'm sorry that it happened."

When he drove his mules back up the mountain road, he went by a number of people who laughed openly at him.

He heard one man say: "You should have heard how he hollered. That was the main thing. The way he hollered!"

And he flushed, as he listened to this. His heartbeat began to quicken. Of course one knew, instinctively, that there is only one curse in the world, and that is to be considered a coward. A man must die rather than. allow this to be said of him.

As the mules pulled him up higher and higher over what was rather a trail than a road, his heart was soothed. The purer air made breathing more easy, and in a little while he would be turning the corner at his Expectation Point, from which he could always look across his little valley. The mules knew his habit so well that when they came to the corner, they halted of their own accord.

Saxon kept on smiling, more and more dimly, for another moment. Something was wrong. Something was so wrong that he would not dare to see what it was, at first.

Instead, he looked up from the valley to the sky, where he was able to see the familiar summits, of shadow and white, going into the blue. But when he looked down again, he was aware that, where his house had stood, there was now only a rising wisp of smoke.

The house was gone, and the barn was gone, too. A wind took hold on its ashes, and whirled the black cinders high into the air. The trees that had stood about the house were now black skeletons. The grass was burned away, also, and left a great dark charcoal mark against the surrounding green.

The whole thing was wiped out!

He drove the mules forward slowly. The world that had been his was shrinking to that buckboard and those two mules. Nothing else was left to him!

He stared about him, and he saw that the cattle had been swept away, also. Fiends had been there, and with a touch, in a single day, they had unraveled eight years of his life! All his labor was wasted. He stood now where he had stood as a boy of sixteen. The gesture was complete.

They had rubbed out the farm, and they had rubbed out the eight years. If it took him another eight years to accomplish what he had just managed, he would be thirty-two. The age seemed very advanced, to him. Mary Wilson could not be expected to wait that long before she married.

He stopped the mules and got out. Here and there a few bits of the smoke were still going up. There were heaps of rubbish, gray and black, and that was all.

Out at the corral, even the two stacks had burned, and he saw the seared bodies of twelve young calves. The flames had hardly touched some of them, but they were all dead. And the killers had not even bothered to cut up the dead bodies for veal!

Yes, there were killers. For a time he felt sure that it could only be that a spark of fire had remained in his stove, and that this spark had blown up through the chimney and lived to reach a haystack, say, and that from this point the fire had spread. But that would not account for the manner in which the cattle had disappeared from the valley. And presently he found the hoof marks of six horses. Where they crossed the little run of water, those hoof marks were printed very firmly on the ground. They were registered in the mud so that he could examine them in detail, and particularly one left fore shoe, with a bar across it, as though the horse might have corns.

One of the mules began to bray, and the horrible sound throttled Saxon.

He sat down on a rock and looked and looked. Every time his eyes fell, the image of the house rose up clearly before him. He could see his ghost inside it, preparing supper. He could hear the cows lowing. But every time he glanced up, the emptiness rushed over his mind again.

It was dusk. The evening increased with rapidity. The empty night which was receiving the mountains was receiving the soul of Saxon, also. He was alone. The cold of loneliness reached to his heart. Even the mules were a comfort to him.

The night itself was now there, black, with many eyes

that watched him. Nature itself asked him what he would do now, and he had no answer.

He was twenty-four. It was a very advanced age. A great part of life was gone behind him. The major portion of hope had been consumed.

Finally he roused himself. Cattle cannot travel quickly. Mules are not fast, but they are a lot faster and more enduring than fat-sided beeves.

He turned one mule loose to graze. He mounted the other, and rode off on the trail of the vanished herd.

CHAPTER IV

THIRTY miles of the moonlit night, of the cold winds above timber line, and the icy snow waters, and the mule gave out utterly.

Big John Saxon dismounted and took off the bridle and threw it into a shrub, and went on. He went faster on foot, as a matter of fact, than when he had been on the back of the mule, because the mule was not spurred as he was by a dreadful anxiety. If Saxon could get back his herd of beef, he would be all right. The house and the rest was chiefly handwork, and there was a plentiful treasure of strength reserved in him, ready to be spent. He felt as though he could work twenty hours a day for endless years to make up for the lost house. It was almost an advantage to have it gone, because now he would make it better and bigger, and more fit to be the house of Mary Wilson.

But with the cattle gone, he was thrown back to the very beginning. There was nothing that he could do, except to resume his daily labor on a ranch, and pile up thirty dollars or forty dollars or even fifty dollars a month of savings, slowly accumulating, saving every penny, starving himself, so that he could get enough hard cash together to begin his purchases of weak and of failing cattle, picking up a starved calf here and a tottering cow

21

there at quarter price, and so building up, finally, a ragged but a salable group of beeves.

Ah, but that needed eight more years, eight more years to reach the point at which fate had so suddenly checked him! And Mary could not wait so long for him.

This inward agony kept him striding, without weariness, all through the night, and under the moon and then under the dawn he still found the thronging sign of his cattle and, now and again, that mark of the horse with the bar shoe.

But he came, now, to a narrow cleft of a valley that split the mountains deep, and out of that valley ran many little ravines, and up each of those ravines, on the left-hand side, rang the sign of some of the cattle. And he saw the rising sun shine along a face of chalk-white cliffs.

When he saw that, he stopped short.

Back in his memory there was lodged a story of rustlers of White Valley, back here among the mountains, fellows who knew how to take in a herd of any size and split it up into sections, and make it disappear in that hole-in-the-wall country. Afterward, it came out for sale at distant points. There would be no chance, therefore, of catching the thieves off guard. They had brought up the herd and already it had dissolved in the hands of the organized rustlers. It was only strange that these experts should have sent out six men to steal a herd of merely a hundred head!

Despair came blackly over him. He began to feel tired. His knees shook, and sitting down on a rock, he looked slowly around him. It was a beautiful valley with a rush of water down the center of it, singing and throwing up thin white arms of spray, and other ribbons of water went over the edges of the cliffs and showered down into white spray that was wind-blown like a mist before it reached the valley bottom, far below. All was a dazzle of brightness, except where groves of big, round-headed trees offered shelter and shadow to the eye. But there was no sense of beauty for John Saxon, in this scene. And every beat of his pulse told him that he was lost, lost, lost.

Six riders were coming up the valley toward him. That made the exact number of the horsemen who had stolen the herd. He had not seen them issue from any of the ravines. It was as if they had been dropped down out of the sky. They came closer, and he saw at the head of them that handsome ruffian, Bob Witherell.

They went straight by him, laughing, each giving him a mock salute. Then, staring down at the ground, he saw that the horse on which Witherell rode left behind, with every stroke of its left forehoof, the impression of a bar shoe.

"Witherell!" he shouted. "You cattle thief! Witherell!"

Witherell turned with a gun in his hand. But Saxon ran straight on at the enemy. There was a madness in him.

"You rustler! You thief!" shouted Saxon.

Witherell held up the revolver for an instant as though about to shoot, but he changed his mind when he saw the empty hands of Saxon, and throwing the reins of his horse to one of his companions, he dropped to the ground.

Saxon, leaning far forward as he ran, came in with a smashing blow. Witherell dodged it, laughing still.

"I'm goin' to teach you something, you fool!" he said.

He stepped in with a lifting punch. Saxon saw the fist only for an instant before the blow landed. It caught him neatly on the point of the chin and made him walk backward with sagging knees. Witherell followed carefully.

"I'm goin' to give you a lesson," he said, and hammered a long, straight left into the face of Saxon.

Saxon rushed in, bellowing with rage. He wanted to kill the man, but all he could meet with was a series of explosive and jarring punches that knocked the wits out of him and dimmed his eyes. The blood began to run from his face over his clothes.

He wiped the thick crimson away from his battered eyes. Two tremendous blows sent him staggering. He heard the men of Witherell shouting with delight. He heard them advising their champion where to hit next. And always Saxon was running forward at a blurring image, and always he was striking against a frightful wall of hard knuckles.

He heard Witherell say: "All right, take it then. Here's a wind-up for you."

It seemed to Saxon that a bullet smashed through his brain. He fell into darkness that only gradually relaxed, and as the world spun vaguely before his eyes, he felt a hard rap against his ribs, and then Witherell's voice was saying:

"You lie there like the swine that you are. And the next time you see me, back up! Sure I stole your cows. Why? Because it pleased me to steal 'em. Just for meanness was why I stole 'em. You get another herd together, and I'll steal those, too. There's nothing that you ever get that I won't come and take. Why? Because that's the kind of an hombre I am. When I find a dog, I kick it, and I keep on kicking it till it howls!"

After a time, Saxon could sit up.

He was nauseated. He crawled to the rush of the water and lay beside it, letting the current ice his face and numb the pain of his battered and torn flesh. One of his eyes was swollen almost shut. Out of the other he saw only vaguely. And his head felt as large as a bucket.

He had been shamed before his girl, he had been robbed, beaten by the robber, and laughed at.

Well, there was justice in the world, and he would have it. There was the law!

It took him two days to get back to Bluewater. And in the early morning, with the blood still in his clothes and his face swollen to blue and purple, he walked into the office of the sheriff.

The sheriff was not there. There was only a young Negro, sweeping up the floor, who pointed out that the sheriff would still be at home, at this time of the day.

"My land, are you John Saxon?" said the lad. "You sure must 'a' fell off of a high cliff, mister!"

Saxon went to the sheriff's house. Two of Sheriff Phil Walker's boys were playing in the front yard and they fled yelling into the building. Those yells brought the sheriff out promptly. He had the face of a bulldog, with mustaches on it. Or he might have been likened to a walrus. He was a fighting man, was the sheriff, and he showed fight now.

"You dirty tramp," he said to Saxon. "You'll scare little kids, will you? I'll fix you so you won't scare *anybody* for a while!"

24

"Wait a minute," said Saxon. "I'm John Saxon. I've come here for justice."

"Where you been drunk?" asked the sheriff. "You John Saxon? Yeah, I guess maybe you are, and you're sure a mess. Where you been drunk, and who rolled you?"

"I've not been drunk," said Saxon. "I never was drunk in my life. My house has been burned, and my cows have been stolen. I'm cleaned out of everything except two mules."

"Yeah? You know who done it?" asked the sheriff calmly.

"I know who did it."

"The devil you do."

"Bob Witherell and five of his friends did it. The same five who were in town with him the other day."

"This here is pretty loud talk," said the sheriff. "Bob Witherell is in town right now. I'll go get that hombre. You go down to my office and wait there."

Saxon went down to the office and sat in the blackness of his misery until he heard footfalls approaching. The sheriff came, and with him came big, handsome Bob Witherell, who stood over Saxon and said:

"You want another licking, do you? What kinda lies you been telling about me, you skunk?"

"He stole my cattle," said Saxon. His voice rose to a shout. "He cleaned out my herd, and he burned down my house. By God, you ought to hang him!"

"All right, all right," said the sheriff. "Lemme have your proofs, now that you been talking so loud."

"He's got a horse with a barred shoe on the left forefoot. I trailed that shoeprint from my house all the way to White Valley, where the herd broke up."

"Well, that sounds like something," said the sheriff, without conviction. "What about it, Bob?"

"Why, it's a stinkin' lie," said Witherell. "What would I be burning down houses for? What's in his house that I would want to burn it down for? Answer me that, sheriff?"

"I dunno," said the sheriff. "It ain't my business to find reasons for things."

"I gotta horse with a barred shoe on a forefoot," said Witherell. "And this rat, he tries to gnaw into me account of that, does he? Why, that ain't any proof. I never seen this hombre till the other day, and I played a little joke on him, and made him howl and dance down the street. That's the only time I ever seen him, till the other day I was takin' a ride, and I meet him and he starts givin' me some lip. So I get down and I give him a fair and square lickin'. I got witnesses to prove it. And if you don't believe it, I'll take him out and lick him again."

It was the sort of a speech that the sheriff could understand. It rang true, to him.

"You talk about prints of horseshoes, do you?" said the sheriff to big John Saxon. "Well, can you take me over the trail of them prints?"

"It rained a regular cloudburst yesterday," said Saxon. "You know that prints wouldn't last under a rain like that."

"Then what in hell are you wastin' my time for?" thundered the sheriff. "Get out of here. And—if Witherell licks you again, I hope he does a browner job than the last one, you big, curly-headed baby! There ain't the makings of half a man inside of you!"

CHAPTER V

WHEN Saxon stood again in the open air, his brain was reeling. The law is a part of each one of us. The law is our right hand, to work for us, to defend us. And the law had failed him, and shamed him.

But there are other powers on which poor, defeated men can lean. So he went straight to the First National Bank and found the president, Jim Tolliver, just swinging up the board walk toward his place of business.

"Hello!" said Tolliver. "Why, what's happened to you, Saxon? What's happened, my lad?"

They had done business together—there had been a few loans given to Saxon on account of his growing herd, to tide him through lean sections of recent years.

The banker had always been friendly, almost confidential.

"Mr. Tolliver," said Saxon. "I'm broke. I'm flat broke. My house was burned by Bob Witherell and his gang. They stole every head of my cattle. I'm down to two mules."

"Infernal outrage!" exclaimed Tolliver. "The sheriff—"

"I haven't the right kind of proof," said Saxon. "The sheriff won't budge. I want to talk to you. I've still got the land up there. You know that I'm a hard working man. I want to know if you'll make a loan to me. A small loan. Something I can make a start on again, and get together a few head of cows, and make the herd grow. You know that I can make a herd grow."

The banker laid his hand somewhat gingerly on the shoulder of Saxon.

"My boy," he said, "I'd like to do what I can, but all I can say is that the bank won't be interested. My personal heart aches for you, but, as a banker, I have to obey banking laws. That land isn't salable. And if we lend you money to start your operations again, how can we tell that you won't be wiped out again by this or some other accident? You seem to have powerful enemies, and all I can do is to give you some good advice—start in a small way once more, go to work, save your pennies, and then make your beginning once more. But as for advancing you hard cash—I'm sorry—banking practice won't let me do it. My partners—they would simply ask me to resign if they knew of such practices!"

Saxon turned wearily up the street.

He had tried the power of the law and he had tried the power of money. There remained love. He could go to that. He could let Mary Wilson see his swollen, distorted face, his blood-stained clothing, and weep over him. But there was no point in that.

It seemed to Saxon that he had come, definitely, to the end of the passage, and there was one deep voice that called to him in words which he could understand—that was the distant shouting of Bluewater Creek.

There was a place just above town where the banks rose in cliffs a hundred feet high, and at the bottom of the cliffs the water rushed in a white froth capable of tearing big logs to pieces. A human body, dropped into that mill, would instantly be shredded beyond all recognition. And it seemed clear to Saxon that his best step in the life that remained to him would be from the edge of one of those cliffs, and so through one stabbing thrust of pain into eternity.

So he walked, slowly, out of the town.

Half a dozen small boys spotted him and danced yelling and mocking around him. They left him on the edge of Bluewater and he went on alone.

He left the road and climbed a fence, crossed a wide field, and reached the edge of the cliff above the white water. The narrow cañon of the creek was filled with shadow, and the voices rose to him in what seemed to Saxon a cheerful chorus. He looked up for his last glance at the world. It was a flawless day of blue and white, with a soft wind blowing, but he had seen a thousand other days as beautiful as this one, and they all led, in the end, to the misery in which he stood.

As for Mary—well, it was much best to step out of her life like this. She would have her freedom. For a few months she would be in anxious doubt. Then she would feel that he had deserted her, and natural resentment would harden her heart against him. A year or two later, nature would assert itself, and she would be married.

So, to John Saxon, the problem seemed solved in the best way. As for that law of God which forbade self-destruction—well, only fools believed in God, not men who had spent their lives in honest labor and seen that labor come to naught, as he had done.

He stepped right to the verge of the cliff, and then he heard, behind him, the voice of Daniel Finlay.

He started. There was even a moment's temptation to fling himself headlong in spite of that voice, but his whole plan went awry if he were seen destroying himself. So he turned, and saw the grim face and the rigidly straight form of Daniel Finlay coming toward him.

"Young man," said the lawyer, "come with me."

"Go your own way and be damned," said Saxon rudely. "I want to be alone."

"Ay," said Finlay. "You want to be alone, like a coward, to dodge a life that's too much for you, to sneak out of it like a thief into a dark alley. John Saxon, because your body has been beaten, is your soul beaten, too? Are you a man or a sneaking cur?"

It was a sharp sauce, that speech, but it gave a sudden relish of hot anger to Saxon. He even made a step toward Finlay in a threatening fashion.

"Don't bluster at me," said Finlay, "because I know you for what you are. You may bluster, but if even an old woman lifted a hand, you'd cringe as you're cringing before the thought of Bob Witherell."

Saxon said nothing. The anger that burned in him was at such a white heat that he could find no words. He could think of nothing to do.

Finlay went on: "You've been beaten, shamed, laughed at in public. You've had your house burned over your head and your cattle stolen. And the town laughs at what's happened to you. And Bob Witherell, with the price of your cows in his pocket, sprawls in the saloon and drinks, and laughs. And you, like a wretched dog, are ready to jump off a cliff and put an end to yourself?"

He made that famous, sweeping, handless gesture which had impressed so many juries.

"I thank God," said Finlay, "that I'm of a different stuff from you! You see me as a man without friends, mutilated, cut off from the happiness of ordinary life. But still I can fight. I can make my way. I can hold my head high! I grow older. There are not so many years left to me, but every one of those years shall be my own. You —you driveling fool—you are throwing away the best part of your life."

And still big John Saxon said nothing. The hot scourge of these words entered his very flesh, but something in him admitted the truth of everything that he had heard.

"Better than to do this," said Finlay, "take a gun. Here. It's a new one and a good one. Take it and learn how to use it. If there is nothing else that makes you want to live, live to revenge yourself like a man on Bob Witherell. Learn how to use this Colt until it is a part of your flesh, until your nerves run down into the steel. And then go and stand up to Bob Witherell and let the world see that you *are* a man. If you want to die, his bullets will kill you as quickly as a jump from a cliff. If you want to live, stretch Bob Witherell dead on the ground before you, and

29

the joy of life and self-respect will come back to you!"

It was a well calculated speech, and Finlay, as he delivered it, was proud of himself. He had seen that down-headed figure dragging slowly out of the town, this morning, and already the story of what had happened to young John Saxon had gone the rounds. The tale was too spectacular to remain a secret. And as Finlay, sneering silently, watched the big fellow go off in defeat, a premonition of what was to happen had come across the lawyer's mind.

He was not unhappy about it. Trouble was what he lived to make, and the fact that a few words from him had armed Witherell with the first malice which had led on to all of these other happenings was not a pain but a rejoicing in the heart of the lawyer. What led him to slip along in the rear of Saxon, what caused him to interfere at the last moment, was that he surmised new and bigger ways of contriving mischief. Saxon was too good a tool to be thrown away. He was worthy of being used. And Finlay saw the way of using him.

So he stood there, holding out with his left hand the big, shining Colt revolver. And the glance of John Saxon went dizzily from the gun to the face of Finlay.

He gripped the weapon with a sudden gesture.

"Finlay," he said, "I always thought you were a mean man and a hard man. Maybe you are, but you've shown me the right way to go about things. I'm going to take the gun. I'm going to do what you advise me to do! By God, I'll make myself fit to stand up to Mr. Murderer Witherell, the thief!"

"You can, John," said the lawyer, with a sudden kindliness. "I know that you can! Self-confidence comes with training. Some men train themselves until they can hit a sapling, and then they are confident. Other men train themselves until they can hit a twig, before they are sure. But the sapling is enough. The man who can hit the sapling can hit the heart—and prove his right to be called brave! Ah, John Saxon, John Saxon, you only need to become familiar with the noise of guns in order to face down Bob Witherell and make your girl stop blushing for shame of you!"

"Mary? Does she blush on account of me?" asked Saxon, heavily.

"How can she help it?" asked the lawyer. "The young people in the town pity her. The girls shrug their shoulders. They give her their sympathy. Do you think it's an easy thing for a girl to have her entire town laughing at the man she loves? Do you think that she can keep on loving a man she begins to despise?"

The word stunned John Saxon so that his bruised, discolored eyes began to blink.

And Daniel Finlay drew out of the pain of the other an infinite joy, a relish more delicious to him than the best of wine. He could already see the picture of Saxon and Witherell standing face to face, ready to draw their guns, snarling insults, or hushed in a deadly, white-faced silence. Witherell would win, of course, but perhaps Saxon would drive one bullet home before he died.

And what would Finlay gain by all of this? Well, he would gain that which was, to him, the keenest of all happinesses—the knowledge that he had stood behind the scenes and pulled the wires that made the puppets dance and prance and talk and die.

Hitherto, he had used his schemes in many ways, but he had not yet advanced his touch to human lives. It seemed to Finlay that he had wasted his other years. Existence would begin for him only when there was the taste of human blood in his soul.

He heard John Saxon saying: "Everything you say is right. Maybe I'm a coward. I don't know. The game will be in giving myself the acid test. Will you do one more thing for me, since you've started by doing so much?"

"Anything in my power, my dear lad," said Finlay. "Tell me what you want? A little cash? You shall have it."

Saxon shook his head.

"Go to Mary and tell her that you've seen me, and that you have a message from me. I'm going to make a new start—and she'll hear from me after it's made!"

CHAPTER VI

THERE had to be cash. Saxon sold his two mules to get it. He turned that cash into ammunition, a heavy load of it. He bought a bit of salt, and that was all. He had never been a hunter, but if ever he was to learn to face Bob Witherell he would have to start shooting straight before long. If he could not shoot enough meat to support him, there was no use hoping to face Witherell.

So, with the Colt revolver, and the heavy weight of ammunition, and the hunting knife at his belt, and the salt in his pouch, John Saxon went back into the mountains.

He stayed there two months. He tramped through the mountains, always hunting, and never once did he remain in the same camp for two nights.

The winds cut him, the rains soaked him, and the snow, above timberline, blinded him with an endless white mist. But he kept traveling, round and round through a small compass, and always hunting, always hunting. If he could not hunt and kill game, he could not hunt and kill his man, when the time came.

The wounds he had received in his beating healed. A rough, triangular scar remained over his right cheekbone, and he used to touch this many times a day. It was just above the upper verge of the beard that had grown out over his face, a reddish, sun-faded beard. He studied that scar with the tips of his fingers until he knew every bit of its corrugations. And every time he touched it, he thought of Bob Witherell, big, dark, and handsome.

After he had killed Witherell, Bob's brother, that remote and famous genius of crime called by all men The Solitaire, would come to find him and would surely fight the battle out.

He would kill The Solitaire, too.

When he was freezing by night or starving by day he used to tell himself that over and over again. He would kill The Solitaire after he had killed Bob Witherell. And then he would wish that there were ten brothers in the family, so that he could destroy them all. Even ten killings would hardly glut his need of blood.

In the meantime, he trained himself with the most perfect care. There was nothing else for him to think about. His mind, indeed, would not go farther forward than the battles which he must fight. As for building up a cattle herd once more, that seemed to him a dream, a vagueness not worthy of a man's attention.

Every waking hour, and in his dreams, he practiced with the gun, or he dreamed or planned for it.

Mere using of ammunition would do little good. A man has to point a gun straight by instinct before he can accomplish anything. And, in a fight, there are sudden necessities, the call for a quick draw, and a shot that goes straight. There is no chance, in a saloon or during a street fight, to level a weapon and take a careful aim. Gunfights have nothing to do with target practice.

So he used to spend hours every day snatching out the Colt and whirling and pointing it at some object which he had selected before. After that he would lean and look down the sights, and see what accuracy there had been in his aim. In order to make that examination he had to keep his hand as still as a rock. But he learned to do that. All the nerves went out of his right hand, except the nerves of speed.

He made a discovery which was of infinite use. He could extend his forefinger along the side of the Colt and point, while he pulled the trigger with his middle finger. It was really very simple. For there is a queer instinct in us that makes us point straight. A man will indicate even a star, very accurately, by pointing, and without sighting down his finger.

The chief trouble was that the middle finger was awkward. There were few brains in it. It had to be trained and taught before the pull it delivered failed to bring the gun out of line. But every day after the discovery of the new method, the skill of that middle finger increased until it could pull the trigger without stirring the gun from the line that had been aimed at.

There was to be no target practice. Finlay, though he seemed a wise man, had talked of fellows who can hit saplings, of others who can cut a twig. But for him, there would be nothing but living game.

He nearly starved in the first week. Then a deer jumped suddenly out of covert, and he crashed a forty-five caliber slug of lead right into the head of the poor brute.

The deer fell without a kick, and John Saxon had roasted venison and all that he could eat of it.

Something rigid and perverse in him kept him from sun-drying or smoking any of that meat. If he was not a good enough shot to supply himself with fresh meat, he was not a good enough shot to face Bob Witherell. So, as the two months went on, he crowded lifetimes of marksmanship, of one sort, into his days.

A fine shot may go hunting for a month out of every year. He may fire two bullets a day, and no more, during that month. But Saxon was crowding months into days. And to make him keen, there was the need of eating, and there was the need of facing Bob Witherell somewhere in the near distance.

If he took a snapshot at a bird on a branch, the name of Witherell hardened on his tongue. If a rabbit dodged across his path, the gun said "Witherell" as it exploded.

Every shot had to be a snapshot. A flashing gesture—for hours and hours he worked on the mere matter of the draw—and an instant explosion of the gun. That was what every shot was during the two months.

His misses ran into the hundreds. He had a hungry time of it for the first month, but after that he began to hit one rabbit in two. He began to hit one squirrel in four. There are trick shots who can do better, but not many. Not many who are using nothing but snapshots.

In the second month his clothes went suddenly to pieces. The constant roughing among the rocks and the prickly shrubbery had worn the cloth and rent it, and the constant soakings rotted the fabric away. So he dressed himself in rags and tatters pieced out with deerskin which he tanned after his own way, and a frightful and stiff thing it made, hard as parchment. He made moccasins, too, that would have made a squaw weep. He made them of deerskin, sewed with the thread of raveled tendons. They were clumsy affairs, but they saved his feet, and his feet were

34

growing as tough as leather. They hardly needed extra protection.

He had been six weeks in the woods when he came to one of the great days of his life. He was climbing among high rocks, above timberline, toward the bee pastures of the uplands where birds big and small may be found, and coming between a pair of great boulders he found himself ten feet from a huge mother grizzly with three woolly cubs about her.

The mother had been investigating an ant's nest, having ripped open the ground with her steel-hard claws. When she was so suddenly surprised by this specter which had come to her up a hard wind, she stood up from her work and then dropped forward to charge.

John Saxon had just time to remember that the descent behind him was practically a precipice. In the next hundredth part of a second he had his gun out and sent a bullet home. That shot smashed the nose of the she-bear to bits. It was a lucky shot, perhaps, but big John Saxon did not call it luck. He had been looking at that bright, moist, pig's-nose as he fired.

The she-bear, in an agony, reared to knock John Saxon off the cliff with one stroke of a forepaw. But John Saxon pumped two bullets through her heart.

She fell with the loose of her jowl right across his feet, and he saw the cubs scamper away into the distance. Then, looking down at the huge quarry, he remembered that the Indians of the old days always considered a brave who had killed a grown grizzly more distinguished than one who had counted coup upon a human enemy.

And there had been no chance about the first shot, he kept telling himself. He had marked the nose, and had fired for it.

He ate tough bear steaks for two days, and then went on, determined to try his hand more and more at small game. There were plenty of mountain grouse, but they were so big and so still and so stupid that they hardly mattered. A squirrel moving hastily about on a high branch, showing himself only by glimpses—that made the best target of all. It meant the keying up of nerves to such a degree that an ache remained in the brain of Saxon for a few moments after he had fired.

Usually he missed, but once in four or five times he began to bring down those impossible little morsels of flesh. And every time one of them fell, he thought of Bob Witherell.

He still had a bit of ammunition at the end of the two months, but then, on a day, he sniped a squirrel off a high branch and, immediately afterward, got one of the squirrel companions as it dodged away into the foliage of the pine tree. Two small, fluffy bodies came softly dropping down, rather like flying birds than falling dead things.

And he told himself that he was shooting straight enough to find the heart of Bob Witherell, so he prepared to return to Bluewater.

He made his toilet with as much care as though he were to be presented to a person of importance. As for his ragged clothes, he could only scrub them thoroughly and make sure that they were clean. He could shave, and he did, though he had only a hunting knife and no soap for the job. But he greased his face with squirrel fat after he had brought the knife to the finest sharpness he could achieve, and gradually, not without pain, he got off the growth of beard.

Then he stared at his face in the still water of the pool that he was leaning over. For it was a new face. All across the brow and the eyes the skin was sun blackened. But below, the skin was snow-white. That whiteness crossed his face like a mask, like a disguise. It would be hard to see and remember the features, he thought.

He had scarcely noticed his image in water during those two months. He noticed it now, in detail, and he saw that not months but years seemed to have passed over him, for no small time could, it seemed, have worn away every suggestion of spare flesh from his features. The very shape of his nose seemed different, with a slight out curve at the bridge that he could not remember having seen before.

And the eyes were smaller. They certainly were more veiled by the lids. The mouth, too, had a smaller curve. It was set in a tighter line, and the cheeks had been thumbed out to hollows.

He was rather amazed to find himself respecting that new image in the water, considering it the face of a man

36

worthy of attention, not to be treated lightly, no matter what happened.

After that, he sat back and made the toilet of the revolver, cleaning it with the oil of some rendered fat, working the parts of it with fingers now so familiar with the precious mechanism that he could take it down and assemble it again in pitchy darkness, bit by bit, swiftly.

Finally, he stood up and started the march for Bluewater. He came out on the brow of a mountain, that day, and saw the town lying in the beauty of its valley, beneath, with the sun glinting on its bright windows as on so many little eyes of fire. And John Saxon smiled, quietly, like a messenger who is bringing home news from the king.

CHAPTER VII

WHEN John Saxon went down into the town, he thought of Mary Wilson and wanted to go to her. But he thought of Bob Witherell and therefore went to the Rolling Bones saloon, run by Lefty Malone. Because when Witherell was in the town he usually patronized the Rolling Bones above all other places.

On the way, a dozen small boys saw Saxon without recognizing him. That face, half brown and half white, was so altered that older eyes might very well have been deceived. This troop did not laugh at the stranger. Instead, they followed at his heels or ran before him as though they found in him something as stirring as the strains of a circus band. When they were ahead, they kept turning, gaping, staring up at him and back at him, for it seemed to them that the spirit of the wilderness had descended out of the mountains into the main street of Bluewater. They had never seen even an Indian so completely in rags, but the tatters hardly mattered. The man underneath them was what counted.

When big John Saxon reached the Rolling Bones, he stared at the familiar face of it for a moment, and considered that sign which for a generation had hung in the window: "Wanted: A Bouncer." People laughed when they saw that sign, because the story was that Bluewater was so extremely tough that no bouncer could hold his job for three days. And that was why Lefty Malone, who had named his saloon so that it would almost rhyme with his own name, kept the placard in the window and a standing offer of twenty-five dollars a week plus keep to anyone who wished to try the job.

Men showed up, now and then, who accepted the chance. But none of them lasted long. John Saxon, remembering that he had not a penny in his pocket, that even the salt in his pouch had been used up, that he carried, for a fortune, nothing but an old Colt and a few rounds of ammunition, shouldered through the swinging doors and advanced to the bar.

All was white hot, outside. All was dim coolness within. But that was all right. Hunting through the aisles of the shadowy forest, he had learned to shoot straight when he had nothing but a half-light to aim by. He would shoot straight now, if he could find Bob Witherell seated either in the bar or in one of the back rooms, playing cards.

Bob Witherell was not there. In the back room there were five men in the mysteries of poker. At the bar leaned three more men. One of them was King-snake Charlie, a freighter of a fearsome reputation, a great and hairy-chested man who purposely left his shirt wide open on his breast.

Behind the bar there was, of course, Lefty Malone himself. It was said that Lefty had the strongest pair of legs in the mountains, for they were capable of supporting his great weight for twenty-four hours a day, so long as there was business to be attended to in his saloon. He got his name from the potent effects of his left hook, a punch which he had learned early in life and with which he had rocked many a loud customer to sleep. One of the points of the bouncer joke was that the proprietor of the place was Lefty Malone.

Lefty said to big John Saxon: "Hello, stranger. What'll you have?"

"A job," said Saxon.

"There's only one kind of a job here," said Malone.

"That's the kind I want," answered John Saxon.

"You want the job of bouncer, eh?" said Malone. "How high can you bounce, then? Hey, King-snake, see how high this hombre can bounce, will you?"

The King-snake laughed. He did not waste time but stepped in from his place with the full sway of his body and the full sweep of his arm. He hit John Saxon fairly on the chin and his knuckles tore loose flesh and skin almost to the bone.

The King-snake stepped back a little, willing to allow room for his victim to fall, and then he saw, with bewilderment, that the stranger was not falling. He merely stood there with a quiet smile, regardless of the blood that trickled down his chin. Then he took King-snake Charlie by one arm and turned twice with him in the center of the floor, and threw him through the swing-doors into the street.

The King-snake did not come in again. He rolled in the dust for a moment, clasping his dislocated shoulder. Then he got up and staggered away.

John Saxon was leaning at the bar, letting his blood drip down on the varnish.

"Is that bouncing high enough?" he asked.

"That's high enough," said Lefty Malone. "But this is a lot higher."

And he tried that famous left hook, from the hip, with the whole sway of his force behind it.

That blow should have knocked John Saxon, whatever white iron his jaw was made of, clear across the room. But he pulled his face just out of the path of the punch and, as Lefty pitched forward behind the wallop, sprawling half way across the bar, Saxon grabbed him by the hair of the head and beat his face into the boards.

At the third bump Lefty said, quietly: "That's enough!"

He was released at once. For a moment each man looked at the blood than ran down the face of the other and each felt that, in a sense, he was staring into a mirror, though the huge, squat image of Lefty was hardly a semblance of that of Saxon.

"I'll take a small beer," said Saxon, finally, and Lefty served him.

The two remaining loiterers at the bar did not remain long after this. They went out of the Rolling Bones and told what they had seen. And the town of Bluewater sat up and cocked its ears.

Lefty said: "You got hands, and you're quick with 'em. Maybe you'll last a week, around here, till some of the real men come in. Your room is the first room at the head of the stairs, on the left."

Saxon went up to it. It was small and dark and opened on the rear yard of the saloon-hotel. So Saxon prospected and found a big corner room that overlooked the main street. He took off his rag of a hat and placed it on the center table of that room and came back to Lefty to report.

"I found a better place," he said. "Down at the end of the hall and front."

"Hey!" shouted Lefty. "That's the best room in the house!"

"It's about good enough for me," said Saxon.

And he tasted this moment, and looked into the eye of Lefty.

"All right," said Lefty, finally. "Maybe that's a better room for you to be buried from. A lot of folks may wanta see you laid out before you go under the ground."

He repeated: "Maybe you'll last about a week!"

But Saxon lasted a month.

He had a fight every day, at least once. It was excellent training, he felt. The other men used their fists, but he used his hands. And he had a good pair of hands. He had built up the strength of them pitching hay, working with a rope, digging in his garden, gripping the reins of hard-mouthed mules, or headlong mustangs. And hands are better than fists when a man has an eye sufficiently fast. The eye of John Saxon was very fast from having shot squirrels out of tree tops. It was a little quicker than the snapping lash of a whip.

Hands against fists seems very easy for the fists, but that is because most hands have not the spread of John Saxon's, and because most men do not train their eyes for two mortal months shooting at small, moving things from the hip and saying, each time: "Bob Witherell!"

If you can tell which way a bird is going to fly after it drops off a branch with a flirt of its wings, if you know which way a squirrel is going to duck its bright little head,

40

or when a rabbit is going to make its spyhop as it flees—
if you can tell these things, it becomes a very simple matter
to tell in what direction a fist is going to shoot. Once you
know, it is easier still to dodge the fist and put hands on
the enemy. John Saxon, like most mountain boys, had
done a good deal of wrestling when he was a youngster at
school. He remembered all of that skill, now, and he in-
vented new ways and means. There is nothing better than
an armlock, when all is said and done, if one knows what
to do with it after it is laid on. And John Saxon knew what
to do with it. He used it for throwing men out through
the swing-doors of the Rolling Bones.

But never once in the month did he have to use a gun.
For that, he walked out in the early morning, beyond gunshot sound of the town, and worked two or three intense
hours with his Colt. But there was never a call for the
weapon. Out there in the West a man can get for nothing
all the trouble that he wants, and he can even specify the
brand. Plainly, John Saxon had specified hand work in
his fighting, not guns or knives. The men who heard
about the reputation of big John Saxon came specially to
try their hands against him.

To be sure, there was a Canuck as huge as a bear and
as fast as a cat who forgot himself in the middle of things
and pulled a long Bowie knife. But his arm was broken
before the knife point slid into John Saxon, and that was
too bad.

Then there was a greaser from the distant regions of
the south who had trained for the prize ring, and thought
that a mystery was overwhelming him when he felt the
paralyzing grip of John Saxon's hands. And he forgot himself and pulled a big knife, also. But a sudden jerk snapped
his wrist bone, and he went howling out of the saloon,
looking down at his dangling hand.

John Saxon stuck those two knives in the wall above
the mirror, not that he wanted to boast, but because it
was a special pleasure to him to drift his eyes over the
bright, dangerous gleam of the steel many times each day.

Up from Casa Nuestra came an Italian giant, a sailor
who had been in the Orient and, it was said, had learned
all the mysteries of jujitsu in addition to the dangers of
his own might of hand. He and John Saxon battled for

41

two hours, and the Italian was iron, but Saxon was yielding steel which, in the end, conquered. The next day the Italian came again, and a third day he returned because he would not believe that he had been beaten by a fellow mortal. But on the third day Saxon secured one of his terrible armlocks, and threw the Italian out the swing-doors with terrible force, so that he rolled four times in the dust of the street.

One day Lefty Malone came in from the street to say: "Out there—you're wanted, Johnnie."

Saxon thought it might be a fresh challenge and he went, hungrily, for he had not put his grip on another man for five days. But when he came into the bright of the sun, with a scowl one of whose purposes was to shadow his eyes, he found himself looking down at Mary Wilson.

There were some idlers out there on the veranda, with their chairs tilted back against the wall, but when they saw how Mary stood with her head thrown back, looking up at Saxon, they suddenly rose and went off to one side or the other, because, in spite of certain roughnesses of demeanor, your Westerner is after all a sensitive fellow.

Mary said: "John, you've been almost a month, here, and you've never come to see me."

He raised his hand with a queer, absent-minded gesture, and touched the jagged scar on his cheek, which the knuckles of Witherell had torn in his flesh.

"I sent a word to you by the lawyer," he said. "I told him to say that I wanted to see you as soon as I'd made a fresh start."

She answered: "Will killing Bob Witherell be a fresh start?"

That remark so staggered him that he could not fix words in his mind; and when he rallied himself, he saw that she was going down the street again, slowly, with her head at such an angle that he knew she wanted to be followed and argued with, but he went gloomily back into the saloon.

"Give me a whiskey!" he said to Lefty Malone.

It was the second time, only, that he had taken a drink since he arrived at the saloon, and Lefty poured out enough to brim the little glass. Saxon took it in sips, and the bartender said to him: "How long you gunna make money for me and take wallops for yourself and leave that poor gal in hell, Saxon?"

It *was* money for Malone, since every man who came to Bluewater was certain to walk into the Rolling Bones and spend time looking at big John Saxon and his formidable hands. But Saxon, when he heard those first words of human consideration from Malone, was unable to make an answer for a time. Then he said: "I know my business, Malone. You know yours. And the best way is to never, never mix the two together."

"Look," said Malone, "I've had enough of your lip. You got a good pair of hands, but if you ever take a crack at me, I'm gunna pull a gun and pay some lead into you, you big ham."

John Saxon smiled down at the whiskey as he finished it. There were so many things that Lefty Malone did not quite understand, and chief among them were certain walks into the woods behind Bluewater, in the dawn of the day.

Half a week after that, Bob Witherell came to the town.

CHAPTER VIII

THERE is something glorious about a rascal who is also a man of might and Bob Witherell was glorious, in a way. He was not like his brother, The Solitaire, but he was glorious. He carried in his eye an infinite defiance. He bore his head like a proud king. And he walked with the step of a young stallion who leads a herd.

There was the usual herd behind him when Bob Witherell came into Bluewater. Boots was his chief lieutenant, his buck teeth shining white in his enforced and perpetual smile. They stopped up the street, by chance, at the blacksmith shop of Wiley Ryan, and Wiley told them about John Saxon in the Rolling Bones. Witherell laughed and came straight down the street.

He said to Wiley a thing that was to be rememb

afterward. "A dog that's been licked knows the hand of its master!"

He had five men behind him, as he entered the Rolling Bones, and John Saxon was not in sight.

"I hear you've got a pretty fine bouncer in here," said Bob Witherell. "Let's have a look at him."

"He don't show himself till there's a need of him," answered Malone.

"Is there need for him now?" asked Witherell. And, pulling out a gun, he shattered with three swift shots, three bottles that stood on the shelf behind the bar.

Malone turned and looked at the liquor that dripped rapidly down on the floor, and he heard the last of the broken glass tinkle as it fell. Then he lifted his eye and looked over the six men.

"He'll be in pretty soon, I guess," said Malone.

In fact, at that moment Saxon came in. He spoke words for Malone, but his eye was upon Witherell, gently, steadily, tenderly, taking in all of the man.

"I thought I heard some noise in here," said Saxon.

"Witherell's gone amuck and shot some bottles off the shelf," said Malone. "I wish you'd throw him out—and make him pay for the stuff!"

"How much should he pay?" asked Saxon.

"Ten dollars," said Malone, generous to himself.

The six Witherells laughed heartily; Witherell himself looked on the face of Saxon, pale below and sun-darkened above, as Saxon stood before him, saying: "Witherell, pay off ten dollars and get out of the place."

"Here's five of the ten," said Witherell, and laid the five fingers of the flat of one hand across the cheek of Saxon. "And here's the other five," he added, slapping him on the other side of the face.

Saxon caught the arm that delivered the second blow. It was the left arm, and by the lock that Saxon put on it he was able to whirl Witherell and jam him into a corner against the wall, with a crash. The blow half stunned Witherell. As he stood there, dazed, Saxon pulled from the vest pocket of his man a small wad of greenbacks and threw them onto the bar.

"Take your change out of that, Malone," he said.

He stepped back.

"Throw him out!" commanded Malone, full of rage and of joy. For he was half afraid, when he saw the bewildered faces of the five followers, that there would be no gunplay. And he wanted to smell powder burning.

"I'll throw him out after he's rested himself a little," said Saxon.

Witherell stood out from the corner.

He had not been badly hurt. It was the shock to his pride that chiefly had amazed him.

"Get out of the saloon," said Saxon, "before I have to throw you out."

"My God," said Witherell, "but I'm gunna take you apart! You—you—"

He broke off, unable to find a sufficient word, and he laughed. He looked around at his followers, but they were not laughing. They were looking from him to John Saxon, and their eyes were like the eyes of rats.

Then he understood, suddenly, that they were doubting him. After all, they had seen him picked up and jammed into a corner like a child, but they forgot that he was something more than a wrestler. They forgot that he was an artist of a different sort.

He merely said to Saxon: "Go get a lift to your feet and—dance for me, damn you!"

He was a little leisurely in his draw. Something made a crooked flash from beneath the coat of Saxon and into his hand, and Witherell had a chance to look down the barrel of a Colt that was held just a shade higher than the hip, and a mere half arm's length in front of Saxon. The ease with which that gun was held meant a great deal to Witherell. It meant a lot to the bartender, too, who had crouched behind the bar, with only the brutal fire of his eyes above the edge of it.

"Let me see how high you can dance, Witherell," said Saxon. "Now you're covered, let me see you jump!"

"Damn you!" whispered Witherell.

"I see," said Saxon. "You don't want to dance. You've got the legs for it, but you don't want to dance. Then let me see you pull out your gun, slowly, and hold it down at your side. We'll have an even start in the other sort of a game, Witherell."

Bob Witherell pulled out his Colt, slowly, as ordered,

45

and let it hang down at his side at the full length of his arm, and Saxon devoured him all the while with a little half smile which he could feel on his own lips. Something like love for Witherell came up in him, a passionate satisfaction as he glanced over this splendid sacrifice to death.

Then he lowered his own gun, suddenly, to the length of his arm.

"Somebody say: 'Go!'" said Saxon.

No one spoke. The silence stretched out to a distance. And a strange thing began on the face of Witherell. His eyes started contracting, as though already he were looking through the sights of a rifle. Then they opened again, suddenly and wide.

Off to the side of the room, behind the bar, Lefty Malone began to curse, brokenly. Off to the other side, Boots began to say: "Yes, and I'll count, Witherell. I've always hated your rotten heart. If you finish him, you can take me on afterward. You're half yellow, you dog! I'll give the pair of you the start."

With that he shouted, suddenly: "Go!"

The two explosions followed almost in one. They were not quite in unison, for Saxon raised his gun not so far as Witherell. He did not need to raise it, since a man can point straight no matter in what position his hand may be. He hardly more than jerked up the muzzle of his weapon, and as the slug from Witherell's weapon went past his cheek, he sent his own bullet home between the eyes of the gunman.

Witherell fell right on his face. His gun banged loudly on the floor, then his body struck. His head recoiled and made the third bump. He lay with one foot turned in, crookedly, and that fine, shop-made boot would never be fitted into a saddle again.

Someone whispered: "My God, he's finished. Witherell's gone!"

There was something impossible about it—grand, and strange. And John Saxon wanted to laugh. He kept himself from laughing and merely smiled, but every breath he drew was a long course of pleasure through his entire soul. He was tasting something—victory—conquest—yes, and death itself.

When a man kills another, he ought to feel a frightful

shock, an utter dismay, a sense of guilt and of loss, a sense, too, of the speed with which a mortal can be beckoned away from this world of ours, and of the fragility of our lives. Three months ago, Saxon would have felt all that shock, but in the meantime he had been hardened. It seemed to him, in fact, that it was not a hardened but a new soul that was in him.

Then he remembered, with a frightful lifting of joy and no sense of danger, that there were five others from the gang standing against the wall, entranced.

One of them had said: "My God, he's finished!"

So he turned his head toward them. They were staring. One was agape. Another had reached out his hand in the very gesture with which he protested against the fall of his chief.

"You fellows—" said Saxon. "Which of you comes next?"

They said nothing to him.

"Then—get out," thundered Saxon. And there was a wild, blind rage in him. He wanted to flash more bullets from that gun. What were rabbits and squirrels for targets compared with the magnificence of human flesh? He was shamed and angered by the fear these men showed. They ought to stand up to him. The guns could all start barking at once—and still he would not be afraid.

But the others? Well, they turned and shambled meekly before him, and went out from the saloon. Only one had failed to go, and that was Boots, who stood against the wall with his buck-toothed smile.

"All right," said Boots, when he saw that he was noticed. "I'm so small that I don't matter. Have a drink with me, will you, Saxon?"

"Get out!" cried Saxon.

"Oh, all right," said Boots. "I know my master's voice!"

And he walked out, lightly, with a quick, short step like that of a woman, in his high-heeled, stilting boots.

CHAPTER IX

WHEN the sheriff came, he looked at Saxon and saw the faint smile still on his face.

"You like it, eh?" he asked.

Any nondescript denial would have done very well, but the truth came rushing up on the lips of Saxon and he uttered it.

"Yes," he said. "I like it. I'd like to put you where he is. You're a bully and a thug. I'll put you where he is, if you'll pull a gun."

They used to say about the sheriff that he was the toughest man in Bluewater and that he loved bullets for their own sake—even the ones that had smashed through his flesh. They used to say that, up to the time that fifty curious men had jammed into the Rolling Bones saloon and John Saxon had said to him: "I'll put you where he is, if you'll draw a gun!"

For the bold sheriff, on this occasion, said not a word in answer and did not make a gesture toward his gun, but instead, tried to pretend that he had not heard, and bent over the body of the dead man.

Saxon, still with that faint smile on his lips, went on: "You're a yellow dog, I see. You're such a yellow dog that you're not worth touching Witherell. He's too good for you. Back up—and get out of here!"

The sheriff jerked himself erect and looked around him. He threw a savage glance around at all those faces of men who had voted for him during the last elections. Then, ready to fight, he glanced at Saxon.

His whole face loosened as he saw that deadly little smile. His eyes wandered. He gave his hat a tug, and turned, and walked out of the saloon with his shame upon him.

"Step up, boys, and have a drink," said John Saxon. "I've been having a good time and I want you all to have the same."

He waved toward the bar, where the crumbled greenbacks of Witherell lay on the varnished wood.

"Bob is paying for another round!" he declared. "But I

won't let him. We don't like his money, in here. Step up, boys, and take your liquor."

Very strange to say, they all stepped up. They were silent. They felt a little guilty, till one of the men said: "Well, Witherell had this coming to him, and he had it coming from Saxon. You done a good job, and here's to you, Saxon."

John Saxon stood at the end of the bar with a glass of whiskey grasped in his hand, but he would not raise it to his lips. He could not raise it. He was too frozen and benumbed with joy that would not cease.

After a time he was able to say: "There's Boot Hill outside the town. Will some of you fellows come to the funeral?"

Yes, they would come to the funeral, gladly. Most of the town would come, and most of the town did come, but all the way out behind the cart that carried the body of Bob Witherell, Saxon wished that the dead man were still alive—so that he could have the joy of slaying him once more!

Twenty picks and shovels opened the soil of Boot Hill readily. In an old piece of tarpaulin the body was wrapped. When it was laid in the grave, Saxon got down into the hole and closed the open eyes.

He made a little speech, standing there in the hole in the ground.

"I'm not sorry about this," said John Saxon. "I wish he were alive still, so that I could have the killing of him again. And if any man wants to bring me to account for what I've done, I'm ready for him, night or day. I guess that's all."

No one said a word of answer, because there was no answer to make—except from the mouth of a gun. When he stood up among the crowd, once more, and looked about him, he saw the pale, staring face of Mary Wilson's father, and he smiled a little more broadly.

After all, now that Witherell was dead and underground, with the big, cruel clods falling down on him, Saxon felt more of a kinship, more nearness to the dead man than to any of the others who were standing about inside the unconsecrated cemetery.

There are, he saw, two types of men. One type is that

of the worker. These are the fellows who slave and keep their noses close to the grindstone and think that with the money they make they may be able to buy enough of the joys of life.

There is another and a more glorious type, and it is composed of the men who want freedom and will have it—freedom to fly abroad like the hawks in the sky and, to prey, when they are hungry, on the lesser and the lower birds of the air.

It was perfectly natural, perfectly arranged.

There was one superior joy, however, and already he had tasted of it and wanted more, and this was the delight of preying on the hawks themselves.

Suppose that a man could tower above even the eaters of flesh, the very hawks. He, then, would have the superior joy. To slay the Witherells and to out-face such bullies as the sheriff—that was to find the purest heaven that a man can find on earth!

He walked back to the saloon, when the burial was ended. In his room he rolled his pack, for he had accumulated a few things during his month of service.

Afterward, he went down into the barroom and found there a thick crowd of people who had been at the funeral and of others who had come into town afterward and wanted to have a glimpse of the slayer.

He walked through them. They gave back before him like water before the prow of a ship, and he said, at the bar: "I'll take my pay for the last two weeks, old-timer."

Lefty Malone looked up at him with a start. His voice rose to a high whine.

"Hey, you don't mean that! You don't mean that you'd walk out on me like that, do you? Hey, Johnnie!"

He came running from behind the bar and led Saxon into the back room.

"You can't go," he said, gripping the arm of Saxon, hard. "Look here—you mean money to me. You've meant money ever since you came."

"Then why didn't you raise my pay, you rat?" asked Saxon.

"Because you didn't ask for no increase," said the other. "I'm not tight, only, you didn't ask for no raise. But I'll give you the raise now. I'll give you thirty-five a week.

That's five dollars a day of any man's money—and you got board and the best room in the place."

"Pay me off. I'm going," said the slayer.

He would have laughed. He wanted to laugh when he thought of confining the future majesty of his life, and his glorious freedom, to this saloon and to this small town.

"I'll make it—I'll tell you what I can make it. I'll make it fifty dollars a week, by God! You'll be the best paid man in the town!" said the bartender.

"Pay me now, and stop the chatter," said John Saxon. "You think that I'll stay on here to draw a crowd, the way a dead horse draws the buzzards? No, I'll take my pay, and I'll go."

He took his pay, straightway, and walked out under the open and the stars, with his roll over his shoulder. There was freedom and space and there was only one thing that he wanted to take with him into it. That was Mary Wilson, and he went straight to her house.

CHAPTER X

HE found the Wilson house as black as a mask, the narrow wedge of its roof making a blunt point among the stars. However, he opened the gate and went up the path, careful that his feet should not make a great grinding among the gravel.

Mary always watered the small garden late in the evening and the good smell of the ground drinking was still in the air, and the fragrance of the flowers was there also. In the darkness, this sense of life from the garden soil seemed to fill the air about him. Then he was aware of someone sitting on the front porch. He knew all at once that it was Mary, and that she was waiting for him.

She got up and came down to the lowest step. He put his arms around her.

"You'd better not be kissing me," said Mary Wilson.

"Why'd I better not?" asked John Saxon.

"I don't want you to," she answered. "I don't want you even to touch me."

He dropped his arms from her suddenly.

"You've stopped caring about me?" he asked.

"No, I care just as much about you."

"You've found another kind of a man that you like better?"

"It's not that, so much. It's because you're bad, John. You've turned into a bad man and I ought not to see you."

"You mean, because I fought Witherell? That's not being bad. That's only being a man. I had to fight him. You know that!"

"Why did you have to fight him?" she asked.

"Why? Are you asking me that serious?" he demanded.

"When you bend down your head at me and glare like this," said Mary Wilson, "I'm almost afraid of you myself."

"Are you serious," said he, "that you don't know why I fought Witherell?"

"You think you had reasons," said Mary Wilson.

"I only think that, do I?" said he. "Having the house burned, and the cattle stolen, and being made to dance like a fool in front of the whole town, and after all being beaten up with his fists—when I name those things over, doesn't your blood boil, Mary?"

"No, my blood doesn't boil," said she.

"I'm shamed to hear you say that!" exclaimed Saxon.

"It doesn't boil so much as when I hear you say that you were glad to murder Bob Witherell."

"I didn't say I was glad to murder him."

"Well, but you killed him, didn't you?"

"I did."

"And you're glad that you killed him?"

"Yes."

"Then I said it right before—you're glad that you murdered Bob Witherell."

"There's a difference between a fair fight and a murder," said Saxon, beginning to breathe very hard.

"How could it be a fair fight?" asked the girl. "You're so big and strong and wild that how could it be a fair fight between you and hardly any other man?"

52

"Mary," answered Saxon, "sometimes a woman says things that drive a man pretty near wild."

"It'd be easy to drive you wild now, John," she replied. "You like being wild."

"I'm trying to hold myself in," said Saxon.

He leaned closer over her, and the starlight let him see her face, delicately made. She seemed so childishly small and very young that he could hardly believe in the bigness of the stubborn nature she was showing now. "I'm trying to hold myself in," he went on, "but you know that Witherell was born with a gun in his hand. It was more than fighting fair to stand to him."

"Bob Witherell wasn't walking out two hours every morning," said the girl, "going through the woods and shooting at poor little harmless squirrels and rabbits and letting them lie dead where they fell. Bob Witherell wasn't practicing like that."

There was nothing particularly wrong in those walks of his in the dawn, but her knowledge of them gave him a sense of guilt and angered him greatly.

"Who's been talking to you about such things?" he asked.

"Nobody," she answered. "But I went out and saw for myself."

"You?" he demanded. "Have you been spying on me?"

"Why would you call it spying?" she asked. "You come back to town for a month, and you don't come near me all that time."

"I told you I wouldn't come back to you till I'd made a new start."

"It's been a long month for me," said the girl. "There's a good many nights that I can't sleep. And some of them I used to go out and take a walk in the cool of the morning. That was how I happened to hear the shooting, and then I saw you slipping along through the woods like an Indian looking for scalps. I wish that you'd never made your new start. You were always a clean-handed man, but your hands will never be clean again, John."

"The way a woman talks, it's a hard thing for a man to stand and take it," said Saxon. "Would you want me to go all my life shamed, and people pointing me out for a coward?"

"I'd rather that than to have them point you out for a gunman and a killer," she answered.

"Are you through with me? Is that what you mean?" he asked her.

"No, but I've got to start waiting again. I'll never be through with you."

He was so touched by this, and so troubled, also, that he threw out his arms around her.

"Will you kiss me, Mary?" he asked.

"If you want me to—yes," said she.

"Only if it makes you happy, too," said Saxon, gloomily.

"Why would it make me happy?" she demanded. "You've been beating and breaking men with your hands. You've killed a man today!"

His arms dropped away from her again.

"Well," he said, "I'll be going along."

She began to cry, softly. And again his big hands went out and hovered about her.

"Don't touch me," she whispered. "I'd rather be unhappy than have you touch me."

"Mary," he asked, "do you love me a little, still?"

"Ay. I'll always love you," said the girl. "You know that. As long as I live. But I've wanted to be proud of you. I'll never marry a man that I'm not proud of."

"You'll never marry me because I killed Bob Witherell?" he asked.

"Not till something has made you clean again," she answered.

"What would that something be?"

"I don't know. The world does things to people. Maybe it'll do good things to you. I don't know a great deal, John."

"Well, I'd better be going," said Saxon.

She was still crying, her breathing making small, hissing sounds. Women cry as easily as they breathe, he thought.

She said nothing to stop him.

"Good-by," said Saxon.

He got to the garden gate, slowly. He still expected a small rush of footsteps and her voice, calling him in a whisper; but nothing happened, and he went, head down, along the street.

54

CHAPTER XI

WHEN Saxon was a block from the Wilson house, the stiffness went out of his lips, though the ache was still in his heart. He paused and looked about him. The weight of the roll on his back was a rather meaningless thing, now. He had intended to see Mary, bid her a tender farewell, and then advance into the world to seek a bigger fortune than that which had been stolen from him. It would not take long, he had felt. This new strength in his hands promised him a quick success, to say nothing of the new strength of his will. If he could be shown a job, no matter how big—well, then he could do it!

But after leaving the girl, unhappily, that sense of surety was gone from him. The heavy Colt—was not that the instrument that had put a distance between him and Mary?

He determined, suddenly, that he would return the gun to the hands that had given it to him. One light shone at him from the house of Daniel Finlay, further down the street, and it was like a guiding signal to him. Somehow he felt that he would find profound understanding in the house of the lawyer.

He went to it at once, as to a harborage. There was no nonsense of a garden in front of it. There was simply a hitching rack at which many a desperate man had tethered his mustang before he climbed up the front steps to ask the advice of the man of the law. The house itself was a mere whitewashed shanty in which there were only two rooms, stifling hot in summer and bitter cold in winter.

Big John Saxon tapped at the front door and heard, instantly, the dry, harsh voice of the lawyer bidding him enter. So he pushed the door open and stepped into the office-livingroom-library. The kitchen-bedroom-diningroom was at the rear. This front room was thickly lined, on all sides, with books of the law, most of them old, most of them in buckram bindings. The desk of Daniel Finlay stood in a corner, crosswise, and on it was a reading lamp with a big circular burner, and behind the burner sat

Finlay with the light strongly on his face, and making his eyes shimmer with the powerful radiance.

When he saw Saxon, he stood up from his chair and came forward. He made a gesture with his handless right arm, as though he had forgotten. Then, hastily, he put forward his left hand and gripped the right hand of Saxon, warmly. In spite of the heat of the evening and the closeness of the room, the skin of that lawyer's hand was dry and cold.

He looked on Saxon with an almost affectionate glance, but what pleased him was the wonderfully harrowing effect of the past three months. They seemed to have been more than three years, and three strenuous years, at that. John Saxon looked actually bigger, but much less soft. The worthless part of the ore had been heated and beaten out of him; only the iron remained. It was strong iron, and one day it might become steel.

Daniel Finlay, who rightly took to himself a major portion of credit for the change, saw at a glance that he now had at hand a magnificent tool, if only he could keep it in his grasp and direct the cutting edge of it.

Saxon said: "I've brought back the gun you loaned to me, Mr. Finlay. Here it is."

He laid it on the edge of the desk.

Finlay picked it up, and cleared his throat.

"I gave this gun," he said, "to a big, soft-hearted boy, a lad incapable of realizing how much evil there was in the world, how much cruelty, how much danger. It is brought back to me by a man of resolution and of courage —the sort of man that an entire crowd shrinks back from, or follows when he decides to lead. I gave a gun," went on Finlay, "to a child who did not know how to use it. Now it is offered back to me by a man who is the master of it. No, Saxon—the gun is no longer mine. It is yours!"

Saxon shook his head.

"It's cost me my girl. I don't want it," he replied.

Finlay wanted to laugh aloud. It was all he could do to keep some of his triumph from glistening in his eyes, at least. This was his handiwork, and he rejoiced. He, with his cunning mind, had already caused the death of Bob Witherell. He had caused the girl and Saxon to diverge

56

from one another. Perhaps he would be able to do much, much more.

"She sends you away?" asked Finlay.

"Yes," said Saxon. "There's blood on my hands, she says."

"There is," said the lawyer, "blood that has washed them clean, blood shed in the service of society."

"I wasn't serving society. I was serving myself," answered Saxon, bluntly. "I hated Witherell and I wanted to get back at him."

"Tell me, then. Were you sorry when you saw him drop dead?"

"No," said Saxon, slowly. "I wasn't sorry. I was glad. I was so glad that I wanted to laugh. It wasn't any shock to me to see him curl up. I liked it."

"The warrior strain in a man," said the lawyer, fiercely, "is the finest strain of all. You have it in you, Saxon. I saw it long ago. That was why I gave you the gun. Do you think that I would have given you the gun if I had not known that you would learn how to use it? I saw that you had in you the sort of metal from which a sword could be forged. And the sword has been made. There is a new gleam in your eyes, Saxon. Whatever you were before, you have become a king of men, now!"

Saxon stared. "I'm a hobo out of a job," he answered. "That's a lot closer to the truth."

"Because a pretty-faced little girl has spoken a few sharp words to you, do you mean to tell me that you are really dispirited?" demanded Daniel Finlay. "No, no! You know that, as you grow greater and greater, as a reputation surrounds you, she will come back to your hand at the first gesture."

"She's not that kind," said Saxon. "You don't know her. She looks small and pretty, but she's as hard as nails! And she's as wise as an old man."

"Was I wrong before, when I talked to you?" asked Finlay.

"No," admitted Saxon.

"Neither am I wrong now. The truth has a singular taste that cannot be mistaken; that is the taste which I find now! I know, John Saxon, that you are meant to do great things—passing beyond and above the reach of a woman's comprehension—lifting you into a nobler and a wider future; the fire is in you—the fire of genius which dissolves the barriers that close in ordinary men."

Saxon listened, bewildered.

That the lawyer was wise, he knew. That he was a good man, he took the common word of Bluewater. That he was a profound hypocrite, John Saxon had no means of knowing. And a shudder of delight and of ambition passed through the soul of Saxon. Perhaps, after all, there was in him a thing that set him apart from other men. Now and again, as he looked back upon his life, he even felt that already he had been aware of it. And the lawyer, of course, had seen all of this clearly!

What was it, in fact, that he was seeing?

"Mr. Finlay," said Saxon, very troubled, "you're an older man than I am, and you know a lot better than I do. What is it that you think I ought to do?"

"Go out into the world with that gun as with a sword. Right wrongs, correct evils. And measure yourself against the thugs and the outlaws and the evil-doers!"

The lawyer allowed a somewhat Biblical strain to come into his speech. His conviction grew; he felt that he was taking in his hand a torch that might kindle a very great blaze, indeed.

"Take from the world," said the lawyer, "what the world has taken from you! Doesn't that impulse come up in you?"

"Ay," said Saxon, "it certainly does. But is it right?"

"How can it be wrong?" asked the lawyer. "It is instinct! An eye for an eye and a tooth for a tooth!"

"But I thought that was wrong," said Saxon, simply.

"Wrong for kindergarten milksops!" exclaimed the lawyer, savagely. "There is only one true law, above printing presses—what a man feels in his heart, he must do!"

"What you say—it seems to set a man free!" said Saxon, honestly. He felt, in fact, a foretaste of liberation.

"When you had been wronged, you went to the sheriff, did you not?"

"Yes."

"And he laughed at you?"

"Well, worse than that!"

58

"And then you went to the banker. He did not laugh in your face. No, but he laughed behind your back."

"Did he?" asked Saxon, gloomily.

"He did! He was willing to use you so long as he could get out of you the regular payment of plenty of interest—so long as you had valuable securities. The moment they were gone, what did John Saxon, the man, mean to him? Nothing!"

"No," agreed Saxon. "I suppose I meant nothing. I could see that I meant nothing to him."

"Is that right?" demanded the lawyer. "Is a man nothing except a title deed to so much property? No, no, we are something more. Even Daniel Finlay, a cripple, a poor man, a despised member of society—even Daniel Finlay feels that he is worth something more than so many dollars —he believes, he hopes, he prays that he may be something more!"

"You are!" exclaimed Saxon, greatly moved as he saw the handless gesture which accompanied the words. "You're about the best man and the best brain in the town, Mr. Finlay. We all know that! *I* know it, for one!"

"If you have the least trust in me, believe that I am advising you for your own good," said the lawyer. And he set his teeth to keep back the smile of triumph.

"I believe it," said Saxon.

"Then go out and spread your elbows at the board. The world owes you a debt. Collect it like a man!"

"Yes," said Saxon, faintly.

"God has made you strong. Use your strength. When Witherell fell before you, a taste of joy went through your entire soul. Well—taste that joy again!"

"Mr. Finlay," said Saxon, very slowly, "I'm trying to follow you. But—one woman already says that I've blood on my hands."

"The blabbling of a silly girl!" said the lawyer. "And if the law should ever touch you—you have *me*. I'll be your shield, my friend!"

He said it so warmly that tears suddenly stung the eyes of Saxon.

"There's nothing for you to gain in all this," said Saxon. "Somehow, I feel as though I ought to follow on,

59

blindly. There would be a lot of happiness in being free—
if it's honest to be free. To trust to what a man's heart
says to him—that would be happiness!"

"Then trust to your heart!" said the lawyer. "Besides,
how long may the happy road be for you? Do you stop to
think of that? Do you stop to think of the danger that
lies ahead?"

"What danger?" asked Saxon.

"The Solitaire!" exclaimed the lawyer.

"Ay! I'd forgotten about him. He'll come as soon as he
knows that Bob is dead!"

"He'll come and his men with him. Leave Bluewater,
my friend!"

"You mean to run away from The Solitaire?"

"Until you're stronger. Bob Witherell went down before
you, but The Solitaire is a stronger man than his brother."

"That's true, of course."

"Go out into the world. I can tell you the path to follow.
Grow stronger. Battle is to be your element. Acquaint
yourself with it. Breathe the atmosphere of danger."

Saxon stood silent.

"Gather around you," said the lawyer, "men who will
look up to you as their natural leader. Men who will
march for you and ward for you. Men who will do your
bidding, freely, because they recognize in you a superior
nature."

"How would I find 'em?" asked Saxon, staring.

"I'll find you the nucleus of the crew," said the lawyer.
"Go out of this town. Take the southwest trail. When you
come to the first forking, turn to the right. You'll come,
presently, to a small lean-to in the woods. In that shack
you'll find a small man with a big nature. You know him.
He has prominent front teeth that make him seem to smile
continually. His nickname is Boots. Only I and a few
others know his real name. Go to him. By night or by day,
he will be glad to see you. Talk to him. He will have something to say."

"I'll go to him," said Saxon. "It seems queer but—
well, I'll go."

"Take this with you," said the lawyer, "and remember
that when you are in any trouble, I am your friend. Is
that clear?"

"Remember it? How could I forget it?" said Saxon, taking the revolver again. "You're the best friend that I've ever had in the world."

Finlay followed him to the front door. He laid his hand on the thick, muscular shoulder of John Saxon and said, quietly: "I would offer you some money to give you a start, but I know that a hungry wolf is the best hunter. Therefore I say: 'Go out and make your way in the world!' Good-by, John Saxon, for a little time!"

So John Saxon went down the steps to the street. There he turned, and made out, dimly, the gesture of Finlay, waving farewell.

As for Finlay himself, he turned back into his room with the smile of a happy devil on his lips and in his eyes. And, for a moment, his exultation was so strong that he was only able to walk up and down, up and down, formulating in his mind the next step which he would take forward in his scheme of things.

Then he forced himself to sit down at his desk, and began to write with a savage speed, the pen point digging deep into the paper, now and then, and making the ink splutter. It was the formless, clumsy writing of a child, because his left hand had never learned thoroughly how to master the fine work of writing.

"Dear Witherell," he wrote, "I hope this letter gets to you quickly. I'll send it off by a special messenger at once. The news I can give you is worth your having.

"You know, by this time, that your brother was murdered by John Saxon in the Rolling Bones saloon, while that precious scoundrel of a Boots stood by, without lifting a hand, and let him go down.

"I warned Bob many times against Boots. I told him that a man who hated The Solitaire must hate The Solitaire's brother, also. I told him that Boots was only attached to him in the hope of seeing him go down in a fight, before long.

"Now comes the proof—and this will be very interesting to you. I have seen John Saxon. He came to my house, and wanted to get my advice, because he was afraid that there might be an arrest following the murder of Bob Witherell. He knows that he took advantage

61

of Bob, and he's afraid that the law might work on him.

"I told him, frankly, that I would not stir a hand to help him. I lost my temper and damned him for a wretched, blood-sucking scoundrel. And he had the effrontery to stand there and laugh at me!

"Ah, Witherell, in all my life as a cripple I was never so moved. I never so wished for the equipment of a normal man. I gripped a paper knife, like a fool, and was ready to jump at his throat. But he saw what I intended, and simply laughed all the more. He twisted the knife out of my weak hand and threw it on the floor.

"Then he told me what he was a fool to confess. He told me that he had joined forces with Boots. That with Boots and the men of Boots he would be able to laugh at the law, after all, and that he really did not need to have my advice and help as a lawyer. He told me that he had killed one half of the Witherell name and that he would never rest until he had taken The Solitaire out of the way, either by a bullet through the back or poison in his coffee.

"I stood there and listened. I was amazed that he had forgotten himself so much as to confess his villainy to me.

"As soon as he left, I sat down to write this letter.

"Witherell, be careful. Saxon is a dangerous man. He has had a taste of blood, and he relished it! He will want more of it, and the next victim in order must be The Solitaire.

"If you wonder why I am taking this trouble to warn you, remember that I was the friend of Bob. Poor Bob is gone. They buried him like a dog in a shallow grave in Boot Hill. I protested, but the brutes waved me aside. Poor Bob is gone, and I pass on to you my good will and my affection. Let me know how I can serve you.

"Ever faithfully yours,

"DANIEL FINLAY."

CHAPTER XII

JOHN SAXON went out of Bluewater down the southeast trail. He turned at the forking as Daniel Finlay had directed him to do, and he came, in time, upon a little shanty of a lean-to which was laid away among the woods.

There was little light. There were stars in a clear sky and a half a moon throwing silver from somewhere, but not much of the bright showering came through the tall shadows of the trees. However, the keen eyes of John Saxon found the shanty, as Daniel Finlay knew that he would do. He stopped there and went up to the door.

A great hound, whose shagginess appeared even by that light, came rushing out of obscurity and recoiled when it saw the size of the man and his steadfastness.

He tapped at the door, and the hound sat down to watch.

After a long moment, he was aware that a human presence had joined him. No one had appeared at the door, but human eyes were watching big John Saxon. He looked askance, and, opposite the dog, he saw a man at the farther corner of the hut facing him, with a glimmering long rifle in his hands.

"Well," said Saxon, "this is sort of like waking up the devil. I'm glad you didn't appear out of the ground at my back, Boots."

The smaller man answered: "Who sent you here, and who in hell are you?"

"Put down your gun, and I'll show you," said Saxon.

"I'd rather have you tell me," said Boots.

"I'm John Saxon, if that means anything to you."

"Ah, and are you Saxon? I was having a dream about you just as you rapped at the door."

"What sort of a dream?"

"I dreamed I was in hell and you told me to get up and turn the spit."

"That's a good dream if you're hungry."

"Ay, or cold," said Boots.

"Which were you?"

"I was cold," said Boots.

He laughed a little.

Then Saxon said: "Well, Boots, I was sent up here to see you by a wise man."

"There are a lot that talk and there are damned few that are wise," said Boots.

"This one is wise."

"You tell me his name, and then I'll tell you."

"His name is Daniel Finlay."

"Hello!" said Boots. "Finlay, eh?"

"Ay, he sent me."

"Well, Finlay never does a thing without having a reason for it. What did he say about me?"

"He didn't say much. He sent me to you. So I came."

"You think he's a right man or a wise man?" asked Boots.

And Saxon could see, or thought that he could see, the faint and glimmering white of Boots' grin, even through the shadow.

"He's a right man," said big John Saxon. "There's not much that I know in the world, but I know that Daniel Finlay is an honest man!"

"Ah, and you know that, do you?" said Boots.

"Don't sneer at me," said John Saxon.

"No?" sneered Boots.

Saxon took a step toward him; the rifle rose to a level.

"I won't have you sneer at me!" said Saxon, and took a longer step toward the rifle. He grabbed the muzzle of it in his fist. And Boots simply laughed as the gun was pushed away from the direction of his heart.

"That's all right," he said.

"Why shouldn't I take and twist the head off your shoulders?" asked Saxon.

"Because you're too big to take on a man of my size," said Boots.

"All right," said Saxon, "and who told you that about me?"

"Oh, I've got a pair of eyes," answered Boots. "Here, you can have the gun if you want it."

"I don't understand it," said Saxon, "and I don't understand you."

"So long as I understand *you,*" said Boots, "that's all right."

"You're a queer fellow," said Saxon.

"Yeah, but I eat three squares a day and never pay for 'em at the end of the month."

"I don't want to talk like this any more," said Saxon. "It's a pretty smart way of talking, maybe, but I don't like it."

"We'll talk any way you like," said Boots. "We've got to talk that way, because you've got my rifle, now."

"There's still a revolver somewhere on you," said Saxon.

"Is there?" answered Boots, letting his good humor appear in a chuckle. "That's a thing that you are not supposed to know. You're a lot brighter than I thought you were."

At that, John Saxon made a considerable pause. He saw that he was being mocked, and he could not quite understand it, because Boots knew something about what he could do with his hands, and yet Boots was capable of standing there within the grip of his hand and chuckling in his face.

Saxon made a quick move and caught Boots by the scuff of the neck.

"I've got a mind," he said hoarsely, "to take and—"

As his grip fastened, he shook Boots. "I've got a mind to—"

He finished in a savage rage.

Boots merely said: "Sure you could do anything you want, but you won't."

"Why won't I?" demanded Saxon.

"Oh, you're too big and too much of a damned fool," said Boots. "But don't you be afraid. I'm not going to tell anybody."

Saxon was silent.

Boots added: "And Daniel Finlay won't say anything, either."

"Then he thinks that I'm a fool, too?"

"He's as wise as I am, anyway," said Boots.

"All right," said Saxon. "I don't know why I don't break your back, but I'm not doing it."

"Of course you're not," said Boots. "You know that I'm the kind of medicine that you can use."

"How can I use you?" asked Saxon.

"Come along! Finlay told you that!"

"No, he didn't tell me."

"The hell he didn't! You expect me to believe that?"

"It's true. Besides, I'm pretty well fed up with you and the funny way you talk, Boots."

"I'm damned near fed up with you, hombre," answered Boots. "And still I've got to keep on talking so long as you have me by the back of the neck, I suppose."

"You're laughing at me," said John Saxon. "Let's say that I'm not bright. Anyway, I've got a hold on you. Well, I give up the hold. And so—so long, Boots. I'm sorry that I came here and waked you up, this way."

He dropped his hand from the neck of Boots, who merely chuckled and said:

"That's the first time that I ever talked my way out of hellfire!"

"I'm tired of your chatter," said big John Saxon.

"Wait a minute," called Boots.

"Well?"

"How did you keep that dog from jumping at your throat?"

"I didn't run—and that's why the dog stood still."

"The same way with me," answered Boots. "I didn't run, and that's why you stood still. Now, let's start and talk sense, Saxon. You mind?"

"Hell, I'm through with you and any sense that you can talk."

"If that's straight, then just take a horse. It's easier riding away from me than it is walking away from me."

"Where'll I find a horse and a saddle and a bridle."

"Back there in the shed."

Saxon could hear the rustling of the hay as the horses ate.

"Which one shall I take?" he asked, sneering, ready to smile in his turn at some sort of a trick.

"Take the best one, because you're the biggest weight." said Boots, laughing again.

Saxon went into the shed. There might be a joke behind all of this, but also there seemed to be a horse, and he was mortally weary of walking.

So he went into the shed and saw by the slant of the moonlight three fine horses and a glorious gray mare

66

seventeen hands tall and made like a statue. He put his hands on her, and she turned her head kindly and shone her gentle eyes at him.

He saddled and bridled her in a wonder of delight.

Then he led the great mare out and mounted her.

"Her name is Mary," said Boots, and laughed in his strange way.

Big John Saxon rode out of view among the trees. There was not even a call after him. He turned the mare suddenly and came back to Boots. There he dismounted.

"All right, damn you," said Saxon. "I won't ride away till we've talked."

"I knew you wouldn't," answered Boots.

CHAPTER XIII

In that outer world of crime where the two Witherells moved, it was plain that men had mysterious impulses, strange and indecipherable to big John Saxon. He dismounted, saying:

"You would have let me ride away on that gray mare —why? She's worth a lot of money."

"You wouldn't have ridden her far," said Boots. "By the time you got into the throat of the pass, yonder, with the moon shining on you, you would have bumped into that big nigger, Arthur William Creston. You know him?"

"No."

"Well, he wouldn't introduce himself except with a rifle bullet—and he can certainly use a rifle. He's right fond of that big mare. Ever since he stole her, he thinks that she belongs to him."

"You mean," exclaimed Saxon, "that you would have let me ride into a murder?"

"Why not?" asked Boots. "If you were hound enough to take the horse and ride away, you were hound enough to deserve a bullet through the brain, the way I see it."

The coolness of this man staggered Saxon again. There seemed no way of getting behind him.

"All right," said Saxon. "Here's the mare back—and good-by to you."

"So long," said Boots. "I'm almost sorry to see you go, but you won't go far."

"Won't I? And why not?"

"Because you'll keep thinking and thinking about me, and pretty soon you'll come back."

"You talk like a book," said Saxon, angrily.

"I see that we could use each other. That's why," said Boots.

"How could I use you?" asked Saxon.

"How could a lion use a fox?" answered Boots.

"And what good would I be to you?" demanded Saxon.

"I want to see the two Witherells dead. You've fixed up one-half of them and now maybe you've got one chance in ten to get The Solitaire."

"You hate the Witherells? Then what kind of a hound are you for riding with them!"

"I never rode with The Solitaire since he did me dirt. He knows that I'd skin him if I could. Bob knew I hated The Solitaire, but he thought I loved *him*. The fool! I was glad when I heard your bullet sock into his skull. He wasn't the man I hoped he'd be!"

"How big a man did you hope he'd be?" asked Saxon.

"Big enough to stand up to The Solitaire, maybe! I hoped that they'd murder each other, one day, and me to stand and look on at the killings!"

He laughed as he said it, and Saxon peered through the dim light beneath the trees at that queer burst of merriment.

"Two brothers?" said Saxon. "You thought that two *brothers* would fight each other?"

"I thought so, and I wasn't a fool. Bob was jealous of The Solitaire. He was apt to start wrangling any time, and The Solitaire will catch fire at a word, any time. He'll shoot as quick as he'll wink. So I hoped, for a time. But after a while I began to see that Bob would never have the nerve to face The Solitaire. Then you came along and settled the question for me. What Bob wouldn't do, maybe you'll wangle for me. That's why I'm apt to turn myself into a slave and do what you tell me to do."

"Boots," said Saxon, "you're the queerest fellow that I ever talked to."

"You'll find me the most useful fellow you ever talked to," said Boots.

"Why do you hate The Solitaire so much?"

"Oh, the same old story. You wouldn't be interested. Just a little matter of a girl. You take a little buck-toothed runt like me, and it's hard to find a girl who'll look at me twice. But I found one. Nice girl. Quiet. She didn't know much about men. Marriage was my idea, and maybe a change all around in my way of living. But The Solitaire saw her. She wasn't very much. She wasn't any beauty. But he felt like wasting a little time, so he took her."

"And kept her?" asked Saxon.

"No, no. He never keeps anything. He likes a change. He took her and he dropped her. I'll tell you what sort of a low hound I am. I would have picked her up even after that; but she wouldn't have me. After she'd known a real man, she didn't have any use for me. And that made me a little sour on The Solitaire."

He laughed again, and this time the sound curdled the blood of Saxon.

"I went to The Solitaire and stood up to him," said Boots. "I thought that I had enough nerve to face any man in the world. But—I didn't! That's all. I wound up by taking water like a Chinaman. And *that* made me a little sour on The Solitaire. You see? Well, you'd better come into the shack and we'll talk things over—that is, if you want me to help."

Saxon leaned his hand against the firm shoulder of the gray mare. He tried to think, but his mind kept whirling. One thing alone remained clear—that he and Boots had a common bond, and that was their mutual enemy, The Solitaire.

Other than that, he knew that Boots was a criminal, worthy of being outlawed, a bloodless and a cruel devil, no doubt. Still, perhaps the man would be useful, and in many ways.

All his instincts told him that it was far best for him to avoid such company as that of Boots and his peers. But he could not help but remember, as a deciding voice in determining his attitude, that Daniel Finlay had specially sent him out here to talk with this very man.

And was not Finlay almost more than a brother to him? Yes, and almost more than a father, also. That was why he said:

"All right. Thanks—I'll stay."

"Good man," said Boots. "Go in and light the lantern. I'll put up the mare."

"That ought to be my job," protested big John Saxon.

"No," said Boots. "You're the boss and I'm the hired man."

"How much do I pay you?" laughed Saxon.

"The blood of The Solitaire," said Boots. "I'm accepting the promise of payment, d'you see?"

"All right," answered Saxon. "I'll make the promise to pay."

He said the thing lightly, but as he went into the house his own words followed him and grew great in his mind. He had promised to kill another man, and that man was The Solitaire!

Inside the door of the shack, he found the lantern and lighted it. The place was a deserted wreck but there were a couple of bunks built against the wall, the blankets of Boots on one of them. He put down his own roll on the other bunk, and Boots came in to ask if he was hungry.

Hungry? He was a wolf!

Boots, in a moment, was working at the rusted ruin of a stove which stood in a corner. He soon had a fire blazing with the rotten boards of the floor; which he ripped up and broke in his hands. And on the stove he assembled frying bacon, and simmering coffee, and a shallow pan of frying bread, also.

He ate not a bite of this food, but served it to John Saxon like a servant to a master. And Saxon, rather embarrassed, accepted this service because he did not know how to refuse it. Besides, even after he had learned exactly why Boots would work for him in this manner, he could not help feeling a bit of gratification.

He ate very heartily and then he lay back in the bunk and smoked a cigarette and felt that he had come to the close of the longest day in his life—a day so huge and embracing that it seemed to him it outweighed all of his years which had gone before it.

Boots put the lantern out, but not till he had asked: "Want anything, Chief?"

"No, I don't want anything, thanks. I only want to know what happened when you faced The Solitaire."

"The same thing happened to me that happens to every man. When I saw him laughing and talking at a distance, I thought that my nerves would be all right. But when I got up close and damned him and got ready to make a pass for my gun, the old yellow hellfire began to burn in his eyes and turned me into a cinder. I was scared. The courage ran out of me. I started to pull my gun, but it wouldn't come clear. I was staring so hard at him that it makes my eyes ache to remember. And there were fifty men looking on, too, seeing me shamed. And The Solitaire, he simply walked up to me and jerked the gun out of my hand, and slapped my face, and marched me right about face out of the saloon. And a couple of bums got hold of me at the door and threw me out into the street. I didn't mind that part of it. I hardly even knew what was happening to me. What counted was the part when I went to pieces in front of his eyes—and he stood there and sneered, and laughed at me. He seemed to know what he was doing to me, and he seemed to wait till I got well paralyzed. I wasn't ashamed, then. I was only ashamed afterward, thinking about it. But just then—well, it was the way a bird must feel when a snake is eating it with its eyes."

Saxon lay still for a long time, thinking over that story. Before he spoke again, he heard a faint snoring that told him his companion was asleep. But, after all, he had not many questions to ask. It seemed to him the most horrible thing that he had ever heard. And when at last he fell asleep, it was to dream all night that out of a crowd of faces, hypnotic eyes had found him and taken possession of him, body and soul.

CHAPTER XIV

WHEN Saxon wakened in the morning, Boots was already outside the shack. Saxon went into the open in his bare feet, guided by the sound of running water that took him through the woods to a little stream that cascaded with a musical plumping sound into a small pool in whose black appeared one rosy finger of the reflected dawn. Saxon had a swim and a shave and came back dressed to find that Boots was no longer alone at the shack. Instead, there was with him, helping at the cookery of breakfast, a vast black mountain of a Negro whose head was dwarfed by the spread of his shoulders. All the features of his face were small, except the mouth, and the huge furrows of his grin made everything disappear except his smile.

Boots said: "This is Arthur William Creston, Chief. I'll tell you what Arthur William can do. He knows how to make 'soup' and take care of it. He can help you run a soft-soap mold around the door of a safe. And when the trouble starts, he won't run away. He's fair with a revolver, good with a rifle when he has plenty of time, and mighty useful in any sort of a crowd. Do you want him?"

The smile of Arthur William Creston grew a little dim as he waited in some tension for the answer, and John Saxon forced himself to look over the candidate for crime with a serious eye.

Want him? Of course he wanted those Herculean shoulders so long as there was such an enemy as The Solitaire in view, but it was only after that moment of delay that he said: "Why, I trust your judgment, Boots. And Arthur looks all right to me." He held out his hand. "If you want to join us," said he, "we're glad to have you."

For answer, the vast grip of Creston almost crushed the hand bones of John Saxon.

"We don't need to be afraid no more," said the Negro. "The three of us, we'd be enough for pretty nigh anything, I reckon!"

Boots merely said: "Don't start telling the Chief his own business."

"No, sir. Excuse me, boss," said Arthur William.

After this, they finished their breakfast, and Boots told the Negro to saddle three horses. Creston went out, singing cheerfully, to execute the order, and that gave Saxon a chance to say: "You're crowding me a little toward something, Boots. What's the direction you want to head for?"

"We need some money, before long," said Boots. "I've got a few hundred. That's all. When it's gone, we'll need a lot of money. And here's the lay of the land."

He took out a letter, unfolded it, and began to work rapidly with his pencil on the blank back of the sheet.

"Here's the Bluewater Mountains," he said as he worked. "Here's the town of Bluewater. Here's Fairfax down in this corner, and Rusty Gulch over here. Banks in all three of them. Here's the railroad running over here, with money shipments on the rails all the time. Here's the Fairfax-Bluewater stage, with a lot of gold in every boot. There are plenty of herds of cattle that we can pick on, too. It's a land of plenty, Chief. But it's a land of trouble, too."

"Go on," said Saxon. "I don't think I'll be a bank robber or a rustler, just yet. Pick out some of the troubles."

"You know the Stillman district?"

"I've never been there."

"Sheriff Cochrane is down there with a big posse, hunting for The Solitaire. But The Solitaire isn't in the Stillman district. He shifted away from there and went up to the headwaters of Bluewater Creek. He's somewhere over there, traveling slow and keeping his head down, because he's loaded down with piles of hard cash that he got in the Stillman raid, and other places. He's hit three times in three weeks, you know. And every time, he's drawn blood! There's nobody like him when it comes to making a fast campaign."

The scalp of John Saxon prickled as he stared at the cross which Boots had last made on the map.

But the idea that had formed in his throat had to come out.

"There's our trouble and there's our money waiting for us in the same spot," he said.

"Meaning?" asked Boots.

73

"The Solitaire is the man you want to get. He's the man I have to get, too, before he gets me. And when we get The Solitaire, we get plenty of cash, too. Does that sound good to you?"

Boots merely stared.

"You mean it," he muttered finally. "You want to tackle that gang barehanded?"

"Yes," said Saxon. "The best way is to get the hard work done early in the week. How many men are with The Solitaire, do you think?"

"He had seven with him," said Boots. "Jack Ransom was killed in Willett's Crossing. Pudge Craven died in the Stillman raid. And Barry died in the woods, later on. That makes four with The Solitaire. And they're four hard ones. First there's—"

"Never mind the names," answered Saxon. "Four and one makes five. Can you pick up three more to go with us? You and I make two. We want the same number to tackle that crowd."

"The same number? We need three times more than they have!"

"Ay, for murder!" said Saxon. "But what we want is the fight."

There was a long silence, after this. Finally Boots lifted his eyes, slowly.

"Partner," he said, "you know The Solitaire, but you don't know him the way I know him!"

"It has to be my way," said Saxon. "If the boys are with me, they have to follow me—and that counts you in with the rest. We don't take odds."

"If that's the way of it," answered Boots, his lips withering back grotesquely over his shining teeth, "why don't you count in Arthur William as our third man?"

"Because Negroes don't fight white men. Not while I'm in the crowd," said Saxon.

Boots smiled, suddenly.

"You're queer," he said, "but you may be right. Only —you've gotta remember one thing."

"Fire away," said Saxon.

"Back there in the Rolling Bones, when you stood up to Bob Witherell, you liked it, eh?"

"Yes, I liked it," admitted Saxon.

74

"Having the life of a man inside the crook of your finger—and your life inside of his—and the best man wins! That was pretty good to you, wasn't it?"

"Yes, that was pretty good."

"Well, the next brawl won't be like that. None of this standing up and being honest and polite. It's going to be dog eat dog, and that's all there will be to it. They'll shoot you from behind if they get a chance. There won't be any flags flying and there won't be any bands playing, either."

"I understand," said Saxon. "But the way I say is the way it has to be—if you want me in. Five of them and five of us. Can you find three more men willing to go with us?"

Boots considered. At last he said: "Ay, three more crazy men—like you! I can find 'em and have 'em here in two days. Will you wait here with Creston?"

"I'll wait here," said Saxon.

And, there he waited, not two days but three, while Arthur William Creston cooked venison and mountain grouse and rabbits. The Negro shot the game that he cooked; except the rabbits and the squirrels which Saxon knocked over with his revolver when he walked out through the trees for three or four hours every day. He no longer said to himself: "Bob Witherell!" every time he fired, but instead: "The Solitaire!"

But the same savagery never came storming up from his heart as he spoke that name. He never had been injured directly by The Solitaire. He had no cause for hate. He was simply preparing himself, from a distance, for the battle which must inevitably occur between him and the outlaw. And always there was lodged back in his heart the memory of the tension of that instant in the Rolling Bones when he had faced Bob Witherell and taken the man's life in his hand, and destroyed it.

Other men could live for other purposes, but it seemed to Saxon that there was nothing in the world comparable with the joy of battle to the uttermost.

He lived very silently with big Arthur William Creston, during those three days. Either he was away, walking through the woods, or else he was dreaming forward to

75

the great fight which was to come. Or sometimes his mind
drifted back to the girl in Bluewater, or to Daniel Finlay.
But about them both there was the melancholy distance
of unreality.

The mountains, the shaggy, great trees, the wild beasts
and the wild men who could be found in the wilderness—
they were the present reality that filled his mind.

And if he had some doubts about the legal morality of
his scheme of things, he could remember the words of the
lawyer, assuring him that society owed him what society
had taken away from him!

Then back came Boots with his three recruits. And each
of them was a young man, all fire and spark. Del Bryan
came off the desert, with sun-whitened hair and eyebrows,
and pale, wolfish eyes. Joe Pike was out of the northland,
a cold, ugly, silent man. Tad Cullen was an old man at
twenty-five, who limped in both legs and who was covered
with scars of bullets and knives; most of his bones had
been broken in a thousand falls from bucking mustangs.
Plainly, he had not won all of his fights, but he had done
a great deal of fighting. And the fire in his eyes never
rested. It burned constantly, all the day long.

Saxon, looking over those men, realized that they were
in fact of the stuff that would stand up to The Solitaire if
enough was to be gained by the battle. There are men in
the West who have been so long familiar with danger and
who have rubbed elbows with death so often that they
feel rather lonely and deserted by life unless they are in
the midst of mortal peril. There are criminals who embrace
a life of crime simply because the savor of it charms them.

These three fellows had been told the purpose of big
John Saxon. They liked the idea. But five minutes after
he had been introduced, limping Tad Cullen said:

"There's only one queer thing about this deal. Our
partner, Saxon, never did anything, so far as I know,
except throw some drunks out of a saloon and then kill
Bob Witherell. But Bob was a bum, when it came to using
a Colt. How come you claim the number one place,
Saxon?"

Saxon smiled on him.

He recognized the danger, but he did not dislike it.

"You see those ears sticking up beyond that rock?" said Saxon.

"Yes. I see 'em. What about 'em?"

"Go and ask the rabbit why I'm the number one man. He may know better than you do. He may have used his ears more."

Cullen looked at him with eyes that were bright little points of fire.

"All right," he said. "I'll ask the rabbit a question."

He flashed a gun as he spoke, and fired instantly. So fast was his hand that the glint of the revolver seemed to be part of the fire of the explosion. The rabbit leaped from behind the rock and high into the air, a big, long-legged jack.

As it landed, Saxon knocked it rolling with a shot from his own Colt.

"Now you can ask the rabbit," said Saxon.

Cullen turned, stared at him again, and then walked over to the rabbit. Pike and Del Bryan went with him, and Cullen lifted the dead rabbit.

"Right through the bean!" he exclaimed.

"That was luck," said Saxon, honestly. "I can't shoot as well as that!"

"You're damn right you can't," answered Cullen. "But you can shoot plenty good enough to suit me. I stay with you hombres, I guess. Now, Chief, you tell us what the big plan is. Boots just opened up the idea for us—and that was all."

"The Solitaire—" said Saxon. "You fellows all know him?"

"I used to have a pretty good left leg, till I met up with The Solitaire," said Cullen.

"My cousin, Harry Feeley," said Pike," he run into The Solitaire and he come away minus the lower part of his face. Chewing without no lower jaw got Harry kind of weary, and one day he walked right on off a cliff. I've done a lot of thinking about The Solitaire ever since that day."

"Me," added Del Bryan, "I never seen him, even, but I've sure done plenty of dreaming about that hombre. It's time for him and me to meet!"

CHAPTER XV

IT was midday when they started. They went along very leisurely, camped in the early evening, and then Boots and Arthur William Creston went off scouting. During the whole of the ride, big John Saxon had not asked a single question, because he felt that questions, on his part, would be a folly, and that what was really important was for him to keep his mouth shut until the time came for action.

In the meantime, these proud and savage riders looked upon him with awe, with curiosity, and with a vast and cruel suspicion. They had seen him shoot a rabbit with a shot which, as he himself had instantly admitted, was a good part of luck. But they had not yet seen him in action against humans, and they wanted to see that before they accorded him any real admiration as a superior being. He was on trial, like a leader of a wolf-pack which is followed until it fails in the kill, when it is instantly torn to pieces by the hungry rivals. If he felt this about the others, he felt it even more about Boots, in whose strange nature there did not seem to be room enough for the slightest affection. Only the big Negro had in him a childish touch of kindness, and the desire for applause, as well as a great willingness to deal out applause to others.

Late that night, Boots and the Negro returned with word that they had found what they wanted. John Saxon lay looking up at the narrow heads of the pine trees around the camping place, and Boots and Creston sat down close to him. The others got at once out of their blankets and came to listen.

Boots said: "We've got 'em cold. I've spotted the hangout. Creston had the idea that they might be there. Creston is as many times right as an old woman. Creston took me there, and we laid out and saw the lights in the house, and heard the boys whooping it up in the hollow. We've seen 'em. We've been so close that I could spot the voices. Somebody got into an argument with another gent and they started singing right up the scale, the sort of a song that means a fight before it's finished, and then we could hear The Solitaire roar at 'em, and the snarling all stopped. We heard him order 'em all to bed, and after a coupla minutes, they were all in bed, except for one gent that was posted on watch. You could see him sneakin' around the house, steady and slow, in the starlight and the moonlight."

"Where's the place?" asked Tad Cullen.

"You know the old Armsby place?" asked Creston.

"Sure do I know it! Do I know the palm of my hand?" asked Cullen. "But what kind of a damn fool is The Solitaire turned into to go to a place like that, with open country all the way around?"

"There's the creek going right past the house," answered Creston. "And that's why it ain't so bad. No, it's pretty good. I like it. Suppose they were all surrounded, they could get out of the house and right down the bed of the creek."

"Suppose that there was men in the creek, too?" asked Cullen.

"Yeah, I didn't think of that," said Creston.

"There's a whole lot you don't think of," said Cullen, scornfully.

"Maybe I ain't so bright, but I wouldn't be needin' none of your ideas, Mr. Cullen," said Creston.

"Don't give me none of your lip!" exclaimed Cullen. "I won't have none of your backchat."

Something touched John Saxon, and it was the toe of Boots. He understood, and before Creston could answer, Saxon growled: "No more of this damn nonsense."

A sudden silence rushed over the little group, but he could hear the quick breathing of Cullen as that crippled young savage prepared to speak again.

Saxon said, calmly: "The first time that there's a fight in my camp, the winner takes me on after he's won. Remember that and keep your snappy talk to yourselves. Boots, you and Creston were telling me something. I want you to go on, and we'll see who has the nerve to interrupt again!"

There was another small breath of the silence. He could see Cullen rise to his feet and stand like a post, tense with excitement, ready at a mere touch to break into furious action, but then the voice of Boots began: "They're in the old house, all right. We can move on up there a little before sunrise and have 'em in a pocket, perhaps. They're sure to have all the stuff with 'em. Unless maybe they buried a little part of it. Boys, this'll make a rich haul for us, and I think we're going to collect. Chief, you give the orders."

Saxon gave them. He would rouse the camp, he told them, at the first hint of daylight. And well before sun-up they would be at the old Armsby house.

Then he concluded: "But mind you, before anything else happens, I'm going to get my fair chance at The Solitaire. Now you fellows turn in."

They turned in, talking quietly for a few moments to themselves. And he heard Cullen say: "Yeah, and he can have his turn with The Solitaire. Only—lemme see him take on The Solitaire hand to hand, and I'll see him five minutes later as dead as hell!"

There was no audible comment upon this, and Saxon lay stiffened with excitement, knowing that he would not close his eyes again before the morning.

One thing at least he had fixed for the next day—he would have to do his best to encounter The Solitaire face to face—he had made his brag and his boast, and unless he carried it through his authority over these men would not be worth a snap of the fingers.

Hardly a moment later, he was aware that the pine trees were visible in the sky above him, but that the stars were dying away to a series of very thin points. The day was beginning.

He got up at once, and in five minutes he had the camp up and ready to be away. Creston took the lead, silently, and for some time they traveled over a series of ups and downs, under trees, through the open, through brush that whipped and scratched and tested the chaps they were wearing, until at last Creston waved the others down and himself dismounted.

The sky was pink with the dawn as Saxon stood on the verge of some second-growth timber and looked down, a mere quarter of a mile away, on the old Armsby house. He had seen it when he was a boy. It looked smaller than on that day long ago. The house itself was not so big, and there was not such an extent of sheds and barns behind it. On a day the Armsby family had put all this narrow valley under the plough and herded their fine cattle over the slopes adjacent. But the soil was too shallow to repay the plough, and some bad seasons decimated the herd. The Armsby attempt was one of those magnificent failures with which the old range is spotted. The range has its own way, and will not take kindly to foreign methods.

In front of the old house, from which most of the paint had peeled, three men were moving from the door to the creek, one of them leading a pair of fine, long-legged horses. All of them were armed; one of them carried a rifle slung at his back. It was plain that they were not hugging to themselves a fancied sense of security merely because they were deep in the mountains.

"There's the place. But I don't see the man, yet," said Boots, at the shoulder of Saxon. "No, The Solitaire wouldn't be up and about, yet. He waits for breakfast to be cooked before he turns out. His lordship takes things pretty easy."

"What's easy," said the voice of Cullen, "is for us to clean up the rest of them—as soon as the—Chief—has put The Solitaire out of the way."

He was openly sneering.

"That's no way to do," said Boots. "The thing for us to do is to hang all together. And when we tackle 'em—"

"Aw, sure, he can back out, that way. I thought he had the nerve to tackle The Solitaire all by himself. That would be a pretty good show. I dunno how many years it is since anybody had the crust to tackle The Solitaire hand to hand, all by himself!"

"You fellows stay back here," said Saxon, squinting his eyes a little for fear lest they should be opened and made staring by the dread that was coming up in him. "Stay back here while I ride down and get at The Solitaire. I'll see if I can invite him away from the house."

"Ay, and up here where we can drop him!" exclaimed Boots.

"No," said Saxon, heavily. I'll go up the valley, there, where everyone can see, and there I'll have it out with him."

"Will you?" said Boots. "Will you?"

He turned his hungry, flashing eyes straight upon his leader.

"Well, maybe!" murmured Boots. "But—it kind of beats me!"

Saxon got to his horse and mounted it. He had been given not quite the best of the mustangs, because the huge gray mare of the Negro was the best of the horses. But his brown gelding was strong enough and fast enough, with the sure-footedness of a true mountain breed.

He said to Creston, in such a voice that all the others could hear him: "Arthur, you're a good fellow and just as brave as ever came over the pike. But you don't take a hand in this job. It's a lot better for white men to fight white men, and the other way around. Understand."

"Yes, sir," said Creston. "I understand that, boss. I come from Georgia and I understand. But down yonder it's a mighty pretty picture, and I'd like to get a hand in it."

"You stay out, and that's all there is to it," commanded Saxon. He turned to the rest and added: "You fellows stay back here. When I've handled The Solitaire, you'll have an easy job to tackle, because those men of his are sure to come out of the house to look on. You can charge down the slope from here with a yell and a volley, and sweep 'em right into the creek. They've done their robbing and killing by tricks, and it's all right for us to use a trick or two on them. But wait till you see what happens between me and The Solitaire."

They looked at him strangely, with narrowed eyes, searching to get close to the fear that, they thought, must be in him. But as he rode out of the woods into the open, he heard someone say, in a stifled voice:

"By thunder, it *looks* like the real thing."

"Ay, a lot of things *look* all right that are rotten inside!" said the voice of Cullen.

There would be trouble with Cullen, later on, even if this thing turned out all right. He was sure of that.

But he could not afford to think of the future, as he backed his horse down that slope.

Yonder came the man with the two horses that he had watered at the creek. He whistled as he walked. He was a chunky, powerful man with his face blackly obscured by a beard of two or three weeks' growth. The two others turned suddenly around, and one of them unshipped his rifle and held it at the ready—then dropped the butt of it to the ground, and waited for Saxon to ride up.

Dreadful fear suddenly poured over Saxon like cold water. He wanted, now, to pull his horse around and flee. But he had come too close. If he attempted to retire, now, he would be drilled full of holes by the accurate rifle bullets.

He had to go on—though there was in him that surety that he was lost.

CHAPTER XVI

THERE were not many steps for the horse to take in coming up to those loiterers before the Armsby place, but in that short distance that was covered, another change came over Saxon. Those three were outlawed men. Otherwise they would not be with The Solitaire. They were murderers and robbers, or they would not have been with him. But whatever they were, they were almost unquestionably less than had been big Bob Witherell.

And he, Saxon, had proved himself the better man of the two! He was better, then, than any of these. And he was very close. If it came to a brawl, perhaps he could ride straight through the lot of them. With swift snapshots to the right and the left, he could drop those fellows, it might be.

As he thought of this, his confidence returned. And, moreover, this was the bright pink of the morning, and the very time when men should live or die. He, John Saxon, intended to live!

And he, John Saxon, might be facing the great Solitaire in another few moments.

"Well? Well? Lookin' for strays?" said the man with the rifle.

Another fellow came into the doorway of the house.

He was carrying a rifle, also. Four pairs of eyes worked curiously, busily, at Saxon. He pulled up his horse close to them.

"I'm looking for a stray Solitaire," he said. "Is he here?"

"I dunno that there's any Solitaire birds around here," said the first rifleman. "Who might you be?"

"My name is John Saxon," he answered. "I'm the man who killed Bob Witherell, and I thought that his brother might want to have the thing out with me this morning."

"Well, I'll be—well, I'll be damned!" said the other.

His two fellows came up close. It was a savage trio— as savage, at least, as the four white men who waited yonder, at the edge of the trees. All of these fellows might be dead, before the sun came over the hills. Saxon looked down upon them from a height of a greater knowledge.

"You're Saxon, are you?" said the rifleman. "Then why shouldn't we shoot you out of that there saddle and take you in to see the Chief before all the blood has leaked out of you?"

"I'll tell you why," said Saxon. He looked straight down into the eyes of the man, and saw the glance of the rifleman waver a trifle. "I'm meat for your master," said Saxon. "And he'll raise hell with the man of you who puts a hand on me before he has his full turn. Understand me?"

He pointed up the valley.

"I'm going up there," he said, "and I'll wait beside that big black rock. That's close enough so that the rest of you can see all the fun. It's far enough away so that you won't be very able to turn loose your guns on me after I've drilled The Solitaire. Now one of you get inside the house and tell him that I've come to finish off the Witherell family."

He turned his horse, as he spoke, and rode it at a walk right up the valley toward the rock which he had seen.

Behind him he heard one of the gang mutter: "I dunno why—"

"Put it down," said another, quickly. "He's right. He may be crazy but he's right in this here. The Chief will want to have his little go at Saxon. My God, what a nerve that gent packs around with him, though!"

John Saxon rode up to the black rock and looked calmly around him.

Off to his right was the dark verge of the trees where his four helpers were waiting with their horses. He himself was the bait which was to lure on the chief hawk of the enemy. And as The Solitaire stooped at him, as the rest of The Solitaire's gang came out into the open, down that slope would pour the charge which ought to scatter the outlaws into the creek.

It was a simple plan. It was so simple that one might wonder why it had not been used before. The novel point was simply that one human life had to be offered as the bait to make the trap attractive. And still, at this distance from the house, he was in danger. Riflemen as accurate as those would not have great trouble in pumping lead into him. At least, they would put the horse down—and after that they could hunt him as he dodged and scampered on foot.

No, he was still held firmly in place. And, if he doubted that, he could take heed of one man who lay out on the ground in front of the house with a rifle carefully trained on the target which Saxon offered to the gun. Even from that distance, he was holding the stranger on a leash strong enough to pull him out of this life and into the next world.

Then The Solitaire appeared.

By the way he came into the doorway of the house and stood there for a moment, turning his head a bit as though the whole landscape were interesting to him, and not simply the enemy in the distance, big John Saxon could have told that it was The Solitaire. His spurs flashed on his heels as he came down the three steps to the ground. The band of metal around his sombrero—no doubt it was Mexican wheelwork—glittered also, and his blue shirt was shimmering silk with a red bandana draped gracefully around his throat. Even the body of the man looked graceful, elegant.

He was as big as his dead brother; he was as big, very nearly, as John Saxon, and it was plain that here nature had been spendthrift and squandered size, strength, speed, grace, elegance all on one body. Even if he had been an unknown, Saxon felt that he would have known at a glance that this was a fearless and a famous man.

One of the band led around the corner of the house one of those gray horses which are stockinged in black to the knees and hocks and so faintly mottled over the rest of the body that they seem white. The saddle shone with silver and gold, and as the horse threw its head proudly, Saxon distinctly and faintly heard the noise of little bells.

That horse, dancing or rearing against the restraining hand of the follower, was instantly quiet when the master leaped into the saddle.

And still The Solitaire did not come directly toward his enemy but first pointed out some things near the house and seemed to be giving orders—before he jaunted off to wipe this small detail of a fighting man out of his path.

His four men came crowding out of the house behind him. They were on foot, all of them, and they came on very slowly, so that it was plain they had been ordered to preserve a little distance and not crowd their chief while he was at work. They could be seen fanning out to this side and to that, each anxious to get as good a view as possible.

And now The Solitaire came, suddenly, at a swinging, grand gallop. The wind caught the brim of his sombrero and lifted it a little. The red bandana blew back from his throat. The pressure of the wind molded that thin silken shirt against his body so that at a distance Saxon could see the muscles.

Yes, this was one of those chosen men among a million!

Should he dismount to meet the enemy?

Saxon could not tell. No, he decided to remain in the saddle, as he was. His gun was in readiness. His right hand stole back just once to make sure that it was loose and all in readiness.

When he fired he would exclaim: "The Solitaire!" He knew that, and even smiled a little.

When he fired? That took for granted that he was able to get his gun out before a bullet from The Solitaire crashed through his brain. He had been confident enough to aim at the forehead of Bob Witherell instead of his body. And no doubt The Solitaire would have a similar confidence. He would shoot for the head.

86

Then it would either be a miss, or else it would be mercifully sudden death for Saxon. On the other hand, suppose that luck favored the challenger—well, that thought made a spring of music well up in the heart of Saxon.

He saw the clots of the turf springing up high above the head of the rider, hanging in the air an instant like birds on the wing, before they fell. Then he saw The Solitaire bring his horse to a sudden halt, a scant ten paces off.

Ten paces, thought Saxon, was a good distance. Ten paces is about the distance that a man uses most often when he slips through the woods, hunting for small game.

He considered his target. The magnificence of this man was such that he had seemed just as big and dominant in the distance as he was at close hand. There was only the glory of the head and face added, and that seemed to Saxon the finest picture that he had ever seen. Bob Witherell had been a handsome man, but he was nothing compared to this olive-skinned hero, this living statue of perfection. The lips of The Solitaire were so red that they seemed to have been painted; and when he smiled, his teeth were wonderfully white. He shone. There was a light inside him, and the central flame burned out through the eyes above all.

It seemed to Saxon that if that fire touched his soul, if he opened his own eyes to it and let it in, it would burn all the manhood out of him. Just so had it burned the soul out of Boots, in that encounter long ago.

Saxon, steadily, with all the strength of his will, centered his own gaze right on the breadth of the forehead under the hatband. That was where he would aim to send his bullet crashing. Right there where the leather of the hatband pressed a little into the flesh!

"You're John Saxon?" said The Soliaire. "I'm glad to meet you, man. I thought that I'd have to postpone this for a little while. I wanted to let you cook a while before I came for you, too. But I see that you got a bit nervous, and you've jumped out of the frying pan into the fire, eh?"

He laughed, as he ended. And it amazed Saxon to hear the golden quality of that laughter, like a flowing music.

Saxon said: "The Witherells were always great talkers. They'll stop their talking today, though."

"Will they?" said The Solitaire. "Well, my lad, I'll do for you what you did for Bob. I'll bury you in the ground and put your name over the grave. Are you ready?"

"I'm ready," said Saxon.

A panic was running in him, however. He felt that if his glance wavered one instant down to the flare of fire in those proud, masterful eyes, he would be lost, utterly. "I'm ready and waiting," said Saxon.

"Fill your hand, then," said The Solitaire.

"I'll see you damned first," said Saxon.

"No? And you won't look me in the eye, either? You fool, you're beaten before you make a move! Wait a moment! There's a cow lowing over the hill. The next time the sound comes—"

That would be the signal. It was a far-away sound. Distance makes into a softly flowing sound even the beating of great bells. It turned the lowing of the cow into a sadness felt dimly on the air, perceived on the edge of the mind.

But when it came again, it shot an electric thrill through the soul and body of Saxon. He twitched out his Colt. It seemed to him that the flash of the eyes and the flash of the revolver of The Solitaire were parts of the same fire—

And then a thunderstroke beat through his brain.

CHAPTER XVII

HE felt himself falling through eternal blackness—he was merely bowing over the pommel of his saddle.

He felt that a cannon had boomed again in his ear— it was merely the second shot from the rapid gun of The Solitaire exploding near by, while the bullet clipped past the down-swaying head of Saxon.

He thought that he had fallen into a seething fire; but it was merely the pain of his torn flesh, for the first shot had glanced along his skull and ripped the scalp up in a huge furrow.

He thought that there was a clapping of hands, a distant applause for this sudden, brief battle, but it was the rattling of many guns in the distance.

The instant that the gun of The Solitaire spoke, and big John Saxon fired wildly into the air, without aiming, down the slope from the trees came first the concentrated volley of Cullen and the rest, then the sweeping charge of their horses.

And The Solitaire, twisting his head about, saw that charge going home, saw one of his men already flat on the ground and the other three flying as fast as they could run!

It meant more than the loss of lives to him. It meant, above all, the loss of the money which he had piled up in the house—one-third of it for himself.

He left the dead body of Saxon to tumble out of the saddle at leisure, and, twitching his own horse around, he charged to the rescue.

That was why, as Saxon's brain instantly cleared, he saw The Solitaire galloping wildly away, as if in flight—and across the valley he saw the riot of the battle proceeding.

No, it was no longer a riot, but a rout.

And Saxon, driving spurs into his horse, rushed it in pursuit. He shouted as he rode.

The Solitaire jerked his head about and saw behind him a man who should be dead, who must be dead with a bullet through his brain, dashing after him, yelling!

Was it that sight which unnerved The Solitaire? Or did he simply see that he had left his rifle at the house, and that with revolvers alone he could not deal with the followers of John Saxon who had driven his own men in rout.

Those fugitives were at the house. They were springing into saddles on the waiting horses. One more of them fell. The other two dashed their mounts around the corner of the building. And of those two survivors, one was clinging desperately, swaying far forward as though he had been terribly injured.

The Solitaire did not need more evidence than this to

89

assure him that luck was against him and that he had lost this day. Already, a rifle was turned towards him by one of the victors. It was little Boots of detested memory, dropping to the ground, letting his horse run free while he concentrated rifle fire on the great enemy.

The Solitaire, swinging his horse sharply to the side, dashed for cover.

Behind him he heard the shouting of John Saxon, begging him to turn and fight it out.

Then a bullet from Saxon's gun hummed close to his ear. He turned and fired rapidly three times at the pursuer, and every shot went wild, as his straining horse flew over the irregularities of the ground.

But he was gaining prodigiously at every leap the gray stallion made, and now the sudden shadow of the forest closed over him. And The Solitaire bent low above the pommel, grinding his teeth, cursing in a stream of oaths, and fled for his life.

Presently he knew that hoofbeats were no longer sounding behind him. He could pull up the gray to a soft trot, and remember in detail the strangest encounter of his life and the first great reverse of his fortune!

And big John Saxon?

He saw that there was no more use in his following The Solitaire than for a linnet to follow a hawk. His horse could never keep that pace. If ever he was to hunt The Solitaire again, he would need under him a far finer specimen of horseflesh!

So he turned back.

He did not really regret that he had failed to overtake his enemy. Man to man, on this day, it had been proved that The Solitaire was the better of the pair. Chance, Fortune, or God, had given to big John Saxon a chance to come away with honor and his life.

He turned his horse, therefore, and rode slowly down the valley to the house. As he came nearer, he first saw his friends go storming into the house, and then he saw, as he pulled up in front of it, how they came charging out of it, dragging filled saddlebags with them, and shouting like madmen.

He saw Pike lift one of those saddlebags and hold it mouth down while a shower of greenbacks fell to the ground. Most of the money was in bundles heavy enough to drop safely to the ground, but a lot of it was loose and blew away in a green shower on the wind.

But Pike did not care for such trifles. He began to leap and bound and yell at the top of his voice. He began to laugh, and choke with hysterical joy. In fact, he had poured out a fortune on the earth, and the other men were screeching and prancing like madmen. Every one of them had found portions of the treasure.

Only little Boots came to big John Saxon and looked up at him with a deadly concern.

"Get down! Get down!" commanded Boots.

Saxon slid out of the saddle.

"I'm all right," he said. "The bullet glanced. I'm all right, Boots."

"Here, some of you yahoos!" shouted Boots. "Get some water ready. Bandages! Lend a hand, here! The Chief's hurt bad!"

The call—or the last name used—operated very effectively upon the rest of them. They stampeded into the kitchen of the house. As a matter of fact, the treasure they had found remained scattered about on the ground in front of the house, while they stormed into the kitchen and each man hurried to do something for the "Chief."

Water was already hot in a big boiler. Coffee was steaming. An ample breakfast of beefsteak and bacon and pone had been prepared before the men of The Solitaire went out to see their master's duel. And now, as soon as the wound of Saxon was cleansed and bound tightly around with a bandage, his men sat down in that same kitchen and ate with a glorious appetite.

Saxon, stunned and ill at ease, only gradually brought his mind back to a realization of what had actually happened. The clearly known world had ended in the flash of The Solitaire's eyes and gun at the same instant.

Now he found himself sitting at a long table in the ruined old house and listening to the clamor of the gang as they ate and drank whiskey. Some bottles of good whiskey had been found among the luggage of The Solitaire, and they were about to broach this, when Boots muttered:

"They'll be drunk as lords in five minutes, if they

91

tackle that stuff. Do you think it's wise, Chief? The Solitaire is a foxy bird, and he may come back here any minute—and with more men behind him! He may be hanging about close, right now."

The very mention of the name stabbed a cold pain through the soul of John Saxon.

He shouted: "Down with that whiskey! Damn you, am I to have a lot of swine rolling around on the ground when you're needed? Give me that whiskey, and if I see a man of you lay hand on a drink without my permission—I'll break him in two and see what the stuff looks like inside his belly!"

He paused, his teeth grinding together, a darkness of rage whirling in his mind. And he saw the others stare at him and then lower their eyes to the table.

He was amazed. He had expected them to rise up in a crowd against him as he damned them. Instead, they sat like frightened children. He felt ashamed, but he stood up suddenly and strode out of the house.

When he was in the open air, he sat down on a rock near the door of the house, and his eye traveled over the mountains and saw the sun come blazing up in the east.

He had a sudden sense of possession. Whatever he saw was his. At least, the dawning beauty of it made the world step into his mind as it never had stepped before, when he was laboring with his hands to make his way.

Behind him, voices wrangled. Well, let them wrangle, for they were suddenly beneath him, apart from him. He had brushed them and their desires aside with an easy gesture. They had bowed their heads like children before an angry parent.

He felt like laughing, but he felt like sneering, also.

Two things were real in this world—the glory of its beauty and full tasting life, and The Solitaire whose bullet had missed his brain by a fraction of an inch that morning.

Would he even be able to face The Solitaire again? Not, he felt, unless he had first gained a great speed of hand and a greater surety of eye. Not, he was certain, until he had steeled himself still more, so that he could face that man as though he were facing, with wide open eyes, the blazing sun in the east. Chance and kind fortune had spared his life on this day. It could hardly be so kind to him again.

Cullen came out bringing the three bottles of whiskey. He put them down on the ground beside Saxon and cleared his throat.

"Chief," he said, "I've been kind of fresh a couple of times around you. I'm sorry. I didn't figger you right. Here's the whiskey. I'm not touching any more booze when I'm on the trail with you, and when you yip at me, you'll see me jump as fast as my bum legs let me. Is that all right?"

Saxon looked into the anxious, rather frightened face of Cullen. The man was overawed.

"Of course it's all right," said Saxon and held out his hand. Cullen took it quickly, eagerly.

"The finest thing I ever seen," said Cullen. "I never seen anything like it. I never dreamed that I'd ever see anything like it. The Solitaire being chased by *one man!*"

Saxon smiled.

There were certain features of that "chase" which could be explained, but what was the use? He said nothing, and saw Cullen go off with the others to pick up the dead.

They had lain there, the pair of them, under the rising sun, unheeded. Now they were dumped like dead dogs into crevices along the bank of the creek, and a quantity of the loose rock and gravel caved in over them.

Saxon did not rise to take part in that ceremony. He remained seated, for the pain in his head was growing blindly great. Then Boots came up to him, after a little time, and saluted.

"The loot's laid out on the kitchen table, Chief," he said. "All ready to whack it up when you say the word."

CHAPTER XVIII

ALL that had been found was laid out on the heavy table, and, though some parts of the treasure might have been pocketed, there remained a great quantity. Boots was rapidly at work sorting the cash into piles of bills of the same denominations; and out of several small sacks of chamois, Pike poured out diamonds, emeralds, rubies, pearls that had been pried out of their settings, together with rings that still contained their jewels, and some fine gold watches. There were other trinkets. There was a woman's penknife in the handle of which was set—a curious vanity!—a pattern of small but very fine emeralds of the true dark sea-green, that green with the blue fire underlying. There was a pair of long, stiletto shaped hat pins with rubies for heads! And big John Saxon saw a good quantity, also, of scarf pins, and such jewelry as men will wear even on the range.

He looked at these things in a dreamy way. He picked up an entire handful of the uncut gems and let them drift carelessly through his fingers, like a precious sand.

That made him think of the running sands of time, and the old metaphor made him smile. Time itself, in fact, had taken on a new meaning, a brighter face, and the moments of his life had a greater importance.

He thought back to the years of hard labor in the course of which he had developed his little property, and gradually built up his herd. Well, all of that start in life, which had so contented him, was now wiped out; but in a moment, at a stroke, he had taken in enough to buy many and many a ranch larger than the one that had been stripped of all his work.

Well, it was a different matter. He was counting his pulse now in pain, as the blood surged against the bullet furrow across his scalp. And in the moment of the battle he had risked his life—in order to gain this? No, not for the money, but for the man, and the man was gone! This was a by-product, an offspring of his action against The Solitaire. This heaped fortune became as cheap as dirt, viewed in such a light, and he thought more of one flash of the eyes of The Solitaire than of all that fortune had now given to him.

The man grew in his mind, not in size but like a light toward which one rides through thick night. All these other people were dim, small, unimportant. The blood that he had lost, the two dead men, nothing mattered compared with The Solitaire, his beauty, his pride, his disdain of danger.

It was a strange trick of fortune that had made The Solitaire turn, and then forced him to flee during the battle. No matter what adventures that famous man had had, it was certain that men had never seen him apparently frightened by a single enemy! It was only an appearance, John Saxon knew. And he knew, also, that he would have to pay in the future for that day's work. The result was that he looked down on the accumulated funds with a perfectly indifferent eye.

Pike announced: "Gents, there's a hundred and seventy-five thousand in this pile, and that ain't saying anything about the jewels. This here haul," went on Pike, gravely, "is one of them things that you don't bump into twice, I reckon. How we gunna divide it, Chief?"

His hungry eyes lifted to the face of John Saxon, who merely said: "Well, there are six of us."

"Hey," said Pike, in violent protest, "the nigger don't come in for a full share, because he didn't do any of the fighting!"

Arthur William Creston looked at his chief and said nothing. He merely shrugged his vast shoulders in submission to fate.

"Creston," said Saxon, "found this place for us. He would have fought as well as the next man, but I wouldn't let him shoot at whites. He gets a full share."

"It's wrong!" said Pike. "There ain't no justice in that! I wouldn't stand for it!"

"Wouldn't you stand for it?" sneered Saxon.

He looked at the man and realized the snaky danger in him, and then mastered that danger by the sheer power of his eye alone.

"If you won't stand for it, sit for it, or lie down for it," said Saxon. "What I say, goes."

"Hold on," put in Cullen. "Is it going to be that nobody has any word except you, Chief?"

"No. Nobody else has a damned word to say," answered Saxon. "Doesn't that suit you?"

Cullen scowled, but he scowled down at the table.

"You're takin' a mighty high road with us," he declared.

Creston stepped suddenly to the side of his chief and

faced the others, silently. It was plain that the camp was divided into two distinct parties at that moment, but Saxon waved the huge Negro away.

"I don't need your help, Arthur," he said. "If these hombres want trouble, they can have all that I can give them."

He saw Pike's hand move suddenly toward his hip; he saw Del Bryan lean over a little like a man about to run forward.

And Saxon merely smiled. Why, if there had been a thousand of them, after facing The Solitaire he felt that he could have laughed at such people.

"Start it, Del," he said to Bryan. "Start it, Pike. I'm ready and waiting."

He stepped back a little and saw that Boots, from the side, was watching with an air of cold amusement and interest. There was plainly no more personal devotion in Boots than in a hawk of the air.

But Bryan and Pike, after staring an instant at their chief, glanced aside toward one another and seemed to realize, after that glance, that they did not want to fight on this point.

"Well," said Pike, sullenly, "you fix things your own way. You done some pretty good work, today, and we oughta humor you a little."

"Nobody humors me in this outfit," answered Saxon. "You're hired hands, the rest of you. Understand? Hired hands. I take you on when I please, and I fire you when I'm ready. This is my ranch," he added, with a sudden and brutal increase of savagery in his breast even as he saw them submitting. He waved his hand toward the windows. "I used to have a ranch, over yonder. It's wiped out. I've got to farm the rocks and the roads, now, and I've got to have my hired hands to help me. But I don't ask what they want to do. I tell them. Does that go down?"

Cullen answered, gloomily: "It's gotta go down. It looks to me like you got us licked. Pike and Del Bryan are takin' water; and I've taken it from you before. Boots don't give a damn what happens, one way or the other, and Creston is with you. That's the lay of the land. How much of the hard cash are you gunna give us?"

This was a humiliating surrender, but Pike and Del

Bryan, though they scowled bitterly, did not raise a voice in protest.

"If there's a hundred and seventy-five thousand," said John Saxon, "one third ought to go to me. That's the way that The Solitaire worked his deals, and that's the way that I work mine. Whether it suits you or not, that's what I get."

He waved toward the jewels.

"There's another seventy or eighty thousand in that pile of stuff. That rock in that stick pin is worth five thousand alone. I've watched the prices in the jewelry windows. Well, I won't bother about all that. The five of you can split up the jewels any way you please. Give me fifty-eight thousand in cash and we'll call it quits. That gives the rest of you something around thirty-five or forty thousand apiece. Boots, bring out my share when it's been divided."

He saw astonishment in their faces. After the tyrannical nature of his opening, it was no wonder that they were surprised by the generosity of this division. No leader of any outlawed crew would have been content with less than two or perhaps three shares for himself. And it was he who had drawn The Solitaire away from the other men, tempted the rest of the crew into a trap, and then stood the brunt of the battle with the great gunman while his men had an easy task given to them.

Amazed, they stared at one another. Del Bryan suddenly jumped up and exclaimed: "By thunder, Chief, that's all damned white of you! If that's the stuff you're made of, you can kick me around as much as you please."

Saxon said nothing. He went out and sat in front of the house and looked again at the mountains. They were, in fact, his ranch. Every road that wound through them was a possible river of wealth on which he might levy a tribute. Immense power would be in his hands. He could strike where he pleased, and success would make him stronger and stronger and gather under him a more formidable band of picked men.

He was in the midst of those thoughts when Boots came out to him. He had a thick sheaf of bills in his hands; Saxon crammed them with perfect indifference into a side pocket of his coat.

"You did it," said Boots, calmly. "I didn't think there was a man in the world that could take Cullen and Del Bryan and Pike and make them eat humble pie the way you've made them. That was a pretty damn slick job. It was as good a bluff as I ever seen."

"What makes you think it was a bluff?" asked John Saxon, and he lifted his glance to Boots. There was new power in his eye. Before, the faces of men had been objects more awe-inspiring than great mountains, prospects more mighty than the loftiest summits could give them. But now, since he had encountered The Solitaire, all other men seemed without force. So he looked straight into the bright, slightly puckered eyes of Boots, and saw them widen, suddenly.

"Why, maybe it wasn't a bluff, after all," muttered Boots. "You got me beat about as bad as you beat the rest of 'em. But I'd like to ask you a question."

"Shoot."

"What made you give Creston such a break? What made you treat him so white?"

"Because he's the whitest of the lot of you, under the skin," said Saxon.

Boots said nothing. He merely stared. And Saxon went on, more calmly than ever: "You're a poisonous snake, Boots. So is Del Bryan. Pike is simply a brute. Cullen is a better cut, but not so good. Any one of you would put a knife in my back if you had a fair chance and thought that there was much to gain by it. But Creston would give his blood for me—just now, at least."

At this abrupt and cruel summing up, Boots said: "If we're such a rotten lot, I suppose you're through with us?"

"Why should I be through with you as long as I can use you?" asked the leader. "You know the ways of The Solitaire. And the others are tools sharp enough to cut."

It seemed to him, as he talked on with Boots, that wisdom and keen insight were given to him increasingly, from moment to moment. He was certain that what he said was the very naked truth.

"What's the next step?" asked Boots, submissively.

"I go to find out if I have a right to this coin," said big John Saxon. "I mean, to the part of it above the price

98

of the cattle and house I lost. The rest of you scatter wherever you please and meet me at that old shack where you and I were together, three days from this."

CHAPTER XIX

THE farewells were brief. Of the horses taken from the men of The Solitaire, one was a long, rather low-built and powerful roan gelding with a Roman nose and a little red-stained eye. John Saxon chose that one to carry his bulk. There were three minutes of savage pitching in the brute before the kinks were straightened out of it; then Saxon waved to the others and rode down the slope.

He would make Bluewater, without much haste, around sunset time, and that, he felt, was the safe hour for him to enter the place. For how matters stood for him in that town or in all the world, at this moment, he could not tell; and how his attack on the great Solitaire and his seizure of this wealth would appear in the eye of the law he could not quite guess. He only knew, by instinct and the actual words of that wise and good man, Daniel Finlay, that the world owed him something. Finlay would be able to tell him just what his rights were.

He had been more than an hour on the way when he heard a horse coming behind him through the thick of a shadowy wood. He pulled back into a thicket and saw, presently, the huge bulk of Arthur William Creston, on the powerful gray mare.

Was the Negro trying to run him down for the sake of the money in his pocket? He waited until Creston had gone by and then called out behind him. What followed was a perfect answer to his question, for instead of whirling about guiltily, Creston called a cheerful answer, then pulled up his mare.

Saxon joined him at once and saw that Creston was grinning, though apparently not totally at ease.

"You ain't sour because I followed along, are you, Chief?" asked Creston. "It sort of hit me all at once that those other gents, they didn't want me, much. They felt I was too much on your side, and then I thought that maybe the best place for me would be right along side of you on the old gray mare. Does that sound to you, Chief, or had I better take my own trail and stick to it?"

"I'd rather have you with me," said Saxon, calmly, "than anybody I know in the world. We'll stay together. Maybe we'll have a need of each other before we're much older."

Creston was delighted. He was so happy that, as they rode on again, he following a few horse lengths behind his leader, he could not help bursting into song in a vast, huskily melodious baritone. It reminded Saxon a little of the howling of a great dog, with the voice reduced to the order of music.

It was Creston's rifle that picked up a mountain grouse; it was Saxon's revolver that knocked over a rabbit. And they camped at noon on the lip of a cliff in the upper valley of the Bluewater, with a ribbon of water flowing over the edge and shaking out into spray, and the forest stopping suddenly on the verge of the rock, so that from pine-scented shadow Saxon could look out over the great valley below, like a bird perched on a lofty cloud.

Creston roasted the meat in generous chunks on the end of splinters of wood. They ate that meat with salt and they had water to drink. That was the meal.

Afterward they lolled for a time, smoking, stretching their bodies on the ground, for a man who lives in the saddle finds no rest in merely sitting down.

"Boss," said the big Negro, "what would you be planning on now, if you don't mind telling me?"

"No matter what I plan," answered Saxon, "the thing I have to do is to find The Solitaire and beat him."

"Boss," said the Negro, "you got a mighty fine eye and you got a mighty fast hand, but you can't stand up to The Solitaire, I reckon."

Saxon stared.

"The other gents," said the giant, "they didn't look none too close. They just seen that you and The Solitaire was shooting at each other; and then there was The Solitaire galloping back as they started shooting up his gang. But I wasn't allowed to use no gun, and I lay on the edge of the woods and saw how the first bullet knocked you down in the saddle. I reckon that The Solitaire thought you was a dead man, Chief, before he went and left you."

"That's what he thought, no doubt," said Saxon. "He was a faster and a steadier man than I was, today. But maybe I can learn to be faster and steadier still."

"That's right, boss," said Arthur Creston, "but when you sat there, close up to The Solitaire, was you able to look him in the eye?"

Saxon drew in a quick breath. He had not expected that question. He countered it with another.

"How much do you know about The Solitaire?" he asked.

"I know kind of a lot," said the Negro. "I was up in the mountains, ridin' range, doin' a regular cowhand's work, and one day I found there was a long stretch on my range that didn't have no cows on it, not even down near the water holes, where mostly I'd find some of 'em loafin' after they come in to drink. And so I looked around and found trails of cows goin' all one way, and the sign of hosses, too, and I followed along till I got in the choke of a valley, and seen the herd gathered and marchin', and heard the clashin' of the horns, and the bellerin', and then I seen gents ridin' point, and when I started lookin' for those in the tail of the herd, all at once a gent comes out at me from around a rock and sticks me up, and that gent was The Solitaire.

"Well, sir, when I seen him I had to throw up my hands, but he was sort of careless with me, and I got a chance to grab him, sudden, and we both rolled off our hosses.

"And I never yet seen the man that could stand a few grips of my hands!"

He held them out and looked down at them, great black engines with the palms worn to a dusky tan. The tendons of the wrist looked as big as fingers, straining hard.

"And I sort of got The Solitaire under," said the Negro, remembering with a dim wonder and horror in his eyes, "and I thought that I could smash him, but all at once I looked into his eyes, and those eyes of his wasn't buggin' out, no matter how hard I was squashin' him, and they burned and glared at me, and the fire blew up higher and higher in them, and somehow the man inside of me caught the fire—and burned to a crisp—and all at once he was on top, and he give me a rap alongside the jaw with the rock that he'd picked up from the ground—"

Arthur Creston paused and shook his head.

"They was camped, not far from there—The Solitaire and some of his gents—and they took me on for a cook, and they ironed me up with the chain out of a bear trap, so's I was hobbled and couldn't go far, and they kept me there in the chain till one day The Solitaire, he come and showed me a newspaper that had been brought in, and in the newspaper there was a reward offered for anybody that got me arrested. Because, you see, I'd disappeared from the ranch the same time the cows went, and folks nacherally kind of thought that I was the rustler.

" 'Now,' says The Solitaire, 'I'm gunna take the irons off you, and you can run free, because the minute you get away from this camp, they're gunna pick you up—and to hell with you!'

"Why, I seen that there was a lot of sense in what he said, and I kept with that camp for another month, and finally I managed to get away. But I never been able to work for honest men since that time, and I been ridin' with this gang, and cookin' for that gang, but I never drawed down an honest dollar to this day!"

He stopped, with a sigh.

"Do you like the life?" asked Saxon, curiously.

"Why, sir," said the Negro, "it ain't a bad kind of a life. It's as free as a bird. You get frost-bit in winter, pretty often; and you get sun-dried in the summer, crossin' a desert now and then, and pretty often there ain't any grub; but it's a free life. Only, even a bird nests once a year, maybe, and I'd be pretty glad to lay up once in a while."

"Matter of fact, Creston," said John Saxon, "you're sick of the business. You were always sick of it. And you'd like to go straight if you could find a chance."

"Yes, sir, I sure would!" said Creston, heartily. "And if your way goes straight, that's how I'd like to head."

Saxon nodded. Where he would be going himself, finally, he could not tell.

"Getting back to The Solitaire," he said, "I'll tell you the truth—that I couldn't look into his eyes, Arthur. I had

102

to look at his forehead, high up, and keep my mind hard against looking into his eyes because there was such a bright devil in them."

Creston, wagging his head, answered: "Maybe you won't have no luck agin The Solitaire till you can look him straight in the eye, Chief."

"What makes you think that, Arthur?"

"I dunno," said Creston. "It sort of come over me when I was standin' in there in the kitchen of the house, back there, and I seen you look at Pike and Cullen and the rest and take hold of 'em with your eyes, and I sort of thought that nobody else in the world could take hold of men like that, except The Solitaire. And he'll never die till he meets a sharper eye than his own, sir."

"Ay, and maybe," muttered Saxon. "How does a man sharpen his eye, though?"

"I don't know, boss," answered Creston. "Maybe by doing what The Solitaire has done."

"Murdering people, you mean?"

"No, but going to hell and back the way he's done."

It was not a very satisfactory answer, but Saxon brooded over it all the way to Bluewater, and as a matter of fact his thoughts were so seriously preoccupied that it was well after dark before he rode into the upper edge of the town.

He came up behind the Rolling Bones saloon, first; and, looking through the end window of the bar, he made out Lefty Malone serving three men.

He tapped on the window, which Malone at once pulled up. The bartender leaned over the sill into the night.

"That you, Mug?" asked Malone, cheerfully.

Then he saw the horseman and started to wince back.

"It's all right, Lefty," said Saxon. "Keep your voice down."

"Sure, kid, sure!" agreed Lefty. "My God, but I been needing you today."

"For what?"

"Because there's been half a dozen thugs here tryin' to make themselves a name by cleanin' up my saloon. Ever since you went away, the boys all seem to think that the place to stage a fight is right in here. I'm gunna lose money on broken glass all the rest of my days, kid, because you been here and give the place a reputation."

"How is it for me to be back in the town?"

"It's not good for you to be anywhere the rest of your life!" growled Malone.

"Why not?"

"You've made your bed. Now go and lie on the damn cactus," said Malone. "You wanted trouble and now you got plenty of it, I guess. Not many nights you'll sleep soft before The Solitaire get to you."

"Who you talkin' to, Lefty?" asked one of the men at the bar.

"The ghost of my father-in-law's uncle's sister," said the barman, without turning his head. "Know him?"

Big John Saxon was asking: "Outside of The Solitaire —I mean about the people in town, how does the chatter about me go?"

"What makes you think that they'd be spending time talking about you?"

"I'm just asking," answered Saxon. "I want to know what the feeling is."

"So's you can come back here and go to work? You always got a home here with me, Johnnie, damn your big blond head!"

"I'm not coming back here, but still I'm asking."

"They talk hard about you," answered Lefty Malone. "They say that you've sure started for hell with a whoop and a holler. But tell me how things are goin' with you, will you?"

"It'd make your heart ache if things didn't go well with me, wouldn't it?"

"You always were a fresh young mug," said Lefty, "but I kind of miss the sight of your mean mug."

"You miss it in the cash register, you ought to say."

"I miss it there, all right," said Lefty Malone. "But listen to me."

"I'm listening, Lefty."

"If you get broke, there's always a handout for you here."

"Thanks. I take that white of you. Can you give me any more news that I need to know?"

"Sure. Your girl has picked up a new fellow."

"Has she, eh?"

"By name of Wilmer Whalen. He's a gent from the

104

outside that's come here to look over the old mill and start the wheels turning again. He says that he's goin' to give new life to Bluewater, and it looks as though he's giving new life to your girl, all right."

"What sort of a looking hombre?"

"Oh, about your size, but good-looking," said Lefty Malone. "There ain't any scars on him, and the sheriff don't want to know where to find him."

"Does the sheriff want to know where to find me?"

"He's going to want to know where to find you before long. It's all in the air for you to take a flop in the jail, brother, or go to sleep in Boot Hill."

Saxon looked away from that broad, dimly lighted face. He saw the stars, and they whirled into thin, brief streaks of light.

"Is that all the news?" he asked.

"Yes," said the bartender. "Now what you got to tell me?"

"Just a little rumor that The Solitaire ran into a snag, got his gang shot up, lost his profits for losses, and had to run like hell to save his hide. That's all I heard. So long, Lefty."

"Wait a minute! Hey, wait! Is that straight?" pleaded Malone.

"Nothing is straight but a left to the chin," said big John Saxon. "So long, partner."

CHAPTER XX

WHEN Saxon pulled back through the darkness and the trees, he rejoined the big Negro, who was waiting patiently at the head of his gray mare. Even in the darkness, she was grazing. The bit clicked softly, with a muffled sound, against her teeth.

Saxon said to him: "Everything goes right along smooth and pretty in the old home town, and the old folks are waiting for Johnnie with a tear in the eye and a joint of lead pipe in the fist. Stay here while I go and see my girl that's giving me the double cross."

"Ah, boss," murmured Arthur William Creston, "I been and seen a girl leave a mighty right-minded colored man for a worthless negro that worked for an undertaker and always smelled of the embalmin' fluid. There ain't any way of figgerin' out which way a girl is gunna jump."

"Was the colored fellow she left named Arthur Creston?"

"Yes, boss, that was his name," chuckled the giant.

"Stay here. Or else you might drift along slowly behind me. Much danger of you being recognized and picked up in this town?"

"God gimme shoulders too wide for my head, and folks never are gunna forget it," answered Creston, with his usual good nature. "I better wait here till I hear guns, and then I'll come for you, Chief."

"There won't be any guns. I'll be back before long," said Saxon.

He went straight to the house of Mary Wilson. Her window, at the back of the little building, was open to the soft stir of the night air. Saxon reached up and tapped lightly against the pane until it gave out a tinny shiver of sound. When he repeated the noise, he heard the rustle of bedclothes, then the squeak of springs. A misty form of pallor grew out at him through the blackness of the room.

"Mary?" he called, quietly.

The form dissolved in the darkness. It was lost to him for a moment and then came on again. He reached in both his big hands for her, but she gave him only her own cool hands to hold.

"Is that all?" asked Saxon.

She kneeled on the floor and so brought her face almost down to the level of his. Leaning forward, she touched his forehead with her lips.

"That's sisterly," said John Saxon.

"You've been hurt!" she gasped. Her hands went out to him and touched the bandage that girdled his head. "*What* has happened, John?"

"You'll hear about it later on—rumors are in the air," said Saxon. "But the thing I want to talk about is more important. I want to tell you that I've got nearly sixty

106

thousand dollars. Is that enough for us to set up house-keeping?"

"John," said the faint, quavering voice of grief, *"what have you done?"*

"I've gotten sixty thousand bucks," said Saxon. "Doesn't that make sense?"

"You can't make that much money!" mourned the girl. "Not in such a short time. Dear old John, tell me what you've done!"

"Sure I'll tell you," said Saxon. "I've gone out and stubbed my toe against a pile of hard cash. I shifted it into my pocket, and there you are!"

"You've robbed someone! John, they'll have you in prison!"

"I'll tell you the straight of it. With some others, I ran into The Solitaire. No need for the details. The Solitaire is still alive. He was tricked or perhaps he would have beaten us. But anyway, we had the luck, and we broke up his gang and got the hard cash. It belongs to us as much as to any people in the world. My share is about sixty thousand. I'm asking you again, is that enough to start housekeeping on?"

"Sixty thousand dollars of stolen money?"

"I'm telling you again, it's as much mine as anybody's."

"It was stolen by The Solitaire—it's stolen money, John!"

"The Solitaire would have kept it, too. I didn't steal it. Taking it from The Solitaire isn't stealing it. It's simply taking a gambling chance and winning cash with guns. Isn't that straight? Listen to me: I'll have to meet The Solitaire some day. I don't know how soon. He might put me down. I might put him down. I want to know if it's fair for you and me to be married. I've got the money here, and we might have a few months of happiness, no matter how things turn out in the end. If you lose me, you'll have something to make life worth while after me. Maybe a child would turn up. That's taking things at the worst. At the best, I beat The Solitaire when he shows his hand. And we go on being happy the rest of our lives."

He saw her rocking back and forth, back and forth, and her head swaying against the rhythm of her body, like one keeping silent in spite of great agony.

"How could I sleep a night in a house built with stolen money, John? Don't you see that?"

"I don't see that. You drive me pretty near crazy when you keep on talking like this, though."

"Will you do one thing for me, John? Will you go to somebody wiser than I am, and ask him whether or not that money belongs to you?"

"Go to someone?" he growled. "I fought for that money. That coin was as good as gone from honest men. The Solitaire and his gang of thugs got it."

"Did you have honest men along with you?" she asked.

"Well, honest enough. What difference does it make?" he demanded.

"Two wrongs don't make a right."

"Mary, I'm not hearing you talk like this. It's someone else! You couldn't talk this way!"

"I'm not talking any way. John, I'm trying to show you the straight thing to do!"

"I don't need any telling about the straight thing to do. I've spent my life working like a dog. I've never taken a penny that I didn't work honest hours for. Now I get some coin from a thug—and you want me to throw it away? Throw it where? That's what I ask you. Throw it where?"

"Back to the people that The Solitaire robbed."

"I don't know whom he took this money from."

"Everybody suspects that he did the Stillman raid, not long ago."

"People suspect—people suspect—yes, but who knows? Nobody knows. Why should I throw that money away on a suspicion after I've fought for it?"

"Because unclean money can't do you any good, John. You'll only lose the money and your honor along with it."

"You're against me," groaned Saxon. "It's because you don't want to see things my way."

"I'm not against you," she pleaded.

"You are!" declared Saxon, with an aching emptiness where his heart should have been. "You're with the rest of the people of Bluewater—all against me! You have me out of sight, Mary, and now you'll have me out of mind, soon."

"But it isn't true," said the girl.

"There's the fellow who's come to start the wheels of the old mill and put new life in Bluewater. You can spend your time on him, now. Isn't that straight? This fellow Whalen—what about him?"

"He's as fine and straight and decent and good a man as I know!" exclaimed the girl.

"Yeah. And I'll bet that he is," said Saxon. "He's the best you know, and that's why you'll have him, eh? Well, that's the wisest attitude. That's what makes women good marketers. They know a bargain when they see one. They know values."

"John," said the girl, "what's happened to you? I've only known him for two days. There's no harm. There's not even been a bit of serious talk between us."

"Enough to make everyone in the town chatter about you, though," said Saxon.

"Who? Who?" she demanded, angrily.

"Even the mobs in the bars," said Saxon.

"Have you been discussing me with bartenders and drunkards?" asked the girl.

"You're *asking* for a quarrel," declared Saxon.

"I've never heard you talk in such a boorish way!" answered Mary Wilson.

"Then I'll get out of your way," said Saxon.

"John, John! Dear heaven, what *is* the matter with you? If you want better advice than mine, go to someone you can trust."

"And who would that be?"

"Well, you've always had a lot of respect for Daniel Finlay. I suppose that he's honest if any man is honest!"

"Finlay? Well, suppose I go to him?"

"If he says that it's all right—if he can say that—then I'll do whatever you say. You know it isn't money that I care about, John. I was always willing to marry you and live in a tent. I don't care about the place. You're the one who always wanted to have me hold up my head as high as other girls can do!"

The truth of this struck home in him. But still he was wounded. And in a sullen anger, which would not pass quickly, he drew back from her.

"I'll see Finlay again. And then I'll let you know. Tomorrow, perhaps."

109

"Mary!" called the sudden voice of her father.

"Yes!" she answered.

"Did I hear you talking in your sleep?"

"No," she answered. "I was awake."

There was an exclamation. Feet pounded on the floor. John Saxon would have withdrawn, but the hands of the girl clung to him. That was how Wilson found them.

He was in a fury at once.

"Who's that. Who's there?"

"I'm John Saxon," said Saxon.

"Sneaking around here in the middle of the night?" exclaimed Wilson. "I don't want you near this place again, Saxon. Mary, close that window and go back to bed."

"If you order him away from the place," said the girl, "I'll go out into the street with him."

"What are you talking about?" gasped Wilson. "Haven't I a right to give orders in my own house?"

"Yes. But I have a right to go with John if he asks me to go."

"True," groaned Wilson. "It's true."

"It's all right," said Saxon, struck with a deeper compunction. "I'm leaving now. I'll be back some time tomorrow, I hope. It's all right, Mr. Wilson. Mary, good-night."

He got away quickly and lengthened his stride as he went down the street toward the house of Daniel Finlay.

CHAPTER XXI

Mr. Daniel Finlay, after his supper, always kept the light burning until midnight or later, and the sheen of the lamp through the drawn shade in front of the room proclaimed to the village the lateness of the hours which Daniel Finlay kept. What percentage of the reputation of Mr. Finlay as a sage and a hermit of great knowledge was due to this lamp of his, it would have been hard to say. On two or three occasions, when neighbors had a chance to break in on him, he was found leaning over a large tome on his desk. As a matter of fact, he kept smaller volumes of far lighter reading always at hand in drawers of that same desk, and a single gesture of his hand was enough to cause the fiction to disappear. On this night, the rap on the door actually roused Daniel Finlay as his head lay on the book he had been brooding over, and he hastily straightened and blinked the sleep out of his eyes.

Then he called out for the stranger to enter.

The door being pushed open, big John Saxon stood on the threshold with his face a little drawn, that pallor still clinging to the lower part of his features like a white mask, and a big bandage wrapped around his head.

He closed the door hastily behind him and his eyes flickered rapidly once to this side and once to that, as though to make sure that he was alone with the lawyer.

For an instant, as he stared at that grim face, the dread that springs out of a guilty heart rose like a fountain of ice through the soul of Finlay, but a single backward glance assured him that the other could hardly know of the treachery of which Finlay had been capable. So Finlay stood up, slowly, with dignity; and with a grave smile and that handless gesture of welcome, he received his guest.

John Saxon accepted the left hand with something that was almost reverence. He said: "It's good to see you, Mr. Finlay. I've been out where there aren't many people like you."

Finlay thanked him.

"You've been hurt. There's been fighting, Saxon!" he suggested.

"The Solitaire," said Saxon, briefly.

Finlay gripped the edge of the desk.

"The Solitaire—he wounded you but you—you killed him, Saxon?"

"I wish I had," said Saxon, ruefully. "The fact is that he had me down. He thought I was dead because his first slug knocked me almost out. And then the crew I was with got to work and cleaned out his gang, and The Solitaire had to go along with the rest of 'em. But—"

"Tell me about it! Who was with you?" gasped Finlay.

"I don't know that I have a right to name 'em," said Saxon. "Not even to you. I trust you. Yes, I trust you a lot more than I trust myself, as I'm about to show you, but I don't think that I have a right to name other men."

"I don't press you," said Finlay hastily. "I wouldn't dream of pressing you. There are, in every good man, certain sacred places of the conscience—"

He made a pause there, and cleared his throat, for sometimes even Daniel Finlay was a little startled by the profound depths of his own hypocrisy. He saw before him as straightforward a youth as he had ever known. It had been his task to start poor John Saxon on a downward path. He saw, with devilish pleasure, that already, on the path which he had recommended, Saxon had rubbed elbows with death and that master purveyor of destruction, The Solitaire; but a chill of awe and something that was even remotely akin to shame pierced the lawyer as he looked upon the handsome, troubled and respectful face of Saxon.

"Let the names go," said Finlay. "You scattered the scoundrels, did you?"

"I drew out The Solitaire. And behind him came his men. My fellows hit 'em from the side and rubbed 'em out. Killed two of 'em and wounded another pretty badly. The Solitaire had to run, finally—though he really beat me. He gave me this—and I didn't scratch him, I think."

"And then?" asked the lawyer, eagerly.

"Well, then we found a lot of loot. A pile of it. And that's why I've come to you."

Finlay looked suddenly down, to keep the devil from appearing through his eyes. He loved money only a shade less than he loved mischief.

"The fact is, Mr. Finlay, that I have a share here. It amounts to fifty-eight thousand dollars. I want to ask you if I have a right to that money?"

Daniel Finlay still looked down, because he dared not lift his eyes. But finally he said: "My dear friend—my dear lad—take the money to another man. You can find plenty who are cleverer than I am. You can find plenty who will give you welcome advice. And in that case, you'll be much happier than if I should tell you what I would have to say."

"I suppose so," sighed Saxon. "I couldn't expect good news. Mary practically told me what you would say!"

"Mary?" snapped Finlay. "Have you told her about this money?"

"Why, of course. And why not?"

"One of the first things that every young man ought to learn," said Finlay, almost angrily, "is to confide in no woman, particularly about money matters."

"Not even in a wife, say?" gaped Saxon.

"Not even in a wife. I might almost say, particularly not in a wife. However—you've done the thing—well, now you come to me and ask me for advice? Advice about this stolen money?"

"You call it that?" asked Saxon, gloomily. "Well, we fought a gang of thieves and we got their stuff. Why does that make it stolen money?"

"Because it was stolen in the first place, and because—"

"Ay, Mary said the same thing. I suppose that it's right. The whole thing has to be given up?"

"Yes!" said Finlay.

"Every penny has to go?" demanded Saxon.

"Ah, well," said the lawyer, "there would be a commission for the recovery of the money. The rightful owners, of course, would pay you a commission for recovering their goods. That's no more than fair and right."

"How big a commission?" asked Saxon.

"Why—five per cent or so. Ten per cent, even, I should suppose."

"Confound them!" growled Saxon. "After a man has spent his blood and taken his life in his hands—ten per cent, eh? I should think that they'd pay twenty and thank their lucky stars that they ever saw a penny. It's the first time that anything was ever grabbed out of the teeth of The Solitaire, and the whole world knows it."

"Ten per cent—almost six thousand dollars—but then, why shouldn't you look on that as a very handsome stake, Saxon? However, let's see the money. Have you the money with you?"

His voice took on, suddenly, such a whining tone that Saxon was startled. For an instant the scales trembled and almost fell from before his eyes to enable him to see the fox in this man. But Finlay was instantly master of himself again.

Saxon, reaching into the deep pocket of his coat, pulled out the worn, crumpled, confused mass of bills and dropped them helter skelter upon the table.

"There's the stuff," he said, carelessly.

Finlay stretched out swift hands to prevent any of the money from tumbling to the floor.

"Loose in your pocket—a fortune like this?" he exclaimed.

"Ah, well," said Saxon, "I'll get little good out of it, anyway. But I'd like to ask you—how are you to find the men that have lost the stuff—the men that The Solitaire robbed?"

"Oh, easily, easily," said Finlay. "It's always easy to find men who have been robbed!"

"I don't see that," said Saxon. "A lot of robberies are blamed onto The Solitaire, and a lot of them he doesn't commit. People don't get much proof to hang on him."

"Therein lies the use of a lawyer," said Finlay, cheerfully. "You needn't worry about that, my lad. I'll look into the case with the greatest care. I'll find out exactly what needs to be done. I'll secure some perfect case against The Solitaire, and then we'll know exactly how much should be paid, and where. Trust it all to me!"

"Thanks," said Saxon. He looked grimly askance at the money. "There's such a heap of it!" he said. "When I think what that would mean, turned all into beef!"

"Ay, ay," said the lawyer. "And when you think what it will mean as a lasting testimonial to you as an honest man—when I think of that, Saxon—ah, that's the thing that stirs my blood, I can tell you!"

"Does it?" muttered Saxon. He was not in doubt, but he was in a good deal of painful reluctance. The stuff seemed his. Something in his nature cried out violently that he had as good a right to it as any man. But there it was, committed to the honest hands of Daniel Finlay, who was so confident that he would be able to find the rightful owner!

"In the first place," said the lawyer, "I want to know exactly what your next steps will be."

"I'm going—well, I don't know where. I see Mary and her father some time tomorrow, though. You know how it is with me, Mr. Finlay, and that when a man has The Solitaire for an enemy, he has to be careful where he shows himself."

"Of course I know that—of course I know that!" said

114

the lawyer. And then, as a thought flashed like a running snake across his mind: "And, as a matter of fact, I'm not so sure that I would even see Mary Wilson. On second thought, I would not see her or anyone else. I would not speak to a human being in this town, my lad, but keep all secrets to yourself. And, in the meantime, I'll look up the absolute law in my books. There *are* lawyers, John, who pretend to have all law on the tips of their tongues, but I am sufficiently honest to admit that I must lean upon these dear and unfailing companions!"

Here he waved his hand toward the shelves of his books. Afterward he went on: "I want to make perfectly sure that I am right in feeling that you should surrender this money. But if I find in my books the least scruple of a rightful claim that you may exert upon the fortune which now lies on my desk, then you may be sure that I shall use all my wits to establish the justice of that claim in the eye of the law—in the eye of that God who is above the law, and sees all the acts of our hands and of our hearts! John Saxon, leave me now to my work, and return at this same time tomorrow night!"

CHAPTER XXII

WHEN John Saxon, thoroughly pledged to see not even Mary Wilson on the next day, had left the lawyer's office, Finlay turned back from the door which he had just shut and stared at the heap of currency which lay on his desk, and such a joy came bursting up in him that it closed his eyes and parted his lips and out of his straining throat brought a faint murmur that was rather like a moan of agony than of exquisite pleasure.

And he thought, as he stood there, that the greatest of all sins is to fail to take from the fool what his folly abandons. That money, he said to himself, was surely abandoned, and therefore he, Daniel Finlay, would be committing the unpardonable sin if a penny of it ever got back to the too trusting possession of John Saxon.

Not only did the lawyer see that the money should be his, but he perceived, instantly, how he could cancel the claim of Saxon to the cash. He could not very well do it by legal means, but he could use the powerful reagent, death, to remove Saxon from this earth and all the goods of it, whatever.

He himself did not care to execute the task, but he knew at once what hand he would employ. He would employ the most fatal hand in the world and yet, instead of receiving a favor, he would seem to be conferring one!

When Finlay perceived this, another burst of joy flooded his soul and body. It left him trembling, but calm and determined.

The money, in the first place, he had to dispose of with care, but he knew exactly what to do in all such cases. He had merely to descend into his deep, narrow cellar, and there he pulled out from the brick foundation wall a pair of loose bricks which opened the mouth of a small cavity. Into that cavity he reached and fondled with a knowing touch a tarpaulin bag which was already inside the hole. It contained the savings of his guilty life of work; it contained the very heart of Daniel Finlay. As for this new accession of wealth, he simply wrapped it in a handkerchief and pushed the parcel inside. It filled the total space. The bricks then were pushed in, and they made the wall, to all appearances, perfectly compact and strong again.

After this, he went up the stairs, got his hat, put out the light in his front room, and retreated to the shed behind his house. He kept there one tough little mustang which flourished like a goat even on the meager rations which Finlay gave it. This horse he saddled, led down the back lane, mounted, and then jogged across the town to the last house on its western edge, a little shanty set apart from the rest of the village by a broad pasture field.

In front of that house he halted the mustang and called cautiously:

"Molly! Oh, Molly!"

He repeated the call. He rode closer and banged on the front door, and then listened to the brief echo go booming through the little place.

116

After a moment, a window screeched up, and a pale form leaned out on the sill.

"Well?" said a girl's voice.

"Hello, Molly," said Finlay.

"Hello, Daniel Devil," said Molly. "What you want?"

"I haven't come from Boots, if that's what you mean," said the lawyer.

"Boots? That poor dummy?" said Molly. "What about him?"

"He's still alive in spite of your friend," said Finlay.

"In spite of my friend? Why, if The Solitaire really wanted to wipe out that little snake, he'd do it in a minute."

"He'd better start wanting, now!" answered Finlay.

He dismounted and stood at the window.

"Don't come too near me," said the girl. "I smell sulphur and brimstone when you're too near. What got you out at this time of the night?"

She was the one person in the world who had seen through the lawyer. Perhaps it was because there was enough evil in her own nature to enable her to recognize the same qualities in Finlay. At any rate, the wall was down, the door open between them. Yet they reserved for one another a peculiar respect, and if she called him Daniel Devil, it was not in the presence of other people, not even in that of her lover, The Solitaire. He, in return, had many times been useful to her, and would be so again. The call of kind worked between them, so to speak, and he felt for her something that was almost an affection. He drew back a little as she spoke, and then said: "Molly, I'm not here to gossip. I want to know where I can find The Solitaire."

"If I knew, would I be fool enough to tell you?" asked Molly.

"Molly, Molly! Not trust old Daniel Finlay?" he asked, in mock reproach.

She laughed heartily at this.

"I'd rather trust the devil, and you know it," she said. "But go on, Finlay. What's eating you? What makes you think that you can play an ace of trumps like The Solitaire in your dirty business?"

117

"I'll tell you something about The Solitaire," said he. "He's nursing a sore head and a sour stomach, just now."

"You'd know, would you?" asked the girl.

"He's been cleaned, Molly," said Finlay. "He's been trimmed of every penny."

"You *are* the devil, or you couldn't know that this soon," she told him.

"Of course I'm the devil," said Finlay.

He made a cigarette, deftly, in spite of the darkness, and lighted a match for it. The flare of the flame showed him the pretty, swarthy face of Molly, with eyes almost too big and lustrous. She was resting her chin on one small fist, and her eyes watched Finlay with a wide open boldness. Shame had no place in her.

"If you're the devil, whistle for your cousin, and The Solitaire will appear," said the girl.

"What's the matter between you and The Solitaire?" he asked. "Are you sour with him?"

"He hasn't had enough time to get tired of me, yet," she answered. "And now that he's flat for a while, he'll be true and good. It's when a man's flush that he gets tired of a girl quick."

"Tell me where to find The Solitaire," said Finlay. "If you don't, he'll be through with you. I've got things to tell him that he has to hear."

"Maybe you have; maybe your friend the sheriff has a lot more. What a dummy you must think I am, Danny!"

"Suppose," said Finlay, seeing that he would have to contribute a bit of concrete information, "that I'm able to put The Solitaire in the way to laying hands on the fellow who made him run like a scared dog?"

"Hold on! You mean to say that The Solitaire ran like a dog?" demanded Molly.

"He didn't tell you that? He didn't tell you that two of his men were killed, either, I suppose?"

"Yes, he told me that. Danny, maybe I can trust you, after all."

"Try me," said Finlay.

"Wait out there, then."

She withdrew from the window. After a time, he heard the rear door of the house open, and then a thin whistle cut the night. It was answered, after a moment, from among the trees, where the forest rolled down the mountainside close to the house.

The expectation of Finlay grew and grew, and he was not surprised when a dark figure appeared silently from among the tree trunks, not ten strides from him. At the same time the girl called from the front door: "It's Finlay, the lawyer. He says that he has something worth saying. Come in if you want to!"

Prepared as he had been by the whistled signals, still Finlay was amazed that the much-hunted outlaw should dare to hide himself so near to the town.

The figure beside the trees came rapidly up to Finlay. "You're Daniel Finlay, all right," said The Solitaire. "What do you want with me, Finlay?"

"I want to do you a good turn."

"How big a turn and what's your price?"

"I'm not selling. I'm giving."

The Solitaire laughed. "I like to hear men talk like that," he declared. "It shows that they think I'm still pretty young. Go ahead, Finlay."

"I've heard about the bad time you've had. I've heard about two of your men being killed—"

"Pretty little Molly has been talking, eh?"

"Not a word. She's a better girl than you think. Also, I've heard how you were run off the ground at the fight. I got that from young Saxon."

"Ah?" said The Solitaire, his musical voice running up the scale a little. "Is Saxon around town?"

"Lying low. Sneaking around by night for fear he might be snapped up by the great Solitaire, like a mouse by an owl. But he's talking pretty big about the way he ran you in front of him into the woods and you didn't dare to turn back and fight."

"It doesn't matter," said The Solitaire. "He has to die anyway. I might as well have another good reason for killing him."

"Perhaps," said the lawyer. "And I suppose that you want to finish off the job in short order?"

"The sooner the better, of course. If people have started talking—I might as well make an example of young Saxon."

Saxon was not, in fact, much younger than The Solitaire, but what a difference between their worlds of experience, thought the lawyer. He added, aloud: "The fact is, Saxon is going to be at a place I could name to you at a certain time tomorrow night."

"If that's the fact," said The Solitaire, "I'll pay for the news—but I won't pay in advance."

"In fact," said Daniel Finlay, thinking of fifty-eight thousand dollars, "you won't pay a penny on any account. I'll donate the news to you."

"Why?" asked The Solitaire. "I've never given a damn for you, nor you for me, the little we know of each other."

"We may come to know each other better," declared Finlay. "And I'm wise enough to know that every man needs a friend in any sort of a pinch. My pinch may come later, and then I'll send you word."

"Very well," said The Solitaire. "You warned me once before about Saxon, and your warning panned out the first time. Tell me why you hate Saxon, will you?"

The voice of Molly suddenly spoke behind them, saying:

"Why does the devil hate everything that's outside of hell?"

"That's an answer," declared The Solitaire. "But get back inside that house and out of hearing, Molly. You know I won't have eavesdroppers."

"Why not?" asked Molly. "All I'm likely to get out of you for a long time is information!"

Finlay expected an explosion of wrath from the outlaw. Instead, The Solitaire merely laughed.

"There's no one like her," he said. "She's tough enough to break the teeth of a saw."

CHAPTER XXIII

BLUEWATER slept and the night was clear and still when big John Saxon stepped down the street toward the house of Daniel Finlay. He was angry because he felt it better to arrive in the town at this hour of the night. No matter what rumors might be going the rounds about him, did it not remain clear that he had not offended the law—as yet? He expected from Finlay, this night, the answer which would make him free of conscience, altogether. And yet he regretted, in a way, having left his money in the hands of Finlay. He regretted it, but, having let Finlay take the coin, his respect for the lawyer was greater than any desire on his part to have it back in his pocket.

He was troubled, now, because he had told the Wilsons that he intended to come to see them this day—and up to this hour they might still be waiting, might they not?

This made him lengthen his stride a good bit, and coming toward the house of Finlay, he saw that nothing lived or moved except one spark, as of a lighted cigarette, which faintly glowed on the veranda of the next house. That would be old Jim Paston, sitting out for his midnight smoke; the old boy was always a bad sleeper, and all his day's work in the blacksmith shop could not close his eyes readily at night.

He was rather sorry that even Jim Paston should be around, but after all, he would be able to get into the house of Finlay without much trouble, and unrecognized.

This was his thought as he turned quickly through the gate and up the steps to the shallow veranda of Finlay's house. But as his hand reached out to knock, he saw the cigarette smoker on the adjoining veranda step off it and then, deliberately, over the low picket fence that divided the two houses. He looked bigger, in the dimness of the starlight, than the outline of the blacksmith should have loomed.

Then that voice spoke which, for three days, had never been entirely out of the ears of Finlay. It had rung like a death-knell in his memory, and now it rose like a ghost from the ground and spoke to him again.

"All right, Saxon," it said. "Step down here and we'll finish things off."

It was a nightmare fear that rushed over Saxon. He wanted to flee, but something told him it would be like a clumsy mountain grouse trying to escape, in the open air, from the pounce of a swift hawk. There was only one way for him, and that was forward. A strange yell rang in his ears. It was his own shout, unrecognizable, as he flung himself past the lighted square of the front window of Daniel Finlay and, reaching the edge of the veranda, hurled himself in a mighty leap straight at his enemy.

He saw the gleam of the gun in the hand of The Solitaire. His own Colt was out, more slowly. A bullet slashed the air beside his face. His own gun exploded— jammed—and as he leaped he hurled it before him at that lofty target.

The Solitaire lightly dodged the flying weight, but he could not quite dodge the bulk of Saxon as he leaped after his gun. A second explosion of The Solitaire's Colt seemed to flare in the very face of Saxon as his shoulder struck the breast of the outlaw and they both crashed to the ground.

He had only one thought, in his desperation.

Strange to say, it was not that he had escaped from two bullets which had been fired at him, and not that he had reduced the battle to handwork, but that in this dim light he would not see the bright, hypnotic eyes of The Solitaire.

The hands of the outlaw were in fact empty. In the fall, he had lost his Colt. He had other guns about him, no doubt, but that did not matter; there would be no time to draw them, for the hands of Saxon were at work.

He tried for a full Nelson, got it, and found the strangle hold suddenly slipped. He grappled with the body of Witherell. It was like grappling with a great cat, made slippery with waves of contracting muscles. The form of The Solitaire escaped him, and he leaped to his feet barely in time to see his enemy erect before him and the wink of steel coming into his hand.

Saxon hit for the head with all his might. Grace, or that penetrating light that springs from despair itself, guided the blow home. He felt it shock heavily against the jaw of The Solitaire, and saw the man go down. The gun exploded as it struck the ground. Saxon kicked at it, and knocked it away, then he dived at the prostrate form.

Lights were streaking the night. Shouts and exclamations rattled through the air. People were trampling out over their porches, drawn by the sound of guns. And he, John Saxon, was striving there with the great Solitaire on even terms!

He tried, as he dropped, to drive his elbow into the face of the outlaw. But the target slipped away from him, and he failed. He tried again, grappling the other with his left arm, to draw them so close together that Witherell would not have a chance to free a hand.

In spite of his effort, Witherell managed to jam up a fist under the chin of Saxon, and the blow knocked sparks through the brain of Saxon. Again and again that shortened triphammer shocked against his consciousness.

He had to get away from it. He threw back his head, and instantly an arm crooked around his neck in a strangle hold.

Despair, again, helped him. He rose to his feet, with the twisting, straining weight of the murderer clinging to him. And the strong flare of a lantern's light fell upon them both.

"The Solitaire!" shouted the voice of the blacksmith, only yards away. "The Solitaire! Get him, boys!"

A faint, snarling cry came from the lips of The Solitaire as he heard that voice. One wrench and he was gone out of the numbed grasp of John Saxon.

Saxon lurched after him. He had the nightmare feeling that if he could lay hands on the elusive ghost it would be better to die outright, now, than to have to dream of another encounter with this monster.

So, rushing after him, he got his hand on the coat of The Solitaire as the latter reached the front fence. The coat came away in his hand, like a skin easily shed, and The Solitaire sprinted straight around the corner of the building.

Three men who were running across the street fired at him as he fled. He dodged like a snipe. Perhaps one of the bullets had hurt him. Then he was out of sight.

Saxon, running in pursuit, from the rear of the house had a fleeting glimpse of a shadowy man leaping on a shadowy horse, and both images instantly disappeared among the shrubbery of the back lot. The drumming of the hoofbeats swung rapidly away.

He was gone.

"Get that man!" the voice of the sheriff was crying. "Get the other one—The Solitaire's gone and you might as well follow a fish in the river as try to catch him in the dark. But get the other one!"

Many hands fell upon John Saxon. He stood stupidly, breathing hard. The dazed mist was leaving his mind. He could feel across his chin the battering received from the fists of the outlaw. And the coat of The Solitaire was still in his hand!

A lantern's light flashed in his face.

"John Saxon!" called someone. "Hey, it's John Saxon."

Then another was shouting: "It's Saxon! He's killed one Witherell and now he's gunning for another in the dark. God, what a man!"

They brought John Saxon up past the side of the house. The sheriff got to him.

"Saxon! By the eternal!" said the sheriff. "I never thought—this is damned strange—"

A calm voice was saying, somewhere in the background: "This is what, my friends? Midnight murder again, in our town?"

That was Daniel Finlay, and at the sound of his words, Saxon was relieved and comforted. There was at least one honest man in the world and that man, in a sense, was on his side, he felt. It gave him an odd feeling of security, even against such an enemy as The Solitaire.

More lanterns were gathered about him. He saw astonished and half frightened faces as he pushed forward into the yard of the lawyer's house. And there, searching the ground, he quickly found and picked up three guns. One was his own trusted Colt and the other pair were similar weapons, but with the triggers and the sights filed away— the real hairtriggers with which The Solitaire had fanned his way to a murderous fame.

So he stood there with the captured coat hanging over his arm and his hands filled with the weapons. The sheriff, gruff and brutal as he could be, on occasion, was slapping him on the shoulder.

"By God, Saxon," he said, "I know you have some hard feelings about me, but I take off my hat to any hombre that'll go mousing at night, when the mouse is The Solitaire! Where are the nerves in you, man? Haven't you any fear of the devil and the dark?"

124

And all of them in fact, were slanting their eyes at John Saxon, as they stood around.

"He's given The Solitaire the run," said a voice in the background. Was not that the voice of Daniel Finlay? "He's killed one of the murdering Witherells, and he's made the other scamper like a whipped dog! Gentlemen, I propose a cheer for a hero and a fellow townsman—John Saxon!"

Why, they split the sky with that cheer. And here was Lefty Malone, grabbing Saxon by the arm and shaking him and calling: "Come over to the old Rolling Bones, son. I'm going to open it up and the drinks are on the house as long as you're inside it. Come on, everybody, and we'll drink the sun up!"

Only a part of the mind of John Saxon comprehended what he heard. The rest of his wits were back there in the immediate past, struggling with the destroying hands of The Solitaire. The outlaw had beaten him with guns, and beaten him again hand to hand. In every possible respect, he was superior to John Saxon.

What, therefore, would the future be like?

There would have to be another encounter, and then the luck which had saved Saxon twice would sure run out and nature and the better man would take their course.

Finlay was beside him, saying: "Come in with me, my son. Or do you want to fill your brain with whiskey fumes —to forget something that has passed?"

"I'll come with you," said Saxon. "You're the one that I want to see."

So he turned his back on the crowd and walked into the house, with Lefty Malone shouting in the street: "Boys, I'm opening up for you all anyway. We got the best man on the range in this town, and we're gunna drink to him, tonight!"

CHAPTER XXIV

INSIDE the house, Daniel Finlay looked over his guest for a moment, with a sense of horror and of hatred combined. He had laid the trap and he had brought the quarry to it. He had provided on the spot the terrible destroyer, the great Solitaire, and yet this big young man had managed to escape destruction again!

There was the grim possibility, it seemed, that Saxon was actually the better man of the two; and on the other hand—a thing that carried the bitterness of death to Daniel Finlay—nearly sixty thousand dollars that might become his own would now have to be shifted back into the possession of this fellow.

There might be some shifts and dodges, however, by which he could avoid that issue. If there were luck in the air, he might manage to turn John Saxon into a different train of thought. Because one thing was certain—that the gull still suspected nothing and looked upon Finlay as his friend.

Finlay said: "This is a frightful thing to me, John. This is a thing that strikes me to the heart."

He stood in the middle of the floor and considered the bandaged head of Saxon. The struggle had opened the wound, somewhat, and the red of blood was staining the bandage. Finlay made one of those handless gestures of his which always served to open the hearts of his fellow men.

He went on: "I ask you to come to my house, John, and in my very yard—"

Here he paused, seemingly overcome.

"Why, you couldn't—help that, Mr. Finlay," said Saxon. "The Solitaire is a devil who knows how to read the minds of men, I suppose—but how he could have known that I was to come here, I don't know. I'd swear that nobody in the world knew that except you and me."

Saxon began to shake his head, and the heart of the lawyer quaked. Saxon, in fact, had reduced the thing to an absurdity. There was no doubt that he had only to go one step forward to perceive that only from the lawyer himself could The Solitaire have learned of the meeting place and the hour of it.

Finlay said, a little hastily: "A fellow like The Solitaire has all the patience of a sailing buzzard or of a hunting cat. For the sake of his fill of blood, he would be willing to wait for a long time, of course, and I suppose he knew —or perhaps he might have guessed—that he would find you coming, sooner or later, either to the house of— Wilson, or to my house, John. Because, as a matter of fact, I've talked a little bit too much about you. I can see that, now. I should not have mentioned you. But I've been unable to keep silence. For the truth is, John, that I've admired your courage and your ability to pick yourself up from the bottom of despair and show yourself the hero—I've admired that so much that I've had to talk a little about you. Enough, perhaps, so that people might suspect that we are friends, and therefore The Solitaire has posted himself beside my house in the hope of seeing you enter it."

"Ay, that's it," said John Saxon. "It's a good thing to me," he added, simply, "that I have a friend like you, Mr. Finlay. I don't know—but sometimes I feel as though I'd be going straight to the devil, if it weren't that I have you to lean on and give me advice."

"Do you?" said Finlay, looking down and drawing a stealthy but a very deep breath. "Is that what you feel?"

And, in his heart, he said: "I'm winning again—and I'll make a worse fool of him than ever. I've got him in my hands, and I'll squeeze the blood and the dollars out of him! I can be sure of that!"

"I feel it," Saxon was saying. "The fact is, Mr. Finlay, that there's something to be said for a free life, of the kind that I've been having for a few days. When I started for your place tonight, I was sorry that I'd turned over that money to you. Mind you, I don't mean that I'm really sorry—not now—but for a while I wanted it for myself. It seemed almost as though I'd earned it with blood and the chance I took. But now that I'm with you, I can open my eyes and see things more clearly. You know how it is? A good friend helps a fellow to come out of the dark and see things right."

"I hope so. With all my heart I hope so," said the

127

hypocrite. "And when I think that a crippled old man, withdrawn from the world, can have influence over a man of courage and force and youth like you, John, I'm amazed and bewildered, a little, and very grateful!"

He was hunting about in his mind for the next step that he would take to assure for himself the possession of the money that had been entrusted to him by Saxon.

Saxon was saying: "There's still The Solitaire. He's still ahead of me, and he's a big hurdle, Mr. Finlay. Except for him, I feel right now that I'd go to work punching cows by the month for regular pay. It was a sort of a shock to have that devil rise out of the dark, tonight, and speak to me!"

He shook his head.

"You've faced him and you've beaten him twice," said the lawyer, "and of course you have no fear of him, now!"

"I've faced him two times, and two times I've had luck," said Saxon. "You know what happened the first time. And tonight I simply happened to surprise him by what I did. My gun jammed—and I had to throw myself at him—and he didn't expect that, you see. But when we were wrestling around, he was a better man that I am, Mr. Finlay. I hate to admit it. I thought, a little time ago, that I could stand up to any man in the world, with bare hands. I've had a life of work behind me, hard work to build up the muscles. I've trained myself like a regular ring fighter. But in spite of all that, The Solitaire is a stronger and a faster man than I am. He would have killed me—he was strangling me at the very moment that somebody recognized his face and shouted—and then he ran. I had such good luck that I even managed to get away from him the two guns that he was wearing. But it was all luck, luck, luck—and the next time that I run into him, my luck will run out!"

Finlay, as he listened to this speech, felt in his heart a vast delight. The honesty and the humility of Saxon meant nothing to him. He had not the slightest feeling for anything connected with this trusting fellow, except the fifty-eight thousand dollars that had come from him. He had begun to despair of finding an agent that could make the money safe to his own hands. If The Solitaire failed,

128

it surely seemed that all other men must fail, also. But now he heard The Solitaire vindicated, and from the lips of the apparent conqueror himself!

A new device was instantly born into that fertile brain of his.

"There will be no next time, my friend," said the lawyer. "If you are wise, there will be no next time. You'll leave the country and avoid the danger."

"Leave the country?" said John Saxon, in sudden pain. "But how can I do that? It's home to me. It's more to me—the face of the mountains, even—than the faces of friends or family, or anything like that. I love it, Mr. Finlay, and I can't leave it."

"Not forever," answered the lawyer. "Of course I don't mean that. But the fact is that a trip away would do you good and also probably save your neck. The Solitaire won't follow you far. And after a short time, you can return, because you know that a man like The Solitaire can't last long. He's reached nearly the end of his rope, and before long he'll reveive his dose of lead."

"I've got no means to leave," argued Saxon. He thought of Mary Wilson and added, desperately: "I can't leave. Everything that means anything to me is right around this place!"

"Your girl?" said the lawyer, with a smile. "Ah, she'll wait for you—perhaps. And as for money to travel with and live on—honest money—I want to ask you what reward you think that the Lumber and Mining Bank in Stillman will offer you when you bring back to them a part of the money that was stolen out of their vault?"

"The Lumber and Mining Bank?" exclaimed Saxon. "But they're a lot of skinflints and robbers and bloodsuckers. I'd rather give back the stuff to anyone except to them!"

"The law," said Daniel Finlay, rather sternly, "is no selector of persons, and you will find in this life, John, that it is not what you want to do but what you ought to do that gives to your life its honest savor that will enable you, in the end, to go down to the grave with a full and an unshaken heart!"

He was rather proud of this impromptu speech, in spite of a certain amount of confusion in it.

Saxon said: "I'm shaken up, Mr. Finlay. I'll do what you say."

"Very well," said Finlay. "Let it be tomorrow. Let it be tomorrow that you start down for the town of Stillman to make that honorable restitution. And that act, my lad, will establish you as an honorable man, a man above suspicion, all the days of your life. Such a reputation is a great deal better than a crown of gold and diamonds."

He added, inspired: "I'll go with you, John. I'll ride all the way with you!"

"Will you?" said Saxon. "Well—not tomorrow. Three days from now, Mr. Finlay, if you don't mind. I have something to do. I have to see Mary Wilson—and there are other things to do. Then—then I'll go along with you. But I wish the money honestly belonged to any other bank than the Lumber and Mining at Stillman! They're famous for sucking the blood out of people! However, it's the way you say. I'm tired of trying to think things out for myself. You can take charge of everything, if you don't mind!"

"With the greatest pleasure in the world!" said Finlay.

CHAPTER XXV

IT was not an hour later, on this night, that Finlay dismounted from his horse before the house of Molly, on the edge of the town. And this time he found a light in the front window, facing toward the mountain. When he rapped on the door, he clearly heard the voice of The Solitaire, bell-like, ominous, and he was amazed. "Go see who that is!" commanded The Solitaire.

"Arthur, don't be a fool!" gasped the girl. "You'll be heard."

"Let me be heard and be damned. I'm damned already with bad luck, and I don't care what happens," said The Solitaire.

The door was pulled open a crack by Molly.

"Hello, here's Daniel the Devil!" said Molly. And over her shoulder she asked: "How about it?"

"Bring him in. Bring anybody in," said The Solitaire.

Daniel Finlay stepped into the rattledown shack and saw the front room furnished in a pleasant Mexican style, with sheepskins on the floor, and a couch that was an Indian willow bed, piled with Indian blankets.

At the central round table sat The Solitaire himself, with dust still on his clothes, and a streak of blood drying on one side of his face. He looked at the lawyer with a sullen and challenging sneer.

"I couldn't bring it off, eh?" he said. "And you're here to ask me why? Well, I'll tell you one thing—I'm just about as glad that I failed, because why in hell should I play my hand into your schemes? Will you tell me why I should?"

He pushed back his chair a little and stared angrily at Finlay who merely responded: "That's forgotten. That's in the past. I've a new idea for you, Solitaire!"

He waved toward the girl.

"Send her out, and I'll tell you what," said Finlay.

She had on a dressing gown of tan wool with a bright Indian design worked over it in red and blue. Her hair was tousled. Her face sadly lacked the paint she usually wore, but her big eyes were as bright and as bold as ever.

"I'll stay here, thanks," said Molly. "Even The Solitaire isn't quite bright enough to read your mind, Daniel. But I'm the little girl for that."

Finlay stared at her with both hate and admiration in his eyes.

"I don't know that I want to talk to you, anyway, Finlay," said the outlaw. "Molly, give me another drink."

She poured whiskey into his glass and offered another to the lawyer. He drank it off, with a single gesture of greeting to her and to The Solitaire.

"I'm here to stay, Daniel," she said, resting her arms on the back of a chair. "So blaze away, if you have anything to say."

"I've offered you Saxon once," said the lawyer. "I'm going to offer him to you again."

"In your front yard, eh, with plenty of neighbors ready to jump down my back, like a lot of hell cats? Thanks, I don't want any more of your schemes!"

Finlay nodded, his eye cold and bright.

131

"You've had enough, have you?" he demanded. "I'm not surprised. He's made you run twice, and I suppose that's enough to shake any man's nerve."

The Solitaire leaped to his feet with an oath.

"What in hell do you mean by that?" he snarled. "I was choking the life out of him when the other fools broke in on us!"

"Go back and say that in Bluewater," said Finlay, calmly. "They're spending the night cheering John Saxon and drinking to him in the Rolling Bones. Go back and tell the boys there what you were doing to Saxon, and they'll laugh in your face."

The Solitaire made a long, catlike stride forward, with a gesture as though he would drive his fist into the lawyer's face. But he checked himself, confronted by the sneering smile of Finlay.

The latter went on: "You're half mad with disgust, and no wonder, because you've been beaten twice by luck; and no matter what the other people in Bluewater think, John Saxon was honest enough to tell me that you're a better man than he is."

"Did he say that?" exclaimed The Solitaire, suddenly shining again.

And the girl, with a frown, muttered: "Did he say that? Then he's a pretty good hombre! It takes a real man to refuse to be a hero when the boys are giving him a cheer."

She turned to The Solitaire.

"Arthur," she said, "mind what I tell you. This fellow Saxon has something to him, if he can talk like that. I know what I'm saying. A man without brag is always mighty dangerous when it comes to a fight!"

"Keep your mouth shut till I ask you to open it," replied The Solitaire.

"Bah!" sneered the girl. "You've had another licking, and now you take it out on your woman. But you're going to find out that I'm not a rag to wipe your boots on. You'll treat me right, or I'll burn hell's lining right out of you!"

Said The Solitaire, softly: "I'm going to have the choking of you, one of these days!"

"You lie!" she answered. "You'll be dead of the poison I give you, first!"

"Molly, be still. You'd best," cautioned Finlay, regarding the white, rigid face of The Solitaire. For there was dark murder in his eyes.

"He's pretty, ain't he?" demanded Molly of Finlay. "Take a look at that hombre of mine and tell me if he's pretty or not, will you? With the blood on his face and the dirt on his mouth and the whiskey in his rotten heart! Oh, he's a pretty boy, all right!"

The hands of The Solitaire worked, but there was a fearless devil in the girl.

"Go back to your little sneak of a Boots," said The Solitaire. "He'll still take you, I suppose!"

"Laugh at him, like a fool," said Molly, "but he'll have the killing of you one of these days, I'm thinking."

"All right," said The Solitaire, pouring out more whiskey and downing it. "I *am* a fool to try to talk you down. Finlay, this is no night to talk to me. I can't talk. I'm half crazy. They say that he gave me the run, do they?"

"He's got your guns. He's even got your coat," said the lawyer, calmly.

The Solitaire beat his fists against his own face. He groaned deeply.

"Look at the poor sucker," said Molly, with a still and judicial eye. "He takes it pretty hard, doesn't he? But maybe he'll think that this was easy—when Saxon gets through with him the second time."

The Solitaire, absolutely maddened, leaped at her and gripped her by the hair. She stood still as a stone, without changing face, without one shadow of fear in her eyes. And the grasp of The Solitaire turned into a caressing stroke.

"By God," said he, "I'm afraid of *you*, Molly, and that's the truth."

"Keep it like that and we'll get on," said the girl, calmly. "Now you go ahead and speak your piece, Finlay; I'll see that the big boy listens to it, right through."

Daniel Finlay said, at last: "Three days from now, I'm riding to Stillman with John Saxon. I'm starting from town just after sun-up. We're riding the old Stillman Pass because it's a shorter cut than the other way. You understand? Also, it goes through wilder country."

"You cold-hearted devil!" said the girl to Finlay. "I

know that pass myself. The best place for a murder that I ever heard of! Even Indians couldn't think up a road with more murder corners on it. You see his idea, Solitaire?"

The Solitaire, rather subdued after his last clash with Molly, sat down in a chair and rested his big, handsome chin on his fist.

"Finlay, what do you get out of this?"

"Hard cash," answered Finlay, instantly.

It was hard for him to confess this, but he had made up his mind on the way to the shack that he had better be as frank as possible with the great outlaw.

"How much hard cash?" asked the outlaw.

"Fifty-eight thousand dollars. That's Saxon's share of the money that he took away from you."

The way this was phrased made the lips of The Solitaire twitch and curl. Then he said: "He's a fool if he didn't take a bigger split than that."

"He doesn't care about the money. The power is all that he wants," said Finlay.

"Is it?" asked Molly. "Then he sounds better and better to me. He sounds like a real man, Daniel. Is he?"

"He's a thick-wit," said the lawyer. "And the poor fool is tempted to live outside the law, just now. He could make a fortune out of it, of course. But he won't do that. No, he won't do that at all. Because Daniel Finlay is persuading him that it's better, for the time being, to be an honest man."

"You're persuading him to be a dead man!" snapped the girl.

"Listen!" said The Solitaire. "Listen to her, will you? She likes this fellow Saxon pretty well, doesn't she?"

"And why shouldn't she?" asked Molly. "He sounds like a right man to me. Maybe he *is* a right man. I've never met one, and I'd like to see his mug. What does he look like, Daniel?"

"Big. Big and blond and handsome," said the lawyer. "Yes, you'd like him, Molly, but you haven't a chance, there. He's picked out his girl."

"He's got her, has he?" sneered Molly. "He's one of the one woman in the world till death does him part, eh?"

"He's exactly that," agreed the lawyer.

134

"Well," said Molly, "a whole flock of those hombres have been parted from their women, at that. Who is she?"

"Be quiet," interrupted The Solitaire. "Now, you talk up, Finlay. You want nearly sixty thousand iron men out of this, and that's a lot of the stuff to pay over for the hide of one thick-head like this fellow Saxon."

"He may be a thick-head," said the lawyer, "but what a lot he means to you, that golden headed little boy!"

The Solitaire appreciated this enough to laugh.

"I don't know. You may be double-crossing me, Finlay."

"Ask Molly," said Finlay. "She knows me, I dare say, a little bit better than you do."

Molly walked up to Finlay and looked straight into his eyes. Then she nodded.

"He means it," she said. "When I give him the acid test, like this, I can always tell when he's on the level, and he means it. Besides, it's the sort of thing that he'd like, anyway. Murder, and another fellow to do the dirty work, while he enjoys the sight of the blood—and collects the hard cash afterward!"

"You like him a lot, don't you?" asked The Solitaire.

"Sure I like him," said Molly. "Because he's all together in one piece. That's why I like him. There ain't a bone in his body except meanness, and there ain't a thought in his head except poison. I like to see 'em that way. That's one reason that I like you, Solitaire. I want my men all white or all black. And you're a damned rotten sort of a murdering devil, Solitaire."

This speech slid off the shoulders of both men, perhaps because they were both attacked with an equal violence and were able to look at one another and smile.

"Let that all go," said Finlay. "Are you satisfied?"

"We'll split that cash two ways," said The Solitaire.

"We'll split it only one way, and that way is all mine. You get the fun," said Finlay.

"Well," said The Solitaire, "I'm pretty busted, just now. But I sort of think this job is worth a big commission. Do we shake on it?"

"Yes," said the lawyer, holding out his left hand.

"No, thanks," said The Solitaire. "I'll take the right one, even if it's only a stump!"

CHAPTER XXVI

SAXON, from the edge of the woods, looked down on Bluewater. It was not a big town but it was his central world and now he was as important to the townsmen as they were to him. He had to look back a vast distance to the time when he had been simply a small rancher on the verge of the place, coming in now and again to buy a few things at the store, and twice a year driving in a small batch of cattle. He had been busy then turning beef into cash and cash back into beef again, making small cows into big ones, as it were, by that margin of labor and care which he personally supplied. His steps up and forward had been so small, so short, that the progress was like that of a snail. No wonder that his years of effort had been wiped out at a stroke! But now he was wanted down there in the town; people were ready to open their hands and their hearts for him.

Of course it would be dangerous to enter the place. Every time he showed himself in Bluewater he would be showing himself, in a sense, to the eyes of The Solitaire. However, he felt the temptation growing up in him irresistibly.

"I'm riding down," he said.

Arthur William Creston, standing just a trifle behind his chief, said gloomily:

"Yeah, and a lot of fish like to come up into the sun, but that's when the kingfisher gets 'em." He pointed down at the town and added: "No matter if you don't see him— The Solitaire is seein' you!"

"Some people," murmured Saxon, "say that he spends most of his time near Bluewater. That doesn't seem possible."

"Boss," answered Creston, "that hombre just begins where we leave off understanding. But don't you go down into that town in the daylight. Ain't you met up with trouble enough there by night?"

"I have to see someone," said Saxon. He thought of Mary Wilson, and his heart poured out to her. "I'm going down now."

He mounted. He barely heard Creston mutter: "Black gals, yaller gals, white gals, they got different colors but they all make the same trouble."

Saxon hesitated no longer, but rode down the slope with the sun flashing on the proud neck and shoulders of his horse. That was a gift, in a way, from The Solitaire. And perhaps, he thought, other good things might come by inadvertence out of his acquaintance with the bandit. Good things—or a bullet through the brain!

When he got near the town, instead of taking the shortest cut behind the houses, and so coming right up to the Wilson place, he entered at the foot of the long, winding main street. And he did not canter his horse. He let it dog-trot, comfortably, and though the eyes of Saxon were fixed straight before him, you may be sure that he was well aware of everything that happened to right and left of him. For one thing, a rifle might peer at him at any moment. But what he hoped for was the thing that happened.

There was a ripple of noise, a babbling of excitement; then a dozen youngsters spilled straight at him out of houses, out of vacant lots. Windows went up with a slam, screen doors flew wide with a jangle. Women stood in doorways, calling out and waving; or they leaned into the sun and laughed and shouted. Men came out, more than a step or two. They waved their hats at John Saxon. They kept laughing, and he knew the reason for their happiness. If one honest man could beat a rogue like The Solitaire, then it made all other honest men seem stronger, more competent, able to meet all others on any plane whatever. It removed from vice and crime its dangerous premium; it made the bee as formidable as the wasp.

He could understand what was in their minds, but he could not help wondering if it were true that he was still honest! Could the leader of Boots and Cullen and the rest really be considered an honest man? He banished that doubt as quickly as he could, and fell to waving cheerfully to faces that he recognized. He spotted a good many who had laughed at him when Bob Witherell had made him dance and run on this same main street. But he could forgive them. Had they perhaps laughed and mocked an honest man and were they now applauding a rogue?

137

When a man abandons all else in order to make of himself a cutting edge—what is his metal good for, then, except to make trouble for others?

The tumult grew every moment. They kept on singing out his name, high and low, from men and women and children, saying, "Saxon, Saxon, Saxon!" over and over. One would have thought that they loved him; instead, they were glorying in the thing they thought he had done.

"If I were honest," he told himself, "I'd explain the whole truth to them. Am I honest?"

Something closed up his throat and stopped thought, speech.

From the window of the Wilson house, Elizabeth Wilson leaned to find out the cause of the uproar. Her daughter stood behind her at the same window, girt with a white apron, a dish towel in her hand. Then, around the farthest corner they could see, they saw Saxon coming. His fine horse shone in the morning sun. Just then he took off his hat and waved to a friend, turning in the saddle, and the fresh white bandage around his head gleamed, in the eyes of Mary Wilson, far brighter than a crown of silver or of gold. There was a dragging troop of children about him. Some of them clung to his stirrups; others thronged in front of his horse, which constantly seemed about to strike them down; and they kept turning up their faces and shouting for their hero, and laughing, and dancing, and calling out pleasant things to John Saxon.

"Look at him!" said Mary Wilson. "Oh, Mother, look at him!"

Mrs. Wilson looked at her daughter, instead. She was a tall woman with a face which had once been small and pretty but which was now largely obscured by a pair of spectacles. She retained a habit of squinting through her glasses and in this way went through life sticking out her chin. When she lost her looks, she promptly discovered a good many other reasons for putting a value on herself. Like her body, her mind was hard and angular. She was one of those virtuous women who will keep on being good even when their goodness is choking the family. She said, now:

"John Saxon is coming to see you, Mary."

138

"Do you think he is?" asked Mary, brightening all at once.

The mother's heart ached with a sudden joy and a sudden pity.

"What else would he be parading up the main street of the town for?" asked Mrs. Wilson. "Of course he's coming to see you, and sounding horns all the way!"

"Oh, how can you say that?" asked the girl. "There's nothing of the show-off about John. Dear old John, he's the most modest man in the world."

"He never had anything to show off, before, except his good looks," said the mother. "But now he'll let them make a noise over him! He couldn't come up the lane and through the back yard. No, he couldn't do that. If he did, who would see him? I tell you what, Mary, a little bit of success gives a man a taste for noise. In six months, Johnnie Saxon may be running for a political job! He's been changed!"

"He'll never change!" cried Mary. "He's good and honest and simple and kind, and you know it!"

"He's good and honest and simple and kind, is he?" said Elizabeth Wilson. "Well, he'll be good and honest and dead, unless he gets out of this part of the country, before long! The Solitaire will have him murdered. You can bet your bottom dollar on that."

The girl took hold of her mother's arm and looked up at her, silently.

"Don't be a great, staring baby," said Mrs. Wilson, trying to frown and succeeding pretty well. "If you think that he's so honest and simple, you ask him, and you'll find out that there are a lot of things that he likes better than he likes you, just now!"

"Do you think so?" asked the girl, sadly.

"Don't wilt and sag like a wet rag," commanded the mother. "Stand up and use your gumption. A man that handles soot soon has black hands. And Johnnie Saxon has been handling soot. Birds of a feather—"

"He's risked his life twice to get the best of a thief!" cried the girl.

Mrs. Wilson smiled, bitterly, as though from a secret knowledge which life had distilled for her, and for her alone.

"There's no proof of the pudding like the eating of it," she declared. "You think that Johnnie would do anything in the world for you, I suppose?"

"I think he would," said the girl, gravely.

"Then you just tell him that you're dying of fear. You just tell him that you want him to leave Bluewater and get out of this country and never come back until The Solitaire is gone—or until he's made a place so that you can come to him."

"Oh, he'd do it in a moment," said the daughter.

"Ay, and would he, though?" challenged Mrs. Wilson. "You try him, and then you'll know!"

"I shall! I shall!" said Mary Wilson. There was a good deal of her mother in her. She had some of those same flashes of grim and sudden insight into the wrongness of men and events.

And that was why, when the babel reached the house, and then footfalls sounded on the steps, and then a hand knocked at the door—that was why she opened the way for John Saxon with only half of her usual radiance of smiling.

As he closed the door, he was leaning to kiss her, but she stood back a little. She said:

"John, my heart was in my throat as I watched you up the street. I kept waiting to hear a gunshot. John, I was sick with fear! And I know what you must do. You've got to leave Bluewater. You've got to go far away, where you'll be safe from The Solitaire and his murderers! Tell me that you'll go!"

His face clouded, at once. She said to herself, turning cold with pride and shame and anger, remembering the words of her mother, that it was true that he cared for many other things more than he cared for her.

"I'd like to get out of it, but I can't," said John Saxon.

"Why can't you?" asked the girl.

"I just can't. You know how it is. I can't run away."

"For your own sake—and for my sake—and for our two lives!" cried Mary. "Is it because you think the crowd will say you're afraid of The Solitaire? Do you care one whit what they say, compared with how I love you and need you, John?"

"That isn't just the way to put it," considered Saxon, rather bewildered.

"It's the *only* way to put it!" exclaimed Mary Wilson. "John, John, John, it's the only way! Don't tell me that you care more about the yelling of a mob than you care about me!"

"Wait!" breathed Saxon. "You're not putting it the right way. I've got a job that I have to finish. I have to do my work——"

"Oh, yes, do your honest work! Go to your work, John," pleaded the girl—and yet there was as much command as entreaty in her voice. "Do your rightful work, and let me come to help the moment we can get married. But give up this wild, horrible life. Why should you be the sheriff? Go away from Bluewater! Please go, John. I'm begging you. I'll go on my knees to beg you!"

He restrained her. She would actually have dropped to her knees. And yet all was not humility and love in her. She had a lot of that stiff-necked American pride working in her blood, and the warning of her mother rang a bell whose strokes were all against her brain.

"You see," said Saxon, "it's this way. I'm as afraid of The Solitaire as anybody needs to be. But just the same, I can't very well run away. You know—people expect me to do something. They don't expect me to run away——"

"People? People? People?" she cried. "Are you telling me about *people?* But, John, I'm telling you about ourselves—our own lives—are you going to throw them away, and all our chances of happiness, just because you like to be followed down a street by a crowd?"

The injustice of this stung him; but the justice of it stung him far more. The only way he could defend himself was by losing his temper, therefore. And he was all the more outraged because he had expected from Mary the sweetest part of his welcome.

"You've no right to say that!" he told her. "Mary, you're talking sort of queer, this morning. I'm going away and let you cool off a bit."

"Go on, then!" said the girl, bitterly. "I expected it, too! Go on out into the street and let them shout and yell for you some more. You'd rather have that! You'd a lot rather have that than my love!"

141

"That's not—" began John Saxon. Then he shouted, suddenly: "Mary, what's the matter with you? What are you trying to do? Drive me crazy, or something?"

"I'm asking you to act like an honest, sensible man, and you say I'm trying to drive you crazy!" wailed Mary Wilson.

"By the holy old jumping thunder!" groaned John Saxon.

"Go on! Swear at me some more. I'm not surprised!" moaned Mary Wilson.

"I'm not swearing at you," said Saxon. "I only—"

"It's true! You *have* changed!" she insisted. "You're not the same man you used to be!"

"Who says I've changed?" demanded Saxon.

"Everybody says so!"

"Who is everybody?" he raged.

"Everybody says that you don't care for anything, now, except guns and gunfighting!"

"My Lord, if I could get 'everybody' by the throat—"

"That's just it!" said the girl, woefully. "The John Saxon I knew never would have thought of taking *anyone* by the throat!"

"I'm going to leave," panted Saxon. "I can't stand it. I'm going crazy."

He was out of the front door and it had thudded behind him before she could gather her wits. She ran after him, but when her hand was on the knob of the door, her mother's dry voice sounded behind her.

"I told you what would happen!" said Elizabeth Wilson. "Don't go bawling after him like a little fool! When a girl starts throwing herself at a man, it's a sign for the man to trample her under foot. Well I know!"

Mary Wilson looked wildly around her, dropped into a chair, and began to weep.

CHAPTER XXVII

ALL that big John Saxon knew was that he wanted to kill something. He did not know what. He hardly cared what, so long as it would fill his hands. He had a vague feeling that women needed a lot of killing. They were too small. They didn't fill the hands. All they filled was the eye—and the ear! There was something unfair about women. They wouldn't talk man to man. They wouldn't see things. Mary Wilson herself—there was something too bright about her—she saw through too much—nobody had a right to say what she had said about him liking the yammering of the crowd, and besides she would only talk on her own side of an argument.

But as Saxon rode out of the town and up the slope, unforgotten moments, like the flashes of sun on the grass, gleamed on his mind, and the sweetness of the past was making his heart ache. He told himself that this was the end—that perhaps he would never see her again, except when she was leading by the hand her children by another man. And then self-pity stung his eyes with tears, and after that he jerked up his head, for he was remembering the bright happiness of other times, in her face. The golden reality of all the other days outweighed, suddenly, this tarnished and leaden moment. "She's only a silly girl," he told himself. "But by thunder, she needs a spanking!" And that made him almost laugh, when he came into the woods and found Creston.

"I follered down a little ways," said Creston, "and I heard them screeching. My Lord, Chief, they sure do think a lot of you!"

This wistfulness, Saxon answered by slapping the wide, muscular shoulder of the Negro.

"You're going to get out of the dark, one of these days," he said. "You wait and see, Arthur. I'm going to fix things for you so that you can go back to punching cows. Now we've got to go back to that shack and find Boots and the rest. Come on, and let's get there!"

They cut off into the trail, therefore, and it was not long before they were in hailing distance of the shack.

The thundering voice of Creston boomed before them, but it brought out only Tad Cullen and Boots from the little old cabin.

"Where's Pike, and where's Del Bryan?" asked Saxon, quickly. "Off shooting somewhere?"

"No, more likely off being shot at," said Boots. "No, about this time they're getting ready to take the train, I guess."

"What train?" asked Saxon.

"The train from Stillman to the capital. They got a bigger and a better prison, up there, to fit Pike and Bryan into."

Saxon, dismounting, threw the reins and dropped his hands on his hips.

"What are you talking about?" he demanded.

"Aw, nothing much," said Boots. "Those dummies went down to Stillman to stage their party, and they begun to spend money so damn fast that their hands got hot. They sure lighted up that little old town, and the first thing you know, a deputy sheriff got doggone curious. He got so curious that he pulled some friends together and they grabbed old Pike and Del. And they found a stack of cash and a lot of sparklers. And the worst of it was that some of the money of the Stillman bank had been wrote down—the numbers, I mean. So it was easy to figger that Pike and Del belonged to the gang that had robbed the bank. So they slammed 'em into jail, and took their stuff—and there you are! It was a good haul for the bank, and a good haul for that deputy sheriff. Willis is his name, and he's a damned hard man! I've seen him! He'll be sticking the pair of 'em on the train, this afternoon, and he'll have 'em in the pen at the big town by the morning. That's all there is to the story, Chief."

Big John Saxon began to walk up and down, up and down, gloomily. He liked Pike and Del Bryan, as men, about as little as ever he had liked humans before, but they had upon him, now, a special claim. They were part of his own thews and sinews. They were his "men."

"That's that," said Cullen. "There ain't any use cryin' about that milk. It's all spilt."

"We'll pick it up again," answered John Saxon. "We'll pick up that spilt milk, or else we'll be spilled ourselves."

144

Cullen whistled. "Hey!" he said, "is that the way it goes, then? All right, boss. You name the drinks and we'll swaller them and help pay, too."

Boots merely said: "It ain't what a man wants to do; it's what he *can* do!"

"Wait a minute," broke in Cullen. "They made some trouble for you. Why do you give a damn about 'em, Saxon?"

"They belong to us, and we belong to them," said the Chief. "That's all there is to that. I've got to go and think it out."

He walked into the woods and sat on a stump that was cushioned by thick and spongy decay. He buried his face in his hands so that he would shut out from his sight the big, brown, honest trunks of the trees and the specklings of yellow sunlight that slid through to the brown pine needles that covered the ground. For he wanted to use the eye of the mind, now.

With it, he glanced back over the map of the country. He knew perfectly well all of the surroundings of Stillman. He knew how the railroad ran through the windings of the valleys toward the state capital. He could name the stations along the way. And the whole picture brightened and broadened in every detail as he considered it.

He went back and called Boots into consultation.

"What'll they do with Pike and Del Bryan on the train?" he asked.

"Well, she's a big train," said Boots. "There'll be a Pullman aboard her. And in that Pullman, there'll be a drawing room. They'll have Pike handcuffed to one guard and they'll have old Del hancuffed to another, and the deputy sheriff, he'll be along, likely, to look things over and ride herd in general. They might have more men along, too, because they'll figure that Del and Pike belong to the gang of The Solitaire, and they'll be looking for trouble along the way. The Solitaire fights for his men when they're in trouble—the same as you do, Chief."

He looked at Saxon with an odd blending of humor and of awe in his eye. Creston and Cullen, in the near distance, were also watching their chief attentively. Now and then Creston murmured something to his companion, and Cullen

145

would nod agreement without ever shifting his gaze from the face of the leader.

And a great sense of pride and of power swelled higher and higher in the breast of Saxon. He had beaten chance several times. He would now make chance serve him. And Pike and Del Bryan, venomous as they were, would have to be set free.

Gradually his plan grew in his mind, developed, came to a sunlight clearness.

Then he thought back to the words of Mary Wilson, and he could not help a sinking of his heart. For, after all, she had spoken a good deal of truth.

Perhaps, before long, he would be able to settle down, and then it might be much wiser to let her rule the roost. But in the meantime there were two tasks before him— The Solitaire, and the delivery of these two men. To save two thieves and to destroy another—no wonder Mary Wilson had spoken as she did!

CHAPTER XXVIII

TOWNS in the West take on their names sometimes with the utmost seriousness, boosters and citizens debating long and loud before they select some sparkling title; but again, and this is the rule along the range, there is the most casual approach. A tin can on a heap of junk may entitle a town Rusty Gulch; a junk dealer at a crossroads is sufficient to christen the place Ragtown; and a desert village where rain never fell may be grimly called Crystal Springs. As for the town of Tunnel, it lay at the mouth of a great six-mile excavation a good distance south and west of Stillman, where the railroad curved away into intense darkness.

The east-bound express was overdue; therefore the Fairmont Express pulled onto the siding and waited, impatiently.

It was twilight, thickened by heavy rain that obscured the windows of the train with a thousand little, intertwisting rivulets. The steam of the interior also condensed in a pale fog that helped to make the train blind for the passengers. And that whistling of the wind, that roaring of the rain kept every soul inside the train. No one was dismounting and there were only two parties getting on.

These were two pairs of men, and it was apparent that they were tenderfeet on an outing with their guides. One was a huge, blond fellow with a curl in his hair, carrying a shotgun in its case, while his guide, a fellow with all the limps and twists of one who has been pitched a hundred times from the backs of fighting mustangs, carried a pair of good jointed fishing rods. He was dressed like any cowpuncher off the range; his big companion wore rough tweeds that made his shoulders seem larger and heavier. This couple went into the length of the Pullman and got seats just in front of the slanting door of the drawing room.

The second sportsman was as well bronzed as the big man, but he wore a blue serge suit that was absurdly out of place, considering the sporting trip which he was making. Well, he had been out in the woods long enough to grow thoroughly brown, and it was strange that he should not have learned better sense. However, he would undoubtedly change before he had been long off the train. With him, he had a huge Negro who carried all the luggage—there was not much of it—and who came in last of the four.

The second sportsman was a slender, lithe man, with buck teeth that kept him smiling. He went into a compartment that had been reserved for "Mr. Cooper," and his huge Negro servant entered behind him.

The eastbound train had just gone thundering by; the Fairmont Express had barely begun to make groaning headway up the grade into the tunnel, when the bell of "Mr. Cooper's" compartment rang, and the colored porter, Bunny Tucker, came at once. He brought up his best smile as he entered the compartment, knowing very well that the first smile is what makes the lasting impression, and is remembered even unto the moment of the tip.

As he came in, he saw the gigantic Negro standing at respectful attention, as it were, and Bunny Tucker stepped by him to inquire of the gentleman what was wanted.

"All right, Arthur!" said the man with the bucktoothed smile. And Bunny Tucker was caught from behind, by one shoulder and his throat.

"Mr. Cooper" pulled out a very long, very shining Colt. Bunny Tucker saw that the sights had been filed from that weapon, and the trigger was gone, also. Mr. Cooper handled it with the most graceful and casual ease, his thumb resting lightly on the hammer.

"Mighty Gawd, boss!" said Bunny Tucker.

"I ain't 'mighty Gawd,'" said Boots, "but you can talk right out just as though I was. Arthur, get out of that coat."

The gigantic Negro, with a grin, stepped back from the porter, who stood enchanted by the sight of the gun, and, throwing off his overcoat, appeared in an immaculate white coat, as a Pullman porter. He leaned and rubbed his wide, black shoes to a polish.

"In that drawing room, next to us," said Boots, "there's how many gents?"

Bunny Tucker worked his mouth vainly. His throat was too dry, and no sound would issue from it.

"Look!" said Boots.

He counted out a hundred dollars in tens. "You get this wad, and you keep your mouth shut. All you know is that you were grabbed and tied. We'll gag you, too, the sort of a gag you can spit out when you want to, but you're gunna be a damn stupid Negro if you get rid of that gag and start yellin' before we're out of this here train. Here—" he closed the money into Bunny's coat. "How many men are in that drawing room?"

"Mister Cooper," said Bunny, "I swear to Gawd that I ain't takin' no bribe, but if I didn't tell you, you could open the door and look. You'd see two poor fellers that are goin' to prison, Mister Cooper, and two deputies hitched to 'em; and then there's Deputy Sheriff Willis that made the capture, and he's in there with two guns, all the time."

"Does he carry the keys for those handcuffs?" asked Boots.

"Yes, sir. He's got on a deerskin vest. He's all dressed up. And in the lower vest pocket on the right hand

148

side, there's a big swelling, and that swelling is all keys, sir."

"That's enough," said Boots. "What's your name?"

"Bunny, sir. Bunny Tucker."

"Tie him, Arthur," said Boots, and then helped to do the job. True to his word, he tied Bunny Tucker firmly, but the gag was a mere inconvenience in the mouth, not a jaw-stretching impediment that threatened strangulation. And Bunny Tucker lay still, counting up to a hundred over and over again.

If people searched him and found that hundred dollars in his pocket he would say that he had been shooting craps just before he got on board for this trip! In the meantime, he smiled a little around his gag. Bunny Tucker did not like officers of the law. He never had since a quick-handed policeman, in bygone days, had fairly cracked his night stick across Bunny's head. Bunny's feelings had been hurt more than his head, and his pride kept him from forgetting. Now he lay very still in the compartment and heard "Mr. Cooper" command the Negro giant to "jimmy those damned lights."

"Then go into the car and tell everybody that the lights will come on in a minute," said Mr. Cooper. "Then open the door of the drawing room and tell them the same thing. The Chief'll be right at your back when you go inside. Have you got that flash ready in your pocket?"

"Yes, sir," said the big man.

"Go ahead, then," said Mr. Cooper.

Arthur William Creston left the compartment but returned in a moment to say: "If I fool with them lights, they'll go out on the whole doggone train, I'm afraid."

"Let 'em go," answered Boots. "Move fast, because we need our minutes counting, brother!"

Creston went out again, and a minute or two later the lights flashed out, even the dim, reddish ceiling light. An instant murmur went like a groan through the train, very faintly audible under the echoing roar of the wheels through the tunnel.

Boots was out of the compartment at once, in time to see the dim, vast bulk of Creston blocking the aisle. He could barely make out the silhouette. The whole car was dimmer than night.

"Just a minute, gentlemen!" called Creston. "There's gunna be more lights in just a minute."

At this, the protest of many voices died out, and Creston opened the door of the drawing room.

"Gunna be lights on in just a minute," said Creston. "I'll just take a look, and see if—"

He started through the narrow doorway.

"Keep out, porter!" snapped a decisive voice.

A flashlight snapped on and splashed white brilliance into the face of Creston and all over his great white coat.

"You're not our porter," said the man behind the flashlight. "Back up, and stay backed!"

"Yes, sir," said Creston. "I was just gunna tell you that I'm the new porter for this car, sir. Bunny is shifted at Tunnel."

"Is he?" answered the other, dryly. "Well, get out and close that door."

"Just a minute, porter," said big John Saxon, stepping to the door. "I can show you gentlemen how to get the light from the reserve batteries, if you wish."

"Who are you?" asked the man behind the steady flashlight.

"I'm the general manager—traffic manager," said John Saxon.

Cullen was behind him, and so was Boots. He felt as though two trained tigers were supporting him. He had only to control their savage fighting strength, not urge it on.

"All right," said the man behind the light. "This is a damned outrage—the lights goin' off on a train like this."

"It is," said Saxon. "Unexpected and astonishing. Flash your pocket torch, porter."

The powerful glare of Creston's pocket torch instantly overwhelmed the other flashlight, and Saxon saw a man with a long, narrow face and eyes set so close together that they seemed to be rubbing the sides of his nose. He sat on the couch. The two seats by the window were occupied by Pike and Del Bryan, and the eyes of Del Bryan, as they turned up to the face of Saxon, opposite him, widened suddenly like the round eyes of a fish. Then he banished all expression from his face.

"I hate to trouble you gentlemen," said Saxon, "but if

150

you budge half an inch, I'll have to start dripping lead all over you." He had a pair of big guns in his hands as he spoke. Then he added: "Come in, boys!"

But Boots and Cullen were already through the door.

As that door closed behind them, they turned on their own flashes. And in that flood of light, like a madman, Deputy Sheriff Willis made his move.

He got out his gun, and he should have died while trying it, except that Saxon was never one for the letting of blood. He simply ran the length of the barrel of his Colt along the side of Willis' head, and the deputy slumped like a sack to the floor.

Boots went at him with rapid hands, merely saying: "I know where the keys are, Chief!"

And the other two guards? That flare of light had taken the heart out of them, and the fall of their chief held them quite unnerved as Creston and Cullen tied them hand and foot together. By that time, Boots had found the keys, and still the train was roaring through the tunnel as the manacles that held Pike and Del Bryan to their guards were snapped open.

A moment later the train was running smoothly beyond the tunnel's farther mouth, and through the window, dimly, they could see the thin pricking of the stars. The emergency alarm caused that train to stop like a mustang on planted, stiffened legs.

Two minutes later, six men were mounting six good horses that had been tethered in the brush near the railroad. They heard the clamoring of the trainsfolk fade out behind them as they headed back toward Bluewater.

CHAPTER XXIX

IT was the morning after that, when the pink was hardly out of the sky, that Mary Wilson faced the sharp edge of the wind of the dawn as she pulled open the gate and turned the two mustangs of her father from the corral into the little pasture behind the house. She was closing the gate and thrusting the bar home when she saw a woman riding out of the woods, a girl with such a carriage that the heart of Mary Wilson lifted as if at a challenge. And then, when the girl came nearer, she felt something between pity and relief, because she recognized Molly. They had been in school together. They had been close friends in the old days. In fact, it did not seem to Mary such a very long time since she and Molly had walked to the school together, holding hands, smiling at one another foolishly, as little girls will do, skipping and laughing on a sudden, mutual impulse.

Afterward, Molly had gone on with her head just as high and her ways just as reckless as on those days when she had defied the teacher before all the class. The time came when the two saw one another no more. Suddenly it was impossible. There was a good deal of friendship in the eyes which Mary turned on her old companion. There was a good deal of cruelty, also, in the way she looked for the effects of the evil life.

There were not many of those effects to be seen. Perhaps Molly was doing her lips a little too red, so that her face seemed a trifle pale; and perhaps her eyes were a shade too hard and fixed. She looked at everyone as though she were prepared against tricks, amused and on guard beforehand. When she came up, now, she waved her hand and sang out, cheerfully. Then she swung down from the horse with the strong grace of a boy and stood outside the fence. She was dressed like a cowboy, but the shirt was the finest silk, and around her little pseudo-sombrero there was a sparkling band of Mexican wheel work, in gold, and her spurs were gold, and the butt of her quirt glistened with the ruddy sheen of rubies. A lot of money had been spent on Molly. And Mary reflected, bitterly, that her own clothing cost for her entire life did not amount to the money invested on that one turnout.

"Come in, Molly," she invited.

"Your ma might see me," said Molly. "Would Elizabeth —Mrs. Wilson—stick out her chin if she saw me talking inside the fence with her precious pet?"

In the judgment of Mary, as on a fine balance, anger and compassion weighed against one another, and then compassion proved the weightier. She went up closer to the fence and looked with kindness into the hard, bright eyes of the other girl. When she stood so near, she could see clearly what had happened, rather by hints and indications than by accomplished facts. There was a little flare of the nostrils and the vicious little wrinkles were incised at the corners of the eyes.

She was being surveyed with equal clearness.

"You're as much of a baby as ever, Mary," said the other girl. "But I see that you've gone and got yourself a man."

"You mean John Saxon?" said Mary.

"How many more have you got—that are real?" asked Molly. "I saw that hombre sashaying up the street, the other morning, with the kids hanging onto his spurs and the crowd shouting for him. He looked real, to me. Like a doggone king he looked to me, with that white bandage around his head. And he only seemed to know partly what the other fellows were thinking. He looked mighty real to me, Mary. How many more have you got like him?"

Mary said nothing. She was wondering if, in fact, she still had John Saxon. Ever since the previous morning she had been wondering. Her mother, of course, was a very wise woman. Her mother always said so, in fact; but now Mary was beginning to doubt more than a little.

Molly went on: "I watched him go into your house, but I watched him come out again, too. He came out pretty fast. If my man came away from me stepping big like that, like he was going to go rope the pet bull and take him to the butcher—why, I'd be kind of worried, Mary. How about you?"

Suddenly Mary confessed: "Yes, I was worried."

"Great Scott!" exclaimed Molly. "Then why not do something about it?"

"I don't know," said Mary. "I didn't know what to do."

"Bah!" snapped Molly.

"Why do you talk to me like this?" asked Mary.

"Because I want to find out something. What's this big hombre to you? Is he just the town hero, or is he your own John?"

"He's my own—" began Mary. But she stopped herself, there.

"If he's your own, why don't you keep an eye on him?"

153

asked Molly. "Why do you give him the run so that he comes out of your place biting nails and looking for more air? There's a lot of bright girls around that are willing to be comforters. Don't you know that?"

Mary looked with horror at her old friend.

"Yeah, and maybe I might be on the list, one day," said Molly. "I don't know. But you step out of the lists and give me a fair shot at your own John, and maybe I'll ring the bell. I don't know."

"Molly, what's making you talk like this?" she asked.

"It beats me. I don't quite know what I've got in my head. But we used to be pretty thick and I thought that maybe I could do you a good turn. Understand? If you really are all wrapped up in this fellow, maybe I could do you a turn. How much do you care for him, Mary?"

"I care for him. I care a lot," said Mary.

"More than you care what people say when you go to church on Sunday?"

Mary said nothing.

"Look!" exclaimed Molly. "Would you cut loose from everything—would you let the family go rip and would you go through hell and highwater for the sake of your own John? Would you be shamed and pointed at and laughed at and mocked and sneered at and damned for his sake?"

"I hope so," said Mary, very faintly.

"You give me the cool gripes," said Molly. "All of you good gals give me the gripes, mostly. There's no more woman in you than there is in a family picture on the dining room wall. You get a man because you've got a pretty little mug, and after you've got him you let him rip the first time there's trouble. That's what you'd do for your own John. Am I right?"

"No," said Mary. "I think I'd try to be—a woman, Molly."

"Wait a minute. Your own John loves you, does he? He grabs hold of you with his eyes when you walk into the room, and he looks like he's eating and drinking, when he's talking to you? Is that the way it is with him?"

Mary thought. She was very honest. And then she could say: "Yes, he's that way."

154

"Then why do you give him the run when he comes to see you?" snapped Molly.

"I don't—the other morning I was wrong. I said a lot of foolish things. I'm sorry about that."

"I hope you are," said Molly, savagely. "I've got a man and a real man, even if I don't have a wedding ring to show for it. But I'm no more to him than an extra good horse or a fine suit of clothes. And you—you've got the real thing both ways and nothing ahead of you to trouble about except the style of your wedding dress—and you—you turn him adrift, do you? You little fool!"

"What do you mean by turning him adrift? I haven't turned him adrift! Molly, what's happening?"

"He's about to start on his way to be murdered," said Molly, with a bitter calm. "Don't gape like that, like a little putty-faced baby. God, I could strangle some of you milk-eyed heifers, with your bleating and your blaaing. Go to Dan Finlay's house, and if you get hold of your own John, get down on your knees and hang onto him, and hold him back, and don't let him ride out with Daniel Finlay today!"

"Molly, Molly! What does it mean?"

"What does it mean? Damn what it means! Go get your man stopped. I'll be somewhere around when you come back. But if you're half a woman, you'll have your tongue torn out before you'll ever tell a soul that the warning came out of me!"

Mary Wilson went around the corner of the house like a running colt. Down the street she went in a flash, and then up the steps onto the veranda of Daniel Finlay's house. She rapped at the door and thought she heard a cessation of dim voices inside the house. No one came. She rapped again, more loudly, and the heavy, empty echoes came knocking back against her brain. "Mr. Finlay!" she shouted.

"Hello, there," called the blacksmith from next door. "You askin' for Finlay? He went off at the crack of day with John Saxon. He went off more'n a half hour ago!"

Somehow, she got back to her house. She was running, but her knees were numb and her whole soul was starved for the lack of air. She could not breathe. Her heart had

155

swelled so that there was no room in her body for the breath of life.

But she had to find Molly—if only Molly had not gone! Molly would know *where* Finlay and John Saxon had gone together. She might know—otherwise—

She saw Molly sitting on top of the back fence, whittling a stick like a boy.

"It's a bust, eh?" said Molly, looking up, calmly, from her whittling. "They've already gone?"

"They've gone—half an hour ago!" gasped Mary. "Where have they gone, Molly? Where? Why? Who would ever dream of—"

"Half an hour ago, eh?" said Molly, lifting her practical head and looking away toward the ragged parting of the mountains that fenced in Stillman Pass. "Well, you've got a good-looking horse in that pasture, Mary. You used to be able to ride pretty well. Pile a saddle onto that horse and come with me. You hear?"

"Where, Molly? Where?" cried Mary Wilson.

"Oh, damn you and all your kind!" shouted Molly, in a sudden fury. "Do you want to save him—or am I going to ride by myself? I've seen him only once—really—but I won't let him die and rot. I'll *fight* for him. What will you do, you little pretty fool? Will you stand there and blubber 'where? where?' or will you jump a saddle onto that horse and come where I show you the way?" All those insults had no power on Mary Wilson, strange to say. They could not stir her anger, but they could scatter the numbness and the darkness from her mind. Suddenly she was alert and alive.

And while she raced to "jump" the heavy saddle on the back of the bay gelding in the pasture, Molly sat by, already on her horse, disdaining to help, watching with a curious sneer and sympathy commingled. Could they overtake two riders who had such a long head start? Well, it depended. When she looked up, she could see swift clouds beating up like a sea on the mountains around the Stillman Pass.

CHAPTER XXX

It had been midnight before Saxon and his five men gained the shack, again. They made a small fire and cooked coffee and bacon and ate the bacon between slabs of stale bread, hungrily, wolfing it down. Then Pike, as they were getting ready for bed, made a speech.

"I woulda done you dirt, Chief," he said. "And then you done this for me. Why, hell, I woulda done you dirt. And then you done this."

He completed this speech with a wide gesture which at once invited wondering comment and at the same time swept aside all words as useless. Del Bryan said nothing, but he watched Saxon with the fond eyes of a dog that will take a beating and return to the master's hand. And Saxon said nothing except, cheerfully: "It's time to turn in!"

But, as he wrapped himself in his blanket and lay down, a king of men and conscious of his monarchy, he said: "Boots, how's the Stillman Pass, now?"

"Always damned rough," said Boots.

But Boots remembered that remark when, in the morning, the chief and one horse were gone from the camp, without a word left behind him. The others, after their long ride of the night before, had slept rather late; the sun was on top of the pine trees before they came out of the shack, and as they looked around vainly for their leader, Creston said, almost to himself: "There's something wrong."

Boots took him by the arm and led him aside.

"What made you say that—that there was something wrong? What d'you know, Arthur?"

"I don't know nothing," said Creston, "but I *feel* something like Christmas morning when there ain't no turkey in the house and there ain't no chicken, neither. I dunno where the Chief went, though."

"Stillman Pass," muttered Boots.

He looked toward those high, ragged mountains and saw the clouds overwhelming them; and something overwhelmed the mind of Boots.

"The last thing that a gent says at night is the first thing in his head in the morning," said Boots. "Stillman Pass— Stillman Pass—Arthur, I'm gunna ride there, and maybe you'd better come along. Don't say nothing to the rest of 'em. Most likely it's a fool idea of mine—but I got prickles up my spine, and that may mean as much as Christmas turkey does to you. Come on!"

Big John Saxon, in fact, had ridden down through the cool brightness of the dawn at that moment when the sky is as beautiful as sunset time, but hope in the place of thoughtful melancholy. And the chill wind carried into his lungs the sweet of the pine trees and into his ears the sound of the waters that rushed and called along the slopes.

For breakfast, he pulled his belt a notch tighter.

A jack rabbit jerked away from behind a rock and ran crookedly, like a snipe dodging down wind. Instinctively he pulled his Colt and blazed away. Two bullets knocked dirt into the fur of that jack rabbit; the third shot smashed his back.

John Saxon rode on, and let the fresh meat lie. He had a strange little working of guilt in his heart, having killed that game out of mere wantonness of spirit, so to speak.

After all, there may be a justice which weighs all things in delicate scales, and balances motives and deeds together, and finds lives of men and beasts akin in value. That queer discontent and trouble remained vaguely in the back of his mind all the way into Bluewater.

He could not look at the place in quite the same spirit that had been his the day before. He had come in like a hero, on that day. He had been able to rejoice and look men in the eye. If there were a crime on his conscience, it was that he had permitted his gang to take the plunder from other robbers; but was that really a crime in the eyes of the law?

He could not tell what the answer might be, but the guilt of it certainly did not weigh heavily on his spirits.

It was another matter to board a train and tear two of his men away from the hands of the law. To be sure, they were seized as robbers of a bank—whereas they had done no more than rob other bandits. But this it would be impossible to prove, no doubt. And, once in the hands of the law, other crimes would probably soon be proved against them. He had taken his men away from the power of the law. Yes, he felt that he would have taken them had they been ten times greater, and of greater crimes than robbery. Pride would have made him try—pride and that odd sense of ruling power which was now in him.

But now, certainly, the law had a definite claim against him. To be sure, very few people had seen his face, clearly. His hat had been pulled well down over his face. The flare of the electric torches in the drawing room had served to show the faces of the deputies and the prisoners, rather than the faces of the rescuers. Only Bunny Tucker, perhaps, would be apt to give damning testimony. And that testimony might be silenced by ten ten-dollar bills which had been lodged in the porter's pockets.

Nevertheless he was glad—very—to be taking this trip with Daniel Finlay, today. He was glad that he was to ride down into Stillman and repay to the bank all the share of the spoils which had fallen into his hands. Perhaps that might still leave him very guilty in the eyes of the law, but human eyes are not as the eyes of the law. And wherein is a man criminal if he will wash his hands clean of the results of the crime and refuse the illegal profit?

When he got to the Finlay place, it was still so very early that the street was empty, but he found that Finlay already had managed to saddle his horse—poor fellow, thought big John Saxon, using his stump of a wrist and one hand!—and now he was prepared to depart.

But when Saxon went into the little shack, he had a new sign of the thoughtfulness of Finlay, as soon as he had shaken the left hand of his host.

"Have you eaten, my lad?" asked Finlay. "I left some bacon and scrambled eggs on the stove, and there's coffee left. The food is still warm. You have a hungry look, John. You'd better sit down and fill up a bit."

Saxon sat down with a smile and ate, rapidly and largely. Suddenly he broke out:

"You think of everything, Mr. Finlay. There ought to be—there ought to be a special sort of a happiness for you, one day!"

159

"Do you think so?" asked Finlay. And there was a sudden and a curious pain in his face. "Do *you* think so, John?"

Then his eyes went wandering, as though a doubt had come to him.

"I have my own sins; I have my own sins!" muttered Finlay, only half aloud.

After that, he got out a packet of money and made Saxon count it bill by bill. His total share of the plunder was there, and Saxon checked off the sum.

"As though I'd doubt you, Mr. Finlay!" he said, laughing.

"Ah, well," said Finlay, "business is business, and doubts are better settled before they begin. Money is like soot, John. It soon is sticking to the hands."

A moment later, they were jogging up the street; and long before the sun was up, they were nearing the pass itself, over which clouds were gathering, crumpling against the sides of the peaks as waves crush in spray against the rocks by the sea; but these aerial waves remained suspended, recoiling a little and then clinging again, while fresh tides of vapor came sweeping in.

Looking up at this scene, it was very much as though they were beneath the ocean, and the force of the wind was as water currents tugging at them. It was very cold, and Finlay was sure that it would soon begin to snow. In fact, the air had a wintry nip to it and drove easily through the clothes and started gooseflesh prickling over the body. And every moment the upper sky filled more with the swirling masses of the clouds.

"Ay," said Saxon, "if I were herding beef toward Stillman I'd begin to hurry them on."

"What do you think?" asked Finlay. "If you had the chance, would you be happy to go back to ranching again?"

Saxon laughed.

"I don't know," he said. "I feel every day, now, as though I were sitting in at a game with high stakes on the table. And that's a good deal of fun."

"Yes, high stakes, high stakes, my lad," said Finlay. "Life or death—life or death!"

He did not say it with the half melancholy tone of a

moralist, but with the hard-lipped savagery of one who knows what he is talking about and has had the relish of the forbidden taste. And Saxon was deeply surprised and a little troubled.

But there had been pain in the life of Finlay. There had been a great deal of pain, and there was little wonder if hardness and bitterness crept into his voice, now and again.

They rode on, now, into the heart of the main pass, a great, rough country with runs of water everywhere corroding the old trail, until they came to the side of the Stillman River itself, running sometimes sleek and dark with speed and sometimes riffling into white down a steeper descent, and sometimes rushing with angry thunder among the jutting rocks that broke up from its bed.

Just above one of these cataracts Finlay, who had been looking about him from time to time, pulled up his horse.

"We'd better water the horses here, John," he said.

"They don't need water, yet," said Saxon.

"Ah, my lad," said Finlay, "how can we tell? The poor dumb fellows have no tongue to tell us. We'd better ask them, John."

Saxon, half smiling, but rather touched by this kindness of heart, dismounted willingly enough and led his horse to the edge of the water. Finlay, by an odd chance, led his down at a good distance and came to the edge of the stream a full ten yards off.

But the horses, though the water was there, and though they spread their forelegs and lowered their heads as though about to drink, merely smelled at the speed of the water and then tossed up their heads again.

Finlay remounted at once and Saxon, about to do the same, heard behind him a sudden shout in that same clear, bell-like voice which he had heard before:

"Saxon, fill your hand!"

Ay, *this* was the end! Colder than the mountain wind that voice of The Solitaire drove through him. He drew his own gun as he spun about, but he had time for no more than the first fleeting glimpse of The Solitaire, not shooting from the hip but standing erect with one hand behind his back and the other arm extended with the gun like a duellist on his mark. He could see the cold cruelty of the smile on that beautiful face. Then the gun spoke, and the weight of the bullet striking into the breast of John Saxon, staggered him backward and sent him plunging into the full sweep of the mountain stream.

CHAPTER XXXI

DANIEL FINLAY, turning in the saddle, saw the man he had betrayed fall back into the water with a quantity of mud and sand from the bank toppling after him. The strong current instantly seized on the dark cloud of the mud and shot it down the stream toward the teeth of the cataract. And now the dark patch was hurled away among the rocks. Daniel Finlay still waited, expecting to see the body flinging this way or that among the rocks, or, at least, a crimson stain in the froth of the current. But he was able to make out nothing at all.

Conscience was no giant in the soul of Finlay, but when he looked where big John Saxon had been standing and saw now the raw margin of the cave-in, and above it The Solitaire with a gloating face and three of The Solitaire's best riflemen, something stirred vaguely in the lawyer. But he was comforted, instantly, by the knowledge that he had nearly sixty thousand dollars in his wallet. He was a made man. He could retire from work when he pleased; he could leave an estate which would make him a solid man in the esteem of the world after him. He had gained at one stroke, through murder, the essence of respectability—a fortune to invest. He called to The Solitaire: "It's better for me to be seen riding furiously from this place, Solitaire!"

He turned his mustang and put it into a dead gallop.

"Wait a minute!" shouted The Solitaire. "Let's have a look at that money!"

The lawyer did not seem to hear.

"Shall I fetch him back?" asked one of the men, raising his rifle.

"I've got half a mind to," said The Solitaire. But then

he shook his head. "No matter what he makes out of it, it's been worth a lot to me. That was through the heart that I slammed Saxon. D'you see?"

"Nope. It wasn't through the heart. He would of fallen on his face, likely, if it had been through the heart," said the man whose rifle was lifted still, as he looked yearningly after the disappearing figure of Daniel Finlay.

A grizzled fellow whose beard looked like a close-growing gray moss on his face, answered:

"He started to fall on his face, and then he pitched back, because the bank caved in."

"That bullet went through his heart. I felt it go through," said The Solitaire, with a queer smile. "But we'll search the stream. Charlie, go down below the rapids and see if you can spot anything. Pete, you walk along the rapids themselves and take a look. I'll give a glance to the water here."

"Thorough is what you are, Chief," said grizzled Pete. But he went off at once to make the search, while The Solitaire stepped a few paces along the bank and paused at the edge of the water just above the spot where John Saxon lay submerged.

The shock of the bullet had left his side and left shoulder numb; the sudden fall had half dazed him; and then the grip of the icy water restored his wits. Blindly reaching out with his right hand—the left hand was fairly useless—he clutched a root from which the soil had been washed away, and so he lay just at the surface of the stream with a small tuft of brush thrusting out to screen his face as he breathed.

The pull of the current, even close in shore, was very strong; the pain from the wound now commenced and grew quickly to a commanding agony. But he could hear the changing voices of the cataract and they poured strength of terror into that good right hand of his which anchored him to safety.

That was how he lay, staring with blank eyes up through the meager screen of the bush and into the whirling shadows of the stormy sky above him, when he heard the voices of The Solitaire and his men; and then a shadow sloped across him, and Saxon submerged himself. Looking up through the water, he could see The Solitaire standing at ease, with the wind whipping his clothes and jerking up the wide brim of his sombrero. He looked more god than man, and Saxon wondered how he had ever dared to stand against such a man.

With one hand resting lightly on his hip, The Solitaire surveyed the stream; and right at his feet lay the watery image of John Sáxon, as the big man stifled in the river. And Saxon was minded to crawl out of the water. Perhaps if he lay wounded at the feet of The Solitaire, he would receive mercy? No, he knew by a perfect instinct that there could be no forgiveness for him!

And now, as his lungs were bursting, and the blood rushing into his staring eyes, he vaguely saw The Solitaire step back.

He pulled himself up to the surface, but the most agonizing part of the struggle remained for him. He wanted to draw in a vast, gasping breath. It would come in with an audible groan. Instead, he had to sip the air noiselessly, like a small bird sipping water. Little by little, gradually, his lungs were filled, emptied, filled again; but the agony seemed as though it would never end.

He could hear voices that cleared as his distress diminished a little. He was growing weak as the blood ran from him. Why did not the bloodstain in the water draw attention like a red flag? He could not know how a riffle in the current covered the stain with a white froth and so concealed it from all except a very careful examination. He could not know, also, that the very surety of The Solitaire was blinding him to what lay at his feet.

For The Solitaire, Saxon was dead and gone through the tearing teeth of the cataract. His men came up to report that there was nothing to be seen but when the water below the rocks was probed, it was found to be very deep, and no doubt the body was down there in the shadows, snagged on some rock. It might be a month before the skeleton broke loose, to be rolled and battered down the length of the stream.

The snatches of words that Saxon heard assured him of these details in the minds of the searchers. Then, distinctly, he heard The Solitaire give the order to mount.

"He rode right into the trap like a blind fool!" he heard The Solitaire saying. "I wish there'd been ten

164

thousand people around to see me cut him down like an ox!"

Afterward came the departing beat of the hoofs of the horses. And still Saxon counted enough seconds to make two minutes before he dared to draw himself out of the water.

Lying flat on his face, he turned his head and looked down the trail, and there he saw, in the vague distance, the disappearing forms of the four riders. There had been no intention of making a fair fight of it. The Solitaire was to try his hand first, but if he failed, his riflemen would make sure of the little job of blasting the life out of the body of John Saxon.

"If ever I meet him again," said Saxon to his soul, "I'm going to be able to kill him!"

But all of that was in the infinite future. Life—the life of the instant was what he had to struggle to retain.

Shelter came first. The sky was black, now, across the whole of the narrow mountain horizon that closed in the gulch; and the wind came in sweeping strokes that made his body shudder with its force. The first snowflakes whirled into his face. They seemed to Saxon like ghostly stones, pelting him. There was a whirling in his mind like the confusion in the sky. And the wind blew him colder than the running ice water of the mountain stream.

He headed for the shelter that first offered—an outcropping of big rocks not far away. But from the signs, he knew that the horses of The Solitaire and his men had been tethered here, and perhaps one or all of them might return to find something that had been left behind them.

Therefore he had to push farther on.

Nausea began to work in him. He had heard that such nausea came to men who were bleeding fast. And he could not get enough air. The horrible air-hunger kept stifling him though he opened his mouth wide and let the pure wind blow into his throat. It seemed to help his breathing, but it did not help enough.

He was going to die. Life was running out of him too fast. Then he remembered that someone had said that bleeding to death was the easiest way of dying. Well, let the theorists try it, then!

The man's part was to keep struggling to the end. He

165

had to get his clothes off, make the bandage, tie up the mouth of the wound, and then, wringing his clothes, drag them on again.

All of these things, he knew that he could not accomplish; but he must struggle on to the end. He dragged off coat and shirt and saw the wound. The horrible furrow began at the breast bone and ripped right across the ribs and then through the flesh of the shoulder. His bones had been strong indeed to sustain the impact, and his body had by chance been turned just enough to make the bullet glance.

For the third time he had stood before The Solitaire, and for the third time his life had been spared by fortune. And a strange confidence grew up in him, a thin fountain of surety which said that he was destined, eventually, to lay The Solitaire dead.

If only he could husband and revive the thin, dying flame of consciousness which remained to him now!

He made the bandage. He could not use his left hand for the work of tearing the cloth, because at the least effort with his left arm the blood burst out in appalling streams. He had to grip with his teeth and his right hand, and so rend the cloth into strips. Holding one end of the cloth in his teeth, he could then wind the bandage around the quantity of moss with which he first padded the mouth of the wound.

The pain was dying out. There was little sensation except that of cold as icy fingers probed the delicate depths of the wound and extended their freezing manipulation to the core of his body.

But he made that bandage hold.

His naked body was blue when he removed the last of his clothes and wrung them. Afterward, he began pulling them on. And the damp clothes clung to his skin and would hardly be persuaded to come over him again.

When they were on, once more, they seemed to give him no shelter. They were simply wet surfaces through which the wind blew, chilling him more and more.

He stood up, determined to run until his circulation was restored, but nauseating dizziness made him drop to his knees again.

He must have a fire. By the grace of God there remained

dry matches inside the pouch of oiled silk in which they were always wrapped. Once he had a fire, the warmth would bring some life back into his body. So he crawled away on hands and trembling knees into the brush.

He was very sick. He was very weak. He was so weak that the air seemed to be filled with slanting lines of gray and white. Then he was aware that these lines were the streaks of the falling snow. The wind had increased; it was whipping the snow down in almost horizontal lines, and that was why the brush was dry.

He tried to pull at and break a dead bush which might give him fuel. But that mighty right hand which never had failed him was nerveless and weak, now. And the horror of the air-hunger was increasing moment by moment.

He lay flat for a moment, thinking only of his breathing. Then he heaved himself to his elbows and laid hold on a branch with his teeth. There was still strength in neck and shoulders and jaw. He tore that branch from the shrub and then sat up, the precious bit of dry tinder between his legs, sheltered from the blast of the wind by his body.

He got out the twist of oiled silk. His fingers were very thick and they were so soft with weakness that it was hard for him to get hold of a thing as small as a match. After he got hold of it, how would he scratch it?

His clothes were wet. The soles of his shoes were wet. But there was the lee side of a boulder just beside him. He scratched the match on that.

The flame spurted blue—and went out. Another died in the same way. He pressed closer to the big stone, and started to take a third match when his clumsy hand slipped and the entire lot of matches showered out into a pool of soft snow. He made a frantic gesture to save them, and only buried them deeper in the snow.

Then, for five fainting seconds, he sat swaying, with eyes closed, surrendering to death.

Afterward, he rallied. Somewhere, in a book or from the lips of his mother, he had heard that only cowards give up the fight. This was a fight—and at the far end of the bitter trail he would win for his reward a chance to stand for a fourth time in front of The Solitaire.

He dug into the snow and picked out the matches. The

heads of them still seemed hard, but when he scraped them, one after another, against the rock, the heads crumbled without giving forth flame.

When they were gone, to the last one, he saw that the face of the rock had become wet. He had been trying to scratch the last matches through a film of water!

At that, he laughed a little, but only a little because his lungs were empty of precious, life-giving air.

He knew, now, that he was to fail. However, he did not want to die like a coward, so he started crawling.

The world was spinning about him, now, and the falling snow covered the mountains with a false twilight. He had lost all sense of direction and all that he had to judge it by was the force of the wind. So he crawled against the teeth of the wind, feeling somehow that this was the better way.

He stretched flat on the ground for a moment, to rest. And after a time, he found himself stiff and cold and knew that he had lost consciousness during the interval.

To die that way, on the ground, like a frozen snake!

He got to his elbows. He got to his knees. He swayed to his feet.

Walking into the wind was somehow the best way. But his knees were buckling under him. He leaned into the wind; he leaned on the hard, quivering arms of it, and went forward until a wall of darkness closed over his mind and he felt himself falling.

CHAPTER XXXII

THAT morning was Sunday, and Daniel Finlay, as he rode swiftly out from under the clouds that covered the Stillman Pass into the bright, hot sun of the lower plain, knew what he would do. He was inspired by the sound of the church bells that chimed thin and sweet from the little steeple, and they spoke cheerfully to Finlay of the best tactics which he could pursue.

The thing was so clear to him that he laughed a little,

and then looked back over his shoulder at the cloud masses which were thickening and lowering over the mountains around the Stillman Pass. In his pocket lay sixty thousand dollars, very nearly, of future comfort. In his heart lay a vast assurance that, having done so much, he could not now go wrong!

So Daniel Finlay felt such cheer within him that it was hard for him to compose himself for the part which he had to play. Only by degrees did he think himself into the proper frame of mind. And, a mile from the town, as the bells had stopped chiming, he put the spurs to his mustang and made it race at full speed, until the froth flew back from its mouth over its breast and shoulders, and the sweat ran down in streams along its sides. Desperately, Daniel Finlay was seen to dash into the main street of Bluewater.

At the doors of the church he drew rein. Inside, he could hear the snoring, dreary notes of the organ, the monotonous sweetness of the hymn lifted by uncertain voices.

Daniel Finlay did not pause. He ran up the steps and cast open the doors. As they crashed back, the organ stopped, suddenly; a scattering of voices maintained the hymn for only an instant, and then there was a silence out of which grew the whispering sound of intaken breaths. Men and women began to rise, for they saw Daniel Finlay striding down the aisle of the church with one arm raised to demand attention; it was his right arm, the handless arm which all of Bluewater knew so well and pitied so profoundly.

"Friends!" cried Daniel Finlay, "if there's courage and honor and faith and kindess among you, I come to demand a rightful revenge—I come to demand justice."

The minister rushed down the aisle. He, good man, had in his great heart nothing but compassion for the sufferings of men and women in this world and the divine hope of offering to them a higher happiness. And when he saw the tall, thin, rigid form of Daniel Finlay standing in the door of his church, black as night against the outer flare of the sunlight, it had seemed to Joseph Hunter that the devil incarnate was on his threshold.

But then, in a moment, he recognized the mysterious and most respected lawyer, Daniel Finlay. He was quickly

169

at the side of the lawyer. Now he cried: "Come into the pulpit, Mr. Finlay. Speak to us where we can all hear and see you. What has happened?"

"No pulpit," cried Finlay, recoiling a little. "Let me call to the manhood of the men of Bluewater, standing among them. I will not be raised in a pulpit above their heads. For God knows that after this day my *heart* shall never be raised high."

"Mr. Finlay," said the preacher, "we know, we all know, something of your goodness and of your secret works of charity and kindness. If you have been wronged, tell us openly, and we will openly try to do you justice."

"Yes!" called many strong voices.

Sunday is a day for best clothes and drowsiness and quiet voices, and dullness infinite; into this Sunday had burst a voice crying for justice, and that voice came from highly revered Daniel Finlay. So every man, young or old, who sat in that congregation on this day, was instantly on his feet, ready for battle.

"Yes," they called. "Tell us what has been done to you. If anybody——"

"Nothing has been done to me, except to make me a witness! A witness, friends, of the foulest outrage that was ever perpetrated in this world," called Finlay.

And he clapped against his forehead that eloquent stump of his right arm, and for a moment he seemed totally overcome. He even reeled a little, as though recoiling from his thoughts, and the kind preacher caught him and supported and steadied him.

The men of the congregation crowded close around him, until the preacher called for more room, and air for Mr. Finlay, and at once the crowd gave back, those in front shouldering strongly against those behind. Every face was determined; grim would be the revenge of these men upon whomever Daniel Finlay denounced.

At length Finlay appeared to recover, and though he had to rest part of his weight, leaning his left hand on the shoulder of the minister, he raised his stub of a handless arm and cried rather weakly, but in tones that passed instantly through the deadly silence of the church: "Murder, murder, murder! They have murdered the noblest soul and the greatest hero we have seen! John Saxon is dead!"

He paused here, his head falling. It seemed as though he would fall to the floor, except for the sustaining arm which the minister instantly passed under those frail, narrow shoulders.

And through the church ran a deep voiced murmur of men saying softly, deep in their throats: "John Saxon—dead! John Saxon—murdered!"

Perhaps at that moment, the picture of Saxon on his horse, surrounded by the shouting children, rose suddenly into every mind. And now he was gone—murdered! The terrible grief of Daniel Finlay, overwhelming that good man, that noble man—was it not to be seen how he shuddered and almost fell to the ground?—took hold on all that congregation. They, too, felt grief. And they felt also a fierce flame of anger. They would know more!

"In the Stillman Pass," cried Daniel Finlay. "There his body was swept down the river and torn to shreds in the rocks of the cataract. And I stood by, weak, helpless, and saw the murder done! Vengeance! Vengeance! God give power to honest men to revenge this foul murder!"

"We'll have it!" called a number of voices in answer. "We'll follow the murderers to the end of time."

But other voices called for silence. "Hush," they said. "Poor Finlay is trying to speak again, if his strength holds out!"

Said Daniel Finlay, his voice so low that only through that stillness could it have made way to every mortal ear and every swelling heart: "Many things about John Saxon, unknown to you, are known to me. I could tell you how he led men against the murderous crew of The Solitaire. I could tell you how he scattered the brigands and drove The Solitaire before him. I could tell you how he brought back nearly sixty thousand dollars which he had torn from the ruffians, the robbers, and how he asked me if he had a claim to it. But when I pointed out that the money should return to the hands of the bank in Stillman, known to have been robbed by the scoundrels led by The Solitaire, instantly John Saxon, that clean-handed, that faultless hero and gentleman, agreed. And to make that restitution, I rode with him this morning from Bluewater. But in the depths of the pass, when we had paused to water our thirsty horses, a volley of shots rang out. John Saxon fell headlong into the river. I saw his body whirled down toward the cataract. In my despair, I rushed into the water. But hands dragged me out. I found myself surrounded by masked men. They searched my clothes. They snatched from me the wallet which contained that money which rightfully belongs to the bank in Stillman. And then they flung me aside and went shouting and laughing on their way, while I, stunned, looked up to the God of heaven and asked how permission could be given for such acts on earth.

"I have come back to you—I have come back to you—to ask—"

At this point, his voice failed entirely. The minister received the limp burden of that falling body. He was lowered into a chair, where he lay gasping.

And that crowd of awed and angry men waited only until the messenger was seen to recover. Then they rushed from the church to find their weapons and their horses.

But Daniel Finlay, presently, walked with bowed head at the side of the minister. And women who saw them go wept with pity for the good lawyer whose heart was broken.

When he came to his house, Joseph Hunter would have gone in with his broken companion, but Daniel Finlay drew himself up with what seemed the last of his strength and said: "Mr. Hunter, you are very kind, but I prefer—I must be alone."

The minister withdrew, reverently.

And that was how it came about that Daniel Finlay sat behind his locked doors listening to the departing thunder of hoofs as man after man, armed to the teeth, swept out of Bluewater toward the Stillman Pass and its thick hood of clouds.

Daniel Finlay, listening, smiled. And he closed his eyes, still smiling, and in his good left hand he clutched more closely the wallet which contained the money.

It was his, now. No man in the world would dare to imagine that he possessed it. No man except The Solitaire, and this day he had served The Solitaire in such a manner that he could never expect harm from the bandit.

All was well. A perfect scheme had been perfectly executed. And there was peace in Finlay's soul.

CHAPTER XXXIII

LONG before Mary Wilson and Molly were in the heart of the Stillman Pass, the snow had begun to fall on them, and looking back they had a strange sight of the brilliant rim of the western sky where the sun was still shining with power, though close over their heads the clouds rushed, and there seemed to be galloping horses inside the mist. But the air grew more and more dim, and as they entered the pass, all their horizon was covered by the dense upper layer of the clouds.

More than once Mary Wilson looked to her companion. They had put on slickers, and the wind rattled and flapped the hard rubber and beat heavily against them from one side or the other. And every time Mary, in her despair, glanced aside at the other girl, she received a smile and a nod of encouragement.

"They'll go slow through a wind like this. Think of that old skeleton of a Dan Finlay. Your man wouldn't let Finlay risk catching a cold in his precious bones. We'll overtake 'em, all right. There! I think I saw something around that shoulder of the hill—"

They galloped on, harder and harder. But when they came toward the center of the pass, Molly turned grim and hard as a stone. At last, they reached the point where the river ran close to the old trail, and here she pulled up her mustang.

It was the place which she had heard Finlay and The Solitaire agree upon, and now it was empty. Ay, but not empty of all traces.

"Horses have been led down to the water, there," said Molly. "Look yonder, where the tracks come out from among the rocks, too—"

The wind drowned her words and blew an air-pocket inside her cheek. She swung down from the saddle and followed the tracks among the boulders, dragging her unwilling mustang into the wind, with Mary Wilson close behind.

They found the sign of the horses. They pushed farther in and the sign disappeared.

"We've got to cut for sign," said Mary Wilson. "We'll leave the horses here and go on foot. You take that way and—"

The wind stifled her again. It was snowing fast. White patches continually appeared on the slickers and were blown away again. The wind staggered Molly, and as she bucked into it, she told herself that she was a fool. Why should she go through this for the sake of another woman's man? And suppose that a whisper of what she was doing or attempting to do, should ever come to the ears of The Solitaire?

But she kept remembering, also, those days when she had walked hand in hand with Mary to the school, and how they had laughed at one another. There was a certain savage faith in Molly. And there was in her that courage which in some people can almost take the place of honor.

Besides, she had seen big, handsome, blond-headed John Saxon waving his hat to his friends, with the white of the bandage like a crown around his head. And he had looked to her like a hero, and something more.

That was why she kept wading through the wind among the rocks and through the shrubbery, though sometimes a snowy gust stopped her like a wall.

Off to the side, now and again, she had a glimpse of Mary Wilson, hunting also, ignorantly, knowing little of the facts that were in the mind of Molly, but blindly doing as she was bidden. And pity and scorn flooded through Molly, again.

They were following a lost trail for a lost cause, she was sure. The thing had happened. Those horse tracks that came out from among the rocks were the tracks of the horses of The Solitaire and his men. They had intercepted Finlay and his gull and they had flung the dead body of the victim into the hungry waters of the Stillman River.

However, it was best to make sure. It was best to take

174

every chance, to the very last before giving up all hope for such a man as John Saxon. And suppose that that big man and The Solitaire were to meet again, hand to hand, how would the thing turn out?

She could not help a cruel wish that she might see the thing. And when it took place, she wondered which man she would wish victory to.

She was in the midst of that thought when she stumbled over a body that lay face down, half covered with a snowdrift. But she saw the blond hair and the bandage around the head.

She screamed for Mary Wilson, cupping her hands, yelling across the wind. She saw her cry take hold of the other girl and bring her at a staggering run toward the spot.

Would Mary Wilson scream when she saw the fallen man? Or would she faint at the sight of the corpse?

Molly, on her knees, thrust her hand under the body and felt the heart. But there was nothing to feel. That heart was still as a stone, and the body was cold—ice cold. It was strange that it should be so cold, and yet not rigid.

But under the tips of her sensitive fingers she felt, now, a faint pulsation—a faint and far-away movement of the dying life.

Mary Wilson, clumping to her knees beside the inert body, put her hands under the head, between the tenderness of the face and the hard rock on which it lay.

No, she did not scream, and she did not faint, but with wild, haunted eyes she waited for the verdict. She was a woman, thought Molly, almost angrily. After all, who could tell? Perhaps the weak, pretty, silly thing had something in her that was worthy of John Saxon.

And throwing up her hands, suddenly, Molly shouted: "He's alive! Mary, Mary, he's living! We're going to save him!"

She thought she was yelling a lie; she felt that the wind was battering her lips because they lied so. But it was worth any pain to see what happened in the face of Mary, when she heard that.

They turned the body, heavily, with labor. He was a big man. My God, what a big man he was! And how could the life of such a monster be such a delicate will-o'-the-wisp, summoned away by the first gesture?

His eyes were closed. His jaw was set. His mouth compressed to a straight line. Up to the moment of his fall he had been striving, and still the indomitable spirit was fighting on, in the thin dream which was all that remained to John Saxon of existence.

His left side was bloodsoaked. Under the coat there was no shirt. There was a great, clumsy bandage drawn crudely over a padding of moss which had been used to check the flow of the blood.

What had happened? Having wounded their man to such a degree, why had The Solitaire and his gang failed to finish him? Or had John Saxon fought with such terrible strength and courage that The Solitaire and all the rest were beaten off?

It seemed incredible.

But thinking was a matter of half a second. Action, action, action, they must have action, now. They must have shelter from that wind, and a fire to thaw the freezing, half-naked body.

"Take that shoulder of him. I'll take this. Drag him!" shouted Molly.

Mary Wilson took the wounded shoulder. Fresh blood squeezed out on her hands, and her face went white. But she gritted her teeth and pulled with all her might.

Yes, there was something in her besides prettiness. The good women, you never can tell what is in them. They seem all surface, but they may be as deep as the blue profound of heaven.

They dragged John Saxon under the lee of a great shell-shaped rock. They laid him there.

"Get brush! Get brush for a fire! Tear off dead branches. Get firewood!" shouted Molly, and ran to start the work.

The tough wood bent, but it would not give. She remembered that there was a little hand ax in a case at the back of her saddle and she raced away to get this. When she returned, she saw that Mary already had gathered a little heap of wood and, with a desperate face, was fighting to break away more.

The ax was the answer to that question. The good steel shore through the shrubs at the bottom of the trunk,

176

cutting the tough wood like butter, in the strong hand of Molly.

They made the pile of firewood low. Some of the branches would have to serve as a bed for the wounded man. Mary, with wonderfully deft and steady fingers, kindled some dead leaves that were luckily dry. The flame blew sidewise, went out in a thin drift of smoke and a glowing coal, then re-kindled under the draft and took hold. The fire began to crackle. They put on more wood. The fierce flame shot up, became a monster, ate, and roared. And the life-giving heat sprang out around them.

Molly piled on wood. Mary, still grimly silent, was gathering more wood, stripping off the soft, small branches, and making the bed on the ground. When there was some shelter from the cold and the damp of the soil, together they rolled the heavy body onto the bed. They pushed the fire closer.

And Mary, on her knees, listened with her head against the breast of John Saxon, counting the dull, small strokes of the heart-beat.

CHAPTER XXXIV

"STAY there close; watch him all the time; keep that fire up; and don't get scared if he starts talking like a loony," said Molly. "I'm going to ride for help. We need men to handle him; we need a doctor."

Mary made a silent gesture of acquiescence. She kept her eyes fixed upon Saxon as though she were reading a book of many pages of fine print. Every instant seemed to be telling her something new and important. And Molly noted that with another strange little qualm of jealousy. She, the past mistress of love—why, it was as if she knew nothing of love!

She was glad to get back to her mustang and mount it and fight its head around into the wind and so get down the pass, half blindly, through the smothering hands of the storm. The snow walked toward her in gigantic images that dissolved under her eyes and rushed by her with a shriek. She could not keep the mustang at more than a hard trot, and even that gait had him slipping and sliding half the time.

Head down, teeth set, she almost failed to see the two dim forms that struggled past her up the grade. She half thought that they were illusions of the mind; then she made sure that they were horsemen, and she shouted to them.

It did not matter who they were. They were not apt to be the men of Solitaire, and any other men in the whole world would be useful to her now. She rode straight at them, and found, first, a gigantic Negro on a huge gray mare, and beyond him none other than the man she had discarded for The Solitaire—the buck-toothed smile of little Boots! She would rather have had anyone other than Boots. Shame moved in her vaguely. But her courage was far greater than her shame when she thought of the need in which Saxon lay. She pushed her mustang right up to the horse of Boots and put a hand out to him. He kept his own hands on the pommel of his saddle and merely stared at her.

"You can hate me and damn me, Boots," she called to him, "but come and help me now, will you?"

She saw the quick response in his face.

In his sullen daydreams he had often begged chance to give him this opportunity—she would come to him haggard and desperate, in the utmost need, and he, with a stony face, listening, would at last consent to lift his hand and help her.

"I'm on a trail, Molly," he told her. "But I'll come along, if it's not far."

"It's not ten minutes," she declared. "Boots, you have the best heart in the world; I know you'll do what you can, because you've got the biggest heart!"

"How can there be a big heart in a runt like me?" asked Boots. "What is it, Molly? The Solitaire?"

He spoke the name hungrily. But she shook her head.

"You've been out in the hills so long you've probably never heard of him," she said. "But you'll want to help. Follow me, Boots!"

Not The Solitaire—but a man—another man! He took

178

the bitter taste deep in his throat and grinned at the wind as he followed her. Big Arthur William Creston pressed on at his side. The wind caught the tails of their slickers and flapped them noisily. The wind pried at their sombreros. They rode through a nightmare of confusion.

And so, twisting up through the rocks, they came suddenly on the flutter of the open fire, the girl bending beside it, and the extended form of John Saxon. And a great cry came out of the throat of Big Arthur Creston.

"Saxon! Saxon!" he shouted at Boots. "It's the Chief! It's Saxon!"

Boots was already out of the saddle and running to the spot. But Creston turned and grabbed the hands of Molly as she was dismounting.

"You know who laid him out!" he said. "You know who did it! Gimme his name!"

She stared at the convulsed, hideous face of Creston.

"The Solitaire!" she said. And, as she said it, she watched hate wrinkle the face of Creston still more.

Well, she was betraying The Solitaire into the hands of many men. But they would have to be men of steel before they could make him pay for what he had done. She herself could not tell, at this moment, whether she hated him more than she loved him, or dreaded him more than she gloried in his fierceness and his strength.

She stood aside, staring down at the scene of Boots, and the girl, and big-handed Creston.

The eyes of Saxon were open, but they were unseeing. His head turned restlessly from side to side and a burning color was in his face.

Boots said: "We've got to get him into better shelter. The woods, up there. We can whack up a lean-to."

"It's cold," said Saxon. "God, it's cold!"

"We're gunna have you warmed up, Chief," said Creston. "You can lay to that. We'll get you fixed up fine. It's me, Chief. It's Creston talkin'."

"It's cold!" said Saxon. "It's terribly cold."

Creston and Boots wrapped him in blankets from head to foot. Still he shuddered and muttered that it was cold. They lifted him. They placed him in the saddle on Creston's horse and Boots led the mare while Creston steadied the slumping figure that loomed above. Mary

Wilson hurried beside, clutching the blanket ends to make them hold about the body of the rider. And Molly? She simply led on the other horses and formed a rearguard. All of those others seemed to have a greater right to minister to big John Saxon.

Ay, but he would have been dead, by this time, except for her!

She felt that she was in the strangest rôle in the world, helping the great antagonist of The Solitaire. Yet she felt that it was almost the only right thing that she had ever done in her life.

The slope brought them into the trees, where the wind screamed with a louder voice than ever, but touched them with muffled hands. Once well inside the woods, they paused in the middle of a thicket and all fell to work. The two girls could care for John Saxon and kindle the fire. The two men with swift hands and a rapid fire of ax strokes cut saplings with which they walled in—using the standing trunks of the thicket—a solid windbreak. They leaned more saplings across the space where Saxon lay by the fire. In a wonderfully short time, all was fast, and Saxon lay in a sort of wooden tent, open at both ends. But a saddle blanket tied firmly over one end stopped some of the draught and now the fire was moved out opposite the open face of the lean-to. The heat of it came flooding in. The wind and the snow were kept out. And the aching weight of Saxon was eased on a deep bed of boughs.

Creston never traveled without provisions. His kit was unlimbered and they began a bit of cookery for the benefit of Saxon. Weakness was plainly his trouble. When they opened the bandage and re-dressed the wound, making use of the underskirt of Mary Wilson for that purpose, all four of them crowded close to consider the hurt, and plainly it was nothing to cause death. Some of the bone of the ribs might have been chiseled away, and the flesh was badly torn, but it was only the loss of the blood that was really dangerous. Long rest and quiet and plenty of nourishing food would put him right. What had seemed desperate an hour before now began to be almost a simple matter.

There was one very strange thing. The wounded man, fully delirious now, could recognize only one name, and this he attached to the wrong person. To Mary Wilson and Creston and even to Boots he never turned his eyes, but he kept looking at Molly and calling her "Mary!" He kept using that name over and over again, and something shrank and shuddered in the soul of Molly as she listened.

She saw wonder and fear, also, in the face of Mary Wilson, whose swift glances kept lifting from Saxon to her friend. Jealous? Well, the best of women can be jealous, of course.

Creston went out to ride off with his mare and get a doctor from a little village back in the mountains. Boots remained there, staring at the woman he loved as she crouched beside Saxon. Saxon wanted to hold her hand, and she gave it to him. Saxon brushed impatiently aside all others, and in his delirium seemed to cling to her. It was she who fed him. The great, inert weight of his head lolled back on her arm and his eyes went up trustfully to her face after every mouthful.

He was very weak, and he was utterly in her hands.

She felt on herself the savage jealousy of the eye of Boots, and the cold, aching jealousy of Mary. And she was content. Her heart was filled.

It was late in the afternoon before big John Saxon at last fell into a sleep, and she felt his forehead with her bared arm. He had eaten; strength was running back into his veins; and he was now far less in the hands of the fever. When he wakened—well, he would be sure to know well enough the difference between Molly and Mary.

Perhaps that was why Molly got up, suddenly.

"I have to go back," she said. "He's going to be in his right mind when the sleep leaves him. He's going to be in the saddle, inside of a week. He's going to be as strong as ever in two weeks. A fellow like that—you can put him down but you can't hold him down!"

She added: "Boots, you don't know anything about me, in this. You didn't see me up here."

"I never clapped eyes on you for weeks," agreed Boots. And suddenly the old yearning admiration burned in his eyes.

"And you haven't seen me today at all, Mary," she cautioned Mary Wilson.

Mary Wilson followed her out of the lean-to.

"Are you going back—to him?" asked Mary. "Don't go, Molly. It's the end for you, if you go back to him. Besides, if he finds out what you've done, he'll hate you. It's you who saved John Saxon. The whole world ought to know that. No, we won't talk—but the whole world ought to know it!"

"The whole world knows such a pile about me," answered Molly, "that knowing a little bit of good wouldn't help any. There's no use in that, Mary. I'm glad I helped your man. You keep your grip right hard on him or one of these days maybe I'll wangle him away from you. So long!"

She mounted and went off down the slope toward the bottom of the pass.

The wind had fallen somewhat; the clouds had lifted, and Molly could see the iron gray of the mountains all the way up against the paler gray of the sky. There was still a little snow falling, and the gusts of wind knocked level sprays of white out of the hollows and down the pass. It seemed to Molly a fitting sort of a day for her return to the old life. For it *was* the old life to which she was returning, an old and dead life since she had tasted something new and better.

CHAPTER XXXV

It was one of the errands of Molly to get word to the family of Wilsons that Mary would not be home—and where she could be found.

That message, slipped on a bit of paper under the kitchen door in the twilight of the day, brought a wave of hope to a very desperate household. It gave the needed clue to the men of Bluewater who had been searching all that day, and out of the town a human river flowed up into the Stillman Pass. That river reached the camp. Mr. Wilson and the sheriff moved at the head of it, and the first thing the sheriff did was to spot big Arthur William Creston and pull down a gun on him.

Creston simply said: "Go and take me and be damned to you. This nigger don't care. I'm kind of tired of hidin 'out, anyways. But ain't you got a doctor with you? There wasn't no doctor up in the hills."

They had a doctor with them, of course.

The doctor spent three days and nights up there in the mountains, not because big John Saxon needed such attention, but because the doctor knew that this was very good for his reputation. He saw that the entire community had fixed upon John Saxon as its pet hero, and the doctor intended to make the most of curing the invalid.

The excitement in Bluewater, in fact, was very great. It is one thing to have a town hero, and it is quite another to have a chance to take care of him. Bluewater had that chance, and it made the most of it.

If anyone wanted a further thrill than the proved heroism of big John Saxon, it was provided by the romantic truth that the girl he loved had found him in the snows of the Stillman Pass and saved his life. There was nothing about that other girl; there was no need of her; she would have spoiled things, in the public eye.

The fact that mattered was that Mary Wilson was at the side of John Saxon up there in the mountains, where the best pair of tents in Bluewater had been sent to house the invalid and the nurse, to say nothing of the other little tents that sprang up, so that there was an entire camp devoted to the care of John Saxon.

We love above all the creatures that depend upon us. Bluewater had respected and looked up to its brand new hero. Now it began to love him, and the more that it did for him, the more affection it felt for him. John Saxon, having been three times brought to the verge of death by The Solitaire, was in two cases considered the victor; in the third case he was considered the victim of a cowardly betrayal. No matter how often Saxon tried to tell the truth about the first two encounters, people merely smiled and shook their heads. They knew a hero when they saw one; they knew a hero's modesty!

Other benefits extended, suddenly, to Arthur Creston, the big Negro. It was true that the law had a case against him, but when Bluewater learned that Creston had been

183

devotedly tending its hero, Bluewater decided that the case against the Negro should be dropped. The sheriff told him so and saw the grin that made the features of Creston all disappear.

But all that Arthur William Creston said was: "They oughta give the boss a shave, sheriff. He can't flourish none when he's got that beard growin' all over his face. You take a clean man and he can't get on none in dirt!"

It was a week before they brought John Saxon back to Bluewater. He wanted to ride in, as he was quite capable of doing, but the doctor laughed him to scorn. Bluewater would not hear of it!

John Saxon wanted to go in quietly, without any blaring of trumpets, but the sheriff himself frowned on this. So did all the other leading citizens who had sent up the tents, and supplies, and all sorts of delicacies to eat. Particularly the banker wanted to ride his horse somewhere in that procession, and a great many others wanted to have a place, here or there. Anyone who could be attached to John Saxon was sure to be forever in the memory of the public of that whole hearted town.

And Finlay?

Oh, he had not gone up into the mountains because he knew that others would do the talking for him, and tell how he had made his impassioned appeal in the church, and how he had practically collapsed at the end of it, broken-hearted.

In fact, Saxon had heard that story not once but many times, and he had been deeply moved. It was not the loss of the money to the bandits. That did not matter. It was the grief and the shock to that preëminently good man, Daniel Finlay, that disturbed John Saxon.

So the entry into Bluewater was made exactly as Saxon did not want it to be made. They had him in a big horse litter. The sheriff rode on one side of it, and Mary Wilson rode on the other, and the banker was just behind her, as pleased as Punch. There were a lot of others in the cortege, including big Arthur Creston, grinning from ear to ear. And Boots was with the rest of them. And the whole population of Bluewater turned out onto the sides of the street to shout and cheer as Saxon went by, propped on

184

pillows, looking a little pale and thin, with that big white bandage again around his head like a crown.

He saw those people laughing and smiling. He heard them clapping hands and stamping and shouting, and it seemed to him that these were the kindest, the gentlest, the most faithful people in the entire world.

And Daniel Finlay?

Oh, he managed to be noticed, too. You may be sure of that. He simply took up his stand at a fence, behind a thick group, and stood there silently, quietly, the way a modest man should do—a fellow who did not in the least want the public eye—a fellow who was there simply to gladden his eyes with the sight of John Saxon.

But of course he was noted down at once. That crowd opened up in front of him. He was at the base of a living funnel when Saxon passed, and a dozen hands were pointing out Finlay to Saxon, who saw him at once and called out to halt the horses.

They were halted. He called to Finlay, and the lawyer came unwillingly, modestly out, and was gripped by the hand of John Saxon, while everyone cheered more loudly than ever before in honor of this meeting between tried friends and true.

Afterward, Finlay walked with downward head beside the litter until it came to the hotel, and he went up the stairs in the hotel and sat among the first with Saxon in his room—the best room in the hotel, and gladly donated to him, free of charge, by the management, which knew on which side its bread was buttered.

Lefty Malone came in among others. He carried his hat in his hand. One eye was black and blue and swollen.

"The boys keep carryin' on just as though you was back there in the Rolling Bones," he said. "They gotta have something to stand up to, still, and I'm the goat!"

Other people kept flooding in until the doctor declared in favor of quiet, and Mary Wilson. It was not until this point in the celebration that Daniel Finlay modestly slipped from the room, and modestly left the hotel, and modestly walked back to his house with his head a little bowed. Everyone noticed him, of course. But not even by side-glances did he need to take heed of their admiration and sympathy and pleasure; out of the very air he could drink in his increased notoriety.

Two or three people called out: "Well, he's back! It's a pretty happy day for you, Mr. Finlay, I guess!"

At that, he would raise his head, as though out of profound thought, and faintly smile on the speaker, and pass on. The good minister stopped him and gripped his hand, warmly, in silence. A bit further on, the banker hurried up and slapped him lightly on the shoulder.

"A welcome day's work for all of us, Finlay," he said. "And I think before the thing's ended that the whole world is going to realize that honesty is the best policy. Always works out that way in the long run. By heaven, what a fine fellow John Saxon is! Who would have guessed—I mean, who would have thought the scoundrels would set a trap for him like that? A lucky thing that the brutes didn't send lead into you, Finlay. A mighty lucky thing! Men without law are without mercy, as a rule!"

Daniel Finlay answered with a vague word or two.

As he reached his home, he was feeling that he had fortified his position as it never had been strengthened before. There were plenty of good citizens in this town who would now fail to believe their eyes and their ears, if testimony against him should appear. He tried to conceive of a way in which they could be convinced of his guilt, but he found that the effort overtaxed his imagination.

So he walked up the steps to his house, pushed the door open, and found on his threshold a fold of paper which, when he opened it, proved to be covered with penciled print.

"Come over where you saw me the last time; come fast; and bring some money."

That was what he read.

He crumpled the paper. He scratched a match and lighted it and saw the paper turn into a tossing flicker of yellow flame. Then a blackened cinder with glowing golden spots on it dropped toward the floor. It turned from black to gray. And on that gray ash he trod with his heel.

The message was gone out of the world of paper and pencils, but it remained in his mind.

He started walking up and down, angrily. He began to compose a speech to his own heart, and he illustrated

186

it with some of his famous handless gestures; but suddenly he realized that he was not dealing with a public audience, but with the profoundly crafty brain of one man. He did not have a throng to influence, but the bright, keen eyes of The Solitaire.

There were many questions which The Solitaire might have to ask him; there were many answers which it might be hard for him to make.

First—there was the matter of the money. He thought, for an instant, of saying that he had abandoned the money on the way, out of fear—that he had cached it under a rock.

But when he thought of the fierce, steady eyes of The Solitaire, he changed his mind about that. He got out the stock of bills. He had to close his eyes as he beheld the fresh beauty of them. They spoke to him more eloquently than any oratory. To part from any of them would be like parting from his own flesh and blood.

And yet he had to make a sacrifice.

At that very time, in the Bluewater Hotel, Mary Wilson was saying: "There's one thing that I have to tell you, John. I promised not to say a word about it to anyone— but that didn't mean you. I've got to let you know that I don't deserve one stick of praise for finding you. There was another girl!"

"Another—girl?" asked Saxon, amazed.

"You know the girl who lives in the old Borden shack on the edge of the town?"

"I know the old Borden shack," said Saxon.

"And you know Molly, too—the one who's living there now!"

"I don't know her."

She was half pleased and half angry.

"The prettiest girl in Bluewater," she said, "the one who—"

"No, she's not the prettiest girl in Bluewater," said Saxon with decision.

"She really is," said Mary Wilson, smiling. "The very prettiest. The one with the bright, bright lips. Sometimes she rides and she has a jeweled quirt—think of it!"

"Ah, I know the one. I know *about* her, too," said

Saxon, darkly. "What are you doing with a girl like that, Mary?"

"She can't harm me. She's all right. She isn't as bad as people say," said Mary Wilson. "She's the one who knew that there was danger to you. She's the one who came to me early that morning and told me to keep you from riding with Daniel Finlay, no matter where Daniel Finlay wanted to go."

"Keep me from riding with Finlay? Ah, she knows The Solitaire!"

"But how did The Solitaire know, beforehand, where you were going to ride with Finlay?" asked the girl.

Saxon started, and stared at Mary Wilson. He said nothing. And she, having planted that one seed of distrust—a seed in which she herself dared not have any belief—went on: "Molly was the girl who urged me to ride on to Stillman Pass. Even she knew that you were going that way. How? Did you tell anyone you were going? Did Mr. Finlay tell anyone?"

Saxon was silent again, and still he was silent. He started shaking his head. It was wrong. It had to be wrong. It was one of those mysteries which, some way or other, are always answered. One word will generally serve to brush the darkness away and give the light.

There was a sort of fear and suffering mixed with a certain brightness in the face of Mary Wilson.

"I've just been thinking it over—for hours—every day and every night," she said. "But the main thing is to tell you about how Molly took me up there into the Stillman Pass. And how she helped. She did a lot more than I did."

"Not more than you did," insisted Saxon.

"Yes, a great deal more. And you know, John, for a time you didn't recognize me. You were delirious. But something about Molly entered your mind. You looked at her and you'd smile and call her 'Mary.' She was the only one who could take care of you. She fed you when you were too weak or too much out of your mind to eat. Afterward, you went to sleep holding her hands."

He closed his eyes, frowning until the old wound in his head began to ache.

Then he said: "I begin to remember. She had a nice

188

voice. I begin to remember a lot about her—out of that delirium."

Mary said, with only a very faint smile: "I hope that you won't remember too much, John."

He looked up at the ceiling, still frowning. After a while be began to smile at his thoughts.

CHAPTER XXXVI

DANIEL FINLAY, before that interview between Mary Wilson and Saxon had ended, was walking across the town in the first dark of the night; and by entangled bypaths and crooked lanes he came, at last, to the old Borden house. It had, as usual, a light in the front room. He stopped at the sight of it, for he knew that somewhere near that light would be Molly. To face The Solitaire would be bad enough; but to face her might be worse.

At last, he rallied himself and went on. There was plenty of courage in Daniel Finlay. Anger, now, was dulling his nerves to other impressions and to other dangers. For one thing, the wad of greenbacks inside his coat pressed against his very heart and caused him pain there.

He carried a bulldog revolver inside his coat. For a left-handed shot, he was not at all bad with a gun. Not that he expected that he would use it, but, in case of a pinch, he might work in even hot lead on The Solitaire. His gun would have the advantage of being totally unexpected by the enemy.

He went up to the front door, knocked, and was invited by the voice of Molly to enter. The voice came from the rear of the shack, so he passed around to the kitchen door and entered there. Molly was cooking. The smell of crisping bacon was in the air, and the smoke of it. She wore rubber gloves. He could see that she hated the fumes and the grime of her work.

She had a pair of little emerald earrings in her ears. They swayed and sparkled as she leaned over the stove.

Somehow, he thought of a great, brutal hand gripping those jewels and tearing them out of the flesh.

"Hello, Danny," she said, without giving him a glance. "How's my old sweetheart?"

"I've been welcoming the hero home," said Finlay.

He walked to the inside door and looked into the front room. A table was set for two, but there was no sight of The Solitaire.

"No," said Molly, "he isn't here, yet. Bring some cash?"

"It was a lot of noise," said Finlay.

"Oh, I was there, and saw the crowd. Saw nice little modest Danny standing away back in the crowd. Just a real good, quiet boy is what our Danny is."

"Stop it, Molly," said Finlay.

She opened the oven door and pulled out a pan of brown-topped biscuits. A thin cloud of smoke rolled into the room.

"Look good, don't they?" said Molly. "Are you going to eat with us?"

"No," said Finlay, shortly.

"All right," she answered. "I'll call in The Solitaire. He's feeling pretty damned solitary, at that. This yelling around for John Saxon burns him up a good bit. Just so you'll know where to step, Danny."

She went to the front and sent the thin, clear note of the signal whistle shrilling across the night. As she came back, she said: "Sort of hard on a fellow like The Solitaire to have to sneak around in the woods while the crowd's all hoarse, cheering for his murdered man. Sort of hard on Danny, eh?"

He said nothing.

"What did you feel like, shaking hands with the hero?" asked the girl. "Little bit giddy? Didn't you wish that The Solitaire had shot a little straighter or that Johnnie didn't have such a tough set of ribs?"

Still Finlay said nothing, but with bent head he was looking down at her.

"Mind you," he said sternly, after she had met his eye calmly for some time, "you play fair with me or I'll raise hell for you where hell will burn the hottest. Understand?"

"I'm sort of tired of a lot of things, Danny," she answered. "But I'm mostly tired of you."

A soft step sounded in the front room. The girl went in, carrying a heaped platter of biscuits.

"Little old Danny, the honest lawyer, is already here, Solitaire," she said, jerking her head over her shoulder. "See if he'll give you enough money to pay the gas bill, will you?"

It was The Solitaire, as Finlay now saw. The big man stood back by the farther wall, smoothing the sleek of his hair.

"Hello, Daniel," he said, and waited.

"Hello, Solitaire," said Finlay, and walked forward, holding out his hand.

"Back up," said The Solitaire.

Finlay halted.

"I want to know a few things," said The Solitaire. "Who did you talk to? How did that damned girl know where to go, straight off, to find the hero, eh?"

"Why, you mean the speech I made in the church?"

"Oh, damn the speech in the church. That was all right. You had to make a speech sooner or later or you'd of choked. Must have been pretty good to make a speech in church, eh? They say the great lawyer was pretty near in a faint by the time he finished. All worked up about the damned bandits, eh? But that's not what I mean. It wasn't the speech in church. An hour before that—yes, two hours before, maybe—Mary Wilson started for the Stillman Pass —and there's where she found her man. If it hadn't been for that, Saxon would have been a dead one, because he would have been frozen, even if lead and water couldn't kill him."

He pointed a sudden finger at Finlay and added, quietly: "Finlay, you talked! Who did you talk to?"

That gesture caused a tremendous reaction in Finlay. He was on the verge of snatching out his gun and making answer with it. But he checked himself.

"Solitaire," he said, "I don't know what to say to you. I'd like to say a lot of words. The truth is that I didn't speak to a human soul."

"Then who did?" asked Solitaire. "Did I walk in my sleep to Mary Wilson and tell her I was going to kill Saxon that day?"

191

"There were three of us on the inside," said Daniel Finlay, but without glancing at the girl.

"Oh, that's the tune, eh?" said Solitaire.

"Danny wants to bring mama into it," said the girl. "He doesn't want to leave mama out in the cold. Nice old Danny."

"Shut up the nonsense and talk," said The Solitaire. "Did *you* talk to Mary Wilson?"

"Well," said Molly, "I was out all that day. I had plenty of time to go talk to her. Ay, and to ride up into the pass, as far as that goes."

"You did," said The Solitaire. "You had plenty of time. There's enough devil in you to make you do a thing like that just to spite me. Or maybe you've had a good look at Handsome John Saxon. Is that it?"

"Good old Solitaire," said the girl. "Of course that was it. I fell in love with Saxon, and that's why I told his girl how to save him. You poor dummy!"

"It doesn't ring true," said The Solitaire, suddenly. "If she wanted to help Saxon, she would have done it herself, and taken all the glory of it. Finlay—you're the one who talked!"

CHAPTER XXXVII

To Finlay, of course, the thing was perfectly open and apparent. Someone had talked. That someone had to be Molly. He turned his head toward her and she, with the assurance of a very devil, merely winked at him without changing the rest of her expression in the very least. She admitted her fault by that wink; she also challenged him to do anything about it.

And he, the master of lying inventions, saw that his hands were tied, and that, in fact, there was nothing that he could say! Having lied a thousand times in this matter, now he was nailed to the cross by another lie. Back in his throat worked his anger, and the words of the denunciation came right up to his teeth, but he took a firm grip and forced back his emotion.

He could see that he was walking on a very narrow ledge between life and death, for The Solitaire was in a killing humor. A man with two hands or one, The Solitaire would sacrifice a traitor. Finally Finlay said: "Solitaire, there's no use talking. You've made up your mind already. But I want to point out one thing to you. The scheme to save John Saxon might have worked; and in that case I would have lost nearly sixty thousand dollars. Does it seem sensible to you that I'd throw that much money out the window?"

The Solitaire's blazing eyes fixed themselves more deeply than ever on the soul of the lawyer. Then, strange to say, it was the girl who said: "It *is* hard to think of Danny giving up a dollar. Eh, Solitaire?"

The Solitaire glared at her, and back again at Finlay. A sudden twitching of the muscles along one side of his face seemed to Finlay the certain prelude to the final action. Death, perhaps, was a split part of a second away when Finlay said: "We made our compact, Solitaire. I was to get the money and you were to get Saxon. I received the money. Through no fault of mine, by chance you failed to receive Saxon. But now you fail to see that I am still willing to carry out the contract and that I am able to do so!"

"Able to do so? Damn you," snarled The Solitaire, "do you think that I'll trust you again?"

"You will," answered Finlay, "because you'll realize that I'm the only man in the world capable of delivering John Saxon into your hands. You know that he has the people of the town around him. You know that he's being watched and guarded day and night. And I'm the one power in this world, Solitaire, capable of making him walk to this house as soon as he's able to leave the hotel room."

As he spoke, he pointed steadily to the front door of the house, as though it might at that moment open and give them a view of the handsome face and the big shoulders of John Saxon. The Solitaire actually cast a glance over his shoulder in that direction. Then he began to walk up and down the room.

"I haven't finished," he said. "I'm going to probe at

193

the thing till I find out the truth. One of you is a traitor and a liar and I'll find out the one!"

He stared at them both; then he continued his pacing through a long moment during which the lawyer began to breathe again. Finlay stared not at The Solitaire but at the girl and she looked back at him, totally unabashed.

Suddenly The Solitaire paused and struck his knuckles against the table. The force of the blow caused the dishes to jump a bit and there was a light shivering tingle from the glasses that died out like an echo.

"I told you to bring money. Where is it?" demanded The Solitaire.

Finlay, in putting up the greenbacks, had made them into two small packages, of five thousand dollars each. Now he rallied himself a little and gathered his courage.

"You haven't a right to a penny of the money," he declared, firmly. "But—since bad luck didn't give you your part of the bargain, I've brought some cash to you. Here's five thousand dollars."

He laid one packet on the table.

"You give me five and you keep fifty-five, eh?" said The Solitaire. "Do you think that I'm a cheap fool, Finlay?"

"I think you're a dangerous man, Solitaire," said the lawyer. "But I know that you want Saxon more than you want cash. This five thousand is a gift to you, not a right of yours."

"Why, a man might think that you're talking in court!" said The Solitaire. "You rotten hypocrite, are you yammering about 'right' and 'wrong'?"

"There ought to be a sort of honesty even among thieves," said Finlay, calmly.

Here the girl put in: "Danny is pretty good at this. He has a steady nerve, eh, Solitaire?"

"I've a mind to steady his nerves for him so that they'll never quiver again!" said The Solitaire.

"I know you've a mind to shoot me down," said Finlay. "I know that, but I'll still stand up for what I think. If you spray lead into me, you're taking me instead of Saxon. Is that the choice you want to make?"

The Solitaire bowed his head a little, in thought. He picked up the packet of money and threw it to the girl.

"Keep this," he said. "I'll take what I want of it later on."

She caught the packet out of the air and hurled it straight back at The Solitaire's head. It whizzed by his cheek.

"Keep your dirty blood money," she said. "I don't want it."

It seemed to Finlay that the outlaw would hurl himself straight at the girl, such a devil appeared in his eyes at that moment. Instead, he caught a breath and then laughed.

"Makes me feel better," said The Solitaire. "You hell-cat!"

"Call me what you please," answered Molly. "You can buy your thugs and your crooked lawyers with blood-money, but you can't buy me."

She turned on her heel and went into the kitchen.

And The Solitaire snapped: "I'll hear from you later on, Finlay. I don't know how long it's safe for me to hang around this place. You may sell me to the sheriff. Somebody might see me. But at any rate, I'll try to stay close to the town for a few days. Mind you, Finlay, if Saxon doesn't turn up—here, inside this house—within a few days, I'm coming to call on *you!*"

"I understand," said Finlay.

"Do you? Then get out!" commanded The Solitaire.

Finlay got.

He went through the kitchen and said softly to the girl: "I remember everything, Molly."

She was pouring the water off some boiled potatoes into the sink. Clouds of steam rolled swiftly up around her. Through those clouds she called cheerfully over her shoulder: "Good old Danny! I'd hate to have you forget."

He went out into the night and walked slowly, very slowly, with a pause in every step, back toward the lights of the town.

Bad luck was in the air for Mr. Finlay, on this night. The events that moved down on him started at a great distance and did not have him in mind at all. They started with the taking of the Stillman loot from the hands of The Solitaire and his men. And this evening some of that loot was changing hands in the back yard of the

195

Bluewater Hotel where the guard which was posted to see that no one climbed up to the window of Saxon's room was composed of his own trusted men. These were, at the moment, Boots, Cullen, and Creston. Pike and Del Bryan were also ready to serve when their time came; they were ready to risk identification as the robbers who had escaped from the train at Tunnel.

Now Creston paced up and down, his little head turning restlessly toward every light and sound, while Cullen and Boots sat on the edges of a blanket which was spread on the ground and played two-handed poker. Two-handed poker is a strange game. The big hands come only now and then; the entire scale of betting is very different; and after a couple of hours in which the fortunes of the game had fluctuated this way and that to the extent of only a few dollars, Cullen grew restless. When he was nervous, his old wounds ached; and now he was in actual pain as he suddenly drew to a pair, got another pair, and shoved five thousand dollars onto the blanket.

Boots looked up quickly. This sign that the sky was the limit did not bother him. He was holding only a wretched trio of sevens, but he instantly covered that bet and raised it five more.

In one minute they had rashly exposed their entire shares of the Solitaire loot and stacked thousands of dollars were heaped on the blanket. Then Boots raised with the whole little heap of jewels that had fallen to his lot; and by the same means, Cullen saw him.

Three sevens beat a pair of treys and a pair of queens. Boots gathered up the treasure without apparent excitement.

"Want any part of it?" he offered.

"Oh, to hell with it," said Cullen. "There's plenty more where that lot came from. I'm going to walk over to the Rolling Bones and get a drink. You two hombres can handle this job, all right."

"Sure we can handle it," said Boots.

So Cullen walked away, but when he came to the street and felt in his pocket, he found that he had bet every one of his paper dollars and that he did not have a single dime in silver. This was annoying. But, in his present mood, he was almost glad to be spurred into action of some sort.

He turned down the first dark cross-street and when he met the first pedestrian, he pulled out a Colt and stuck it into the stranger's stomach.

Under the dark of the night and the shadowing trees which grew along the way, it was hard to make out any features of the stranger, except that he was rather tall, with thin shoulders. But it was easy to make out his left-handed gesture inside his coat.

Cullen was tempted to put lead into this fool. Instead, he struck down with his own gun across the forearm of his victim. A weapon slithered down to the ground and landed with a heavy thump.

"Damn you!" breathed the voice of Daniel Finlay.

"All right, brother," murmured Cullen. "That was a fool play of yours, but I'm a simple and kind sort of a dummy. Are you Daniel Finlay? Just shove up your hands before you talk back."

Finlay, after grinding his teeth for an instant, answered calmly:

"My poor fellow, if it's money you want, I can give you—let's see, I think there's fifteen dollars in my pocket."

"Yeah?" answered Cullen. "Only fifteen bucks?" Would you try to make a gun-play when another gun was rammed into your belly—and just for the sake of fifteen bucks?"

"The instinctive reaction," said Finlay, "of a man taken violently by surprise—"

"Instinctive bunk," said Cullen. "You've got a bale of coin on you. Stick up those hands and I'm going to have a look-see."

Finlay drew in his breath. It came out slowly with the words:

"What do you gain by this, my friend? You insult a helpless man and you'll get no cash. As a matter of fact, however, rather than endure this humiliation further I'll take you to my house and give you as much as—"

"What a sweet old gag that is!" said Cullen. "Look, Finlay—you gotta reputation for brains. I've heard a lot about you. And I hate to do this because you been a friend to a friend of mine. But—I didn't like that gunplay, brother. It sure didn't make any hit with me. If I'd delayed action a little, you would of salted me full of lead. Now—get those damned hands up in the air, and get them quick!"

In his voice, though he spoke quietly, there was something which made Finlay forget even the other five thousand in his inside coat pocket. He hoisted his hands, and the touch of Cullen went rapidly over him.

Those practiced fingers found the spare change in the pocket of the lawyer's trousers and the little fold of bills in his vest. Then they touched the paper wrapping of the inside coat pocket and drew it out.

"What's this, brother?" asked Cullen.

"That?" said the lawyer. "That's nothing but a few loose notes I've been taking on a recent case."

"Yeah?" said Cullen, fingering the packet and finding something familiar in the dimensions of the papers it contained. "You sure that it ain't some notes that you got *out* of a recent case? I'll keep it and see. All lawyers are liars, and I guess you're a lawyer, all right. Now, walk along and spread the alarm. So long, Finlay. Sorry as hell that you happened to be the first gent I bumped into here."

CHAPTER XXXVIII

WHEN Finlay had walked on, muttering savagely, Cullen turned the next corner, scratched a match, and looked down at the uncovered contents of the little parcel. When he saw the greenbacks, he smiled. He flicked up the corners of them, and, assured that he had several thousand dollars in that thick sheaf, he jammed the money into his pocket and chuckled aloud.

"Lawyers—they're all liars," said Cullen. "Even this bird Finlay, that's a friend to the Chief."

He was a good deal ashamed of having robbed a friend of his boss, but shame could not live long in a heart like Cullen's. When he cast about for what he would do next, he remembered that he had wanted a drink; and now he

198

wanted it more than ever. Any sensible man, having raised such a wind, would have taken himself out of the town, but there was no savor for life in Cullen unless the days were freely sprinkled with danger of one sort or another. He simply trusted that his face could not have been recognized by the lawyer's eyes in the dark beneath the trees, and therefore he rounded the corner and walked straight into the Rolling Bones.

There were half a dozen men in the place, and big Lefty Malone, with a black eye and a grin on his face, was serving the drinks. Cullen ordered a whiskey and paid for it with the top ten dollar bill from that thick sheaf he had taken from Finlay.

He was thinking: "Four or five thousand dollars in a lump! It sure pays to be a lawyer!"

And, while he pursued this thought and sniffed at his whiskey and then swallowed it, he did not notice that the bartender, instead of dropping the ten dollar bill into the cash register when he rang up the change, stared intently at the bill and then pursed his lips.

He made the change, with an absent-minded look of a man in thought. And the bill itself he laid on the shelf under the bar beside a long printed list of numbers.

Part of the money stolen from the Stillman bank could be identified by the numbers printed on the bills, and it was a similarity in the number on this ten dollar bill that had caught the attention of Lefty Malone. For he had a peculiar interest in the ways of the law. Lefty had been on the verge of prison, in the very shadow of the bars, so to speak, more than once in his younger days. Now that he was out of trouble himself, he did not mind seeing others get into it. And now, in half a minute, he spotted the identical number that he was looking for!

When he had done that, he cheerfully filled two or three orders for drinks, stepped from behind the bar, and went into the back room of his place, where six men were at a poker game. He closed the door and said: "Gents, one of the Solitaire gang is outside at the bar. I've spotted one of the numbers of the bills that have been advertised. What'll we do about it?"

"Ay, it may be the right number but the wrong man,"

said one of the gamblers. "It might of passed through a good bit of circulation before it wound up in his hands."

"It's as fresh and straight as a playing card just out of a case," said Lefty Malone. "Boys, I reckon we'll take this gent in."

"If that's the lay of the land, sure we will," said they, and rose from their chairs.

That was why a little procession of men filed in from the cardroom, while Lefty himself went around behind the bar, and busied himself at once with the washing of glasses.

It was a big man with a full front and a flow of pale mustaches who came up to Cullen and held a gun close to his head.

"Brother," he said, "how long's it been since you seen The Solitaire?"

Cullen turned from the bar and faced the leveled Colt squarely. He felt that he was two-thirds gone, but not entirely. Besides this fellow, five others had weapons in their hands, but, as though they trusted their comrade to conduct affairs safely and easily, none of those guns were pointed. It left, for a moment, only one weapon to deal with. And Cullen took note of the fact.

"I dunno what's eating you," said Cullen.

"Put up your hands, and you'll begin to find out," said the stranger.

Cullen, obediently, lifted his hands above his head. But in his eyes there was a waiting shadow that was not entirely reflection.

"There's my hands touching the sky," said Cullen. "Now talk to me about The Solitaire."

"You bought a drink with a ten buck note, just now," said the stranger.

"It's a lot of money," said Cullen, "but cowpunchers have had that much before."

"Not with a number on the ten spot—not with one of the numbers of the stolen cash from Stillman," said the stranger.

The eyes of Cullen opened very wide. It was not entirely of his own predicament that he was thinking. He was more troubled about another thing that bewildered him. If there was a number of a stolen bill in that heap of money which he had taken from Finlay, then how did it come into Finlay's hands?

To be sure, everyone knew that a certain amount of the stolen greenbacks had been in Finlay's possession on the day when he rode with John Saxon through the Stillman Pass. But all of that money had been taken from him by The Solitaire's gang. That was the story which Finlay had published—and now—

The thing kept Cullen staring, wide-eyed. He could see echoing and re-echoing possibilities extending, so to speak, through the open window at the end of the bar and into the dark of the night. If Finlay retained part of that money, then he had it all! If he had it all, then he never had been robbed; if he had not been robbed, he had lied about the Solitaire gang. If he lied about that gang—might he not have worked hand in glove with them?

The story grew in the mind of Cullen. It staggered him. Finlay, men said, was the best and the nearest friend of John Saxon. Such treachery was surely impossible and yet—

Said Cullen, aloud: "All lawyers are liars, by God!"

"Yeah, that may be true, but you're gunna need one of them liars to work for you," said the stranger. "Terry, step up and fan this gent. There's a couple lumps under his coat that might be extra bandanas but they might be guns, too."

"All right, boys," said Cullen, "but take it easy!"

Then he acted. The thing was not so hard. As the surety of the fat man increased, he had allowed the level of his Colt to decline until the hand which held it was hardly more than hip high. And Cullen kicked up with all his might, accurately, and knocked that gun spinning up to the ceiling.

It exploded in midair and crashed a bullet through a bottle behind the bar.

The sudden act, the roar of the gun, the total surprise made every man in that barroom jump; but Cullen jumped farthest of all. He went by the astonished face of the fat man like a streak. For the window he headed and dived into the dark of the night as into a soft depth of water. The fall on the hard ground nearly knocked the wind out of him. He went on staggering hands and knees to a patch of brush, near by, and sat down in the middle of it as a stream of angry, shouting men poured out of the saloon.

They came through the back door. They came through the front door. Some of them leaped into saddles and rode vaguely up and down the street. Some of them ran over the empty field behind the saloon, but no one thought of looking into the heart of the little shrub that stood alone so close to the side of the saloon.

For an hour the excitement continued. After it died down, a good crowd had assembled in the Rolling Bones to drink to the pleasant occasion, and through the window Cullen could see the worthy sheriff lifting his glass with the others.

So Cullen stood up, stretched himself, and walked in leisurely fashion back to the hotel. He merely took care that, as he crossed the street, there was no one else in view.

In the back yard of the hotel he found his two companions, and Boots gave him an ugly greeting:

"Where you been all this time? Drinkin' a barrel? Is that what goin' to get a drink means to you?"

"I've been sitting in a bush watchin' the boys hunt for me," said Cullen.

"You been what?"

"I'm a wanted man," said Cullen, carelessly. "And now don't ask me no more questions. I gotta see the Chief, and I can't go up the stairs inside without bein' spotted by gents that might know me. Here. Gimme a boost and I'll climb up to the window from the outside, here."

Creston it was who lifted him up.

"You're the gent that started the ruction on the street a while back? What you thinkin' about, anyway?" demanded Boots.

"Nothin'," said Cullen, as he reached for the sill of the window of Saxon's room. "Only thinkin' that all lawyers are liars—and some of 'em are murderin' sneaks, too!"

CHAPTER XXXIX

SAXON was not asleep in his room. Now that he was alone, with his light out, he faced in the darkness the thought of The Solitaire, and that thought made him get out of his bed and begin to manipulate his revolver. The familiar weight of it, gliding comfortably over his fingers, made him seem far stronger than he was in fact. He was still very weak, but the right hand of a man is the last part of his body to succumb to weariness or the actual lack of strength. Therefore he could manage the heavy Colt almost as well as ever.

It was a great reassurance. He flashed the weapon at the dull glimmer of the doorknob. He aimed at the thin highlight that touched the back of a chair, and at the gilded rim of the mirror. And every time he felt sure that the bullet would have flown true. His spirits were therefore rising when he heard a soft sound outside his window, and then saw the head and shoulders of a man outside the window frame, against the stars.

He covered that form with his gun.

"Chief!" said a whisper. The voice became faintly audible as that of Cullen. "Hey, Chief!"

Big John Saxon put away his gun.

"Come in!" he invited.

He reclined on the bed, half dressed as he was, and saw Cullen quickly slip through the window.

"There's a lamp on the table, here," said Saxon. "What's the matter?"

"I don't want any lamp for showing you what's the matter," said Cullen. "It's the kind of thing that you won't thank me for telling you. This is what it is."

He came close, and crouched down into a chair beside the bed.

"Here," he said, "is a wad of money. Five thousand lacking a mite. It's your money."

"How can it be mine?" asked Saxon.

"It's money that you started taking to Stillman that other day."

"It can't be that money," said Saxon. "Finlay was carrying it all, and the thugs grabbed it all from him."

"Then you explain this to me," said Cullen. "I got busted in a poker game a while back. Boots cleaned me. I wanted a drink and I was flat. I went around the corner and stuck up the first man I saw. It was Daniel Finlay. He tried to pull a gun with a left-handed draw, but I tapped him on the wrist and he dropped it. I fanned him. He said he only had fifteen bucks on him. I pulled out this wad of five grand. I go to the saloon and there I try to buy a drink, and Lefty Malone, he spots the number on the ten spot. It's one of the numbers that the bank in Stillman advertised. Malone gets a crowd and they jump me; I manage to wriggle out. And that's why I'm here handing you the package of dough."

Saxon lay back on the pillows, stunned. His brain picked up the ideas one by one, rejected them, refused to put them together.

"If that were true," he said, "then it would mean that Daniel Finlay— But he can't be! Finlay's almost the only honest man in the world."

"Yeah, that's what I thought," said Cullen, and said no more.

"But what does it mean?" asked Saxon.

"I dunno," said Cullen. "I get the story and I hand it on to you with the evidence. You can make up your mind about it better than I can!"

"I've got to see Finlay!" declared Saxon.

"Do you?"

"I've got to see him. Ask somebody to go to his house. He may not be in bed, yet."

"I'll damn well bet he ain't in bed," said Cullen. "Nobody puts up with a loss of five thousand iron men all on the easy. He's awake, all right, if damning can keep him awake."

"Send somebody for him. You'll have to get out of town."

"Yeah, I'll have to move."

"I wish, before you go, that I could have you handy when Finlay comes."

"I'll be any place you say."

204

"It's too dangerous for you. Go back to the shack. Do you need money?"

"I got some change, now, that'll do me; and there's plenty of grub at the house. I don't need any money. None of that marked poison, anyway. There's skulls and cross-bones all over it."

"So long, partner."

"So long, Chief. Good luck."

He slid through the window and was gone as he came, merely murmuring from the window: "I'll send a gent for Finlay."

Afterward, John Saxon lay back on his pillows again and tried to think the thing out. Suppose, he thought, that one of the thugs who robbed him had gotten into trouble in the meantime. What a queer freak of fortune if one of the very men who had taken the money from Finlay had afterward got into a jam and had to come to the lawyer he had wronged and had had to give him part of the stolen money as a retainer?

But the thing was impossible, he decided. There had hardly been enough time for such events to happen. Besides, honest Daniel Finlay would not be found in the criminal courts very often. He would pick his cases.

The long minutes went slowly by. He lighted the lamp beside his bed, and presently a slow step came up the hall, and a hand tapped at his door.

"Come in!" he called.

The door opened, and Daniel Finlay stood tall and lean on the threshold.

"Ah, John!" he said, and gave Saxon his smile.

He crossed the room and held out his left hand, which Saxon grasped. Intimately, gently, with the eye of a friend he smiled down on John Saxon.

"You need something?" he asked.

The heart of Saxon melted.

"I had to see you, Mr. Finlay," he confessed.

"I'm glad you sent for me," said Finlay. "Sleep, as you know, does not come easily to me at night. My books keep me up, John. Study, and thoughts that do not come often in the day. Solitude, after all, is the happy region for the mind. And all evening I've been sitting there."

"Without going out at all?" asked Saxon.

"No. I kept at home," said Finlay.

Saxon sickened.

"Then it's a lie that I heard," said Saxon. "I heard that you'd been stuck up and robbed on a side street an hour or so ago."

Finlay received the shock by merely lowering his eyes. It was his way. With his eyes veiled, he could defy any glance, because his face in itself would never change color, would never betray him.

Where had Saxon heard the news? He himself, of course, had not dared to speak a word about his loss. For if it were recovered, how many questions would be asked?

"I'm sorry that you heard about that, John," he said. "As a matter of fact, I told a little fib, just now, in the hope that you wouldn't be upset."

"Is this the money that was taken from you?" asked Saxon. And he laid the sheaf of bills suddenly under the table lamp.

Finlay was shocked as by a bullet. For a wild instant, he dreamed that Saxon himself might have performed the robbery. His brain whirled. Merely lowering his eyes would not serve him, now. He would have to do something more, so he leaned far forward and brought his face very close to the sheaf of bills.

What should he say? What should he do?

There was a frightful temptation for him to snatch out his gun and empty it into the body of this man whom he had betrayed. But in that case, he would have no escape. Too many people knew that he had entered that room.

"Yes, John," he said. "That's the money that was taken from me."

"Is it?" said Saxon, vainly searching the face of the lawyer, praying that he might find no guilt there. "And you know what money it is, Mr. Finlay?"

There could be only one reason behind that question.

And Finlay said, though it cost him strength out of his very soul to speak the words: "Yes, I know what money it is. Part of the money that you and your men took from The Solitaire's outfit."

"Mr. Finlay," said Saxon, with something like a groan

in his voice, "isn't it part of the money that you were taking to Stillman for me? Part of the money that you were robbed of?"

"That?" said the lawyer, opening his eyes in surprise. "Tut, tut! Could they have exchanged it as soon as that? I don't think so. I really don't think so! It really couldn't be."

He shook his head, calmly.

"It's strange," he said, "that this has come back to you."

"Ay," said Saxon. "It's strange. It's too strange, Mr. Finlay. And—it makes me a little sick."

He closed his eyes, and while they were shut, Finlay allowed one flash of hate to cross his face. For it was too absurd that this clumsy-witted dummy, this stupidest of men, this most malleable of tools, should have been drawn by chance or speculation, or by both combined, to suspect him. There was treachery in fate, if this was the case. But it would be strange indeed if he did not manage to hoodwink the gull again.

"Great heaven, John," he cried, suddenly, "is it possible that you suspect—that you dream—no, no, my dear lad! You don't doubt Daniel Finlay! You don't think that I could ever—"

"I don't want to doubt you," said Saxon, looking up with a real agony in his eyes. "I certainly don't want to doubt you, Mr. Finlay. I'd rather do anything than doubt you. This thing sticks into me like a knife. I can't help wondering how you happened to have that money on you!"

"Shall I tell you, John?" asked Finlay.

"Ay, tell me, for God's sake!"

"I wonder if I should?" said Finlay. And his eyes wandered away toward empty space and the stars beyond the window frame. His mind was all as empty, at that moment, and no possible expedient appeared to him.

"I have to know," said Saxon. "No matter what it costs, I have to know the truth!"

That instant the device came readily into the mind of Finlay. Joy burned through him.

"The fact is," he said, controlling the exultation that worked the muscles of his throat, "the fact is that I think I *shall* tell you, John. It's a very strange thing, but

207

I'm going to try to explain it to you. Your nerves are quite steady, John?"

"Ay, steady enough."

"But wouldn't it be better if I were to show you the mystery as well as talk about it?"

"Can you do that?"

"Yes. Are you well enough to take a short walk—a very short walk?"

"I'm well enough to walk miles if I can get rid of the doubts that are in me, Mr. Finlay."

"It's only a matter of going to the house where that friend of your Mary lives—do you know where Molly lives?"

"I've heard about her, yes, and I know where the house is. Do you know her, Mr. Finlay?"

"In my business," said the lawyer, "you know it is necessary for me to meet many strange people. She is one of the strangest, John!"

"What can you show me there?"

"Ah, I can show you at once—no, if you are able to take the walk, it's better for you to wait and see with your own eyes a thing that will astonish you—but it will make all clear."

"I'll go," said Saxon. "I'd go if I had to crawl on my hands and knees. Mr. Finlay, if I can't believe in you, I can't believe in anything!"

"My dear lad!" said Daniel Finlay.

He added: "I'm going home. I must do that, first. Then I am going to return in an hour's time, and I'll meet you in the lane beside the hotel. It will be easy for you to get there. Just turn on the stairs and go out the side door, and no one will see you. Good-by for a moment, John!"

CHAPTER XL

BUT it was not to his home that Finlay went. With his left hand still tingling with the parting grip of Saxon, he left the hotel and walked straight to the old Borden house.

They were still there. When he knocked on the front door the voice of Molly called out: "Who's there?"

"Finlay," he answered.

Her quick, light step approached. She unlocked the door and held it open.

"Come in, Danny Devil," she said. "Nice to see your jolly old mug again, twice on a night."

Finlay gave her not a look. He went to the table where The Solitaire was lounging aslant in his chair, still sipping coffee. The man was as beautiful, as graceful as a fine black panther. His steady eyes, fearless as the eyes of a beast, considered Finlay with interest, but with no kindness.

"Well, Finlay?" he demanded.

"I've got him in a bag," said Finlay. "I've got him ready for you. I'm ready to bring him here and pop him into the house."

"Saxon?"

"Yes."

"You mean you'll bring him here tonight? But he's still sick in the hotel."

"He's well enough to walk—and handle a gun. I wanted to show you that I really live up to my engagements, Solitaire. I feel that you've robbed me of five thousand dollars tonight. Now I want to finish off my old share of the bargain—I want to wash my hands of it by bringing him to you here!"

"That's right, Danny," said the girl. "Wash your hands in blood. That's the best way. That'll make 'em clean."

Finlay turned on her in a rage.

"You black-hearted devil!" he said to her.

"My, my, listen to Danny talk!" said Molly. "What a little gentleman he is!"

"Shut up," said The Solitaire to the girl. "You—Finlay—my God, you mean, really, that you can walk the swine into this house tonight?"

"I can."

"But he'll have twenty men with him, eh?"

"He'll come alone. He'll come if he has to crawl!"

The Solitaire leaped to his feet, exultant.

"Finlay," he said, "you're one of the great men of the world. You're the greatest man that I ever knew. Bring him here, of his own accord, and I'll call you the champion devil and wizard of the world!"

He began to laugh.

Finlay said: "You'll have your man. You haven't been drinking, Solitaire?"

"No."

"Have you got other men around here—in whistling distance?"

"Yes."

"Get 'em in here. Because—Saxon has to die!"

"Even John Saxon is on your trail, is he?" said the girl. "Even honest John is opening his eyes and watching the fox a little?"

"By God, Solitaire," protested Finlay, "it chokes me to have to listen to her. Will you get more men in? Will you make sure of Saxon?"

"I'll make sure of him. I'll get 'em in," said The Solitaire. "How long before he'll be here?"

"Forty minutes—or less."

"Forty minutes? Only forty minutes?" The Solitaire threw both hands above his head in a glory of triumphing.

Then he cried in a great voice: "Get out—and bring him, then! I'll have the trap ready."

Finlay, for some reason, hesitated for one instant, staring dubiously at the girl. Then he turned and left the room.

The Solitaire, after the lawyer had left, began to pace up and down, his shoulders cleaving the fog of cigarette smoke which rippled together again in his wake.

"Forty minutes! And already they're passing. By God, Molly, when I think of laying that rat dead on the floor —when I think that he's going to lie there—on the floor —dead—dead!"

He laughed joylessly, went to a front window, and threw it open.

"Going to call in the hounds, Solitaire?" said the girl.

"I'll whistle in a couple of the boys," said The Solitaire.

"That's right," she answered. "Don't take chances. It doesn't pay a man to take chances, when there's the old chill in him."

"What chill?" asked The Solitaire, turning toward her.

"Fear, boy!" said Molly.

"Fear? Of Saxon? I've stretched him out three times, and three times the luck has saved him!"

"That's it," answered Molly. "You're not afraid of Saxon. You're just afraid of his luck!"

"I'm not afraid of any part of any man living," said The Solitaire. "You know it, too. What's the matter with you, Molly?"

"No, you weren't afraid a month ago. You weren't afraid before Saxon came up to you. But it's different now, Solitaire."

He stared at her. His eyes wandered over her beauty with an evil intent. She was calmly indifferent to his glance.

"I've seen it working in you for a long time," she told him. "I know how those things go. They start small, but they grow big. First time, you said that Saxon had had a lot of luck. Second time, you called it luck, too, when he got away from you. But you had the marks of his hands on you, just the same. There still are some black and blue spots on you. And you know that twice you'd been made to run. That puts the cold in a man's blood—to have to run. You may not be afraid when you start sprinting, but you've got the ice on the back of your spine before you've gone two jumps. Then comes the third time—and your nerve is running out. You can't stand up to him alone!"

"You lie!" shouted The Solitaire. "I faced him alone."

"Ay, with two rifles at your back—just to make sure."

"Why not? I did the real fighting!"

"You're going to do it again tonight," said the girl, sneering. "You're just going to get a couple of rifles in—to make sure!"

He slammed the window down with a crash.

"I won't call 'em—if you think I'm afraid of any man—"

"I hope not, but I was sure beginning to wonder."

He came up to her, slowly. "You think a good deal about this John Saxon, eh?" he asked her.

"Sure. I think a lot of him," she said.

"If he got me—you'd be mealy-mouthing around him in a minute!"

"That claim is all staked out," she said," "A better looking girl than Molly has it. One of the real good girls, Solitaire—and he's one of the real good boys."

"By God," said he, "I've really got an idea that you've been thinking a lot about him!"

"I have," she said.

"You're going to see a lot of him tonight, then," answered The Solitaire. "You've got a regular heart interest in him, and I'm going to hand you his heart—on a platter!"

"That's the way to talk, boy," she told him. "You do your best, too. It won't be any walkover. You're getting him pretty weak and just out of a sickbed. But it won't be any walkover. That right hand of his will be able to flash a gun."

"You sort of beat me," said The Solitaire, lowering his head and staring out at her from beneath his bent brows. "You've always beat me, one way or another. But—there's nobody like you."

"Not yet, Solitaire," she answered.

"One of these days, you know what? I'm going to take and marry you," said he.

"That's the way to talk," she nodded. "Just as if you already had jumped Saxon and left him behind in the dust. But he's not dead yet, old son. Not by a long shot. Sit down and pull yourself together. Go back there in the kitchen and sit down, and pull yourself together. You'll want steady nerves for this game."

He hesitated for an instant, as though in doubt of her motives. But finally he nodded.

"You're right," he said. "You nearly always *are* right. I'm going to pay a lot more attention to you from now on, old girl."

With that, he left the room and walked into the kitchen, closing the door gently behind him.

And the girl lay back in her chair with her head far tilted, staring at the ceiling, trying to make up her mind. The doubt lasted a long time, and she was still in a quandary when she heard the two pairs of footfalls approach the house. After that came a gentle tapping at the front door.

"Come in!" she called.

And, as the door opened, she saw Finlay and big John Saxon, looking drawn and pale, against the black velvet of the night.

CHAPTER XLI

To Saxon, that red-lipped, dark-eyed girl was like something re-seen from the past. She had changed from his picture of her, but not a great deal.

As he saw her there, reclining in the chair, only beginning to rise, slowly, he tried to fit her into the other picture which Mary Wilson had given him, of the white storm, and the mountain cold, and his own great body helpless, his mind lost in the wild sea of the delirium, and this girl taking charge of him.

He went across the room with awe in his face. When he took her hand he said: "Mary has told me a good deal. Not as much as you could tell. But she's told me a good deal."

She glanced at Finlay and shook her head at Saxon. "Never mind," she said.

"I'm not to thank you, even?" asked he.

There was in her eyes such a curious expression as he never had been before in the face of any human being. She seemed to be surveying him in flesh and in spirit. There was something at once affectionate and cold about her, something kind and cruel.

"Thank me?" she cried. "Thank me?"

She began to laugh in a manner stranger and wilder still. "Thank me for what?" she repeated. "For this?"

She pointed toward the door at the back of the room, as she spoke, and then Saxon, turning, saw that that door was opening softly and slowly—on blackness.

And suddenly he knew everything.

He spared one lightning glance aside, at Finlay, and saw a face like a yellow stone, with a sneer carved on it. The left hand of Finlay was sliding inside his coat. His deadly eyes were glued to the face of Saxon.

213

"God! God!" breathed Saxon. "You—Finlay! Not you!"

He saw the girl, too, standing back against the wall, with her hands spread out against it. She leaned forward a little. Perhaps there was some passion in her face, but above all there was a vast animal interest. It was as though she expected a most interesting play to commence—a scene wherein she might be summoned to the center of the stage!

Once—it was long, long ago, in his childhood—Saxon had seen by moonlight two he-wolves battling savagely, and a she-wolf lying sleek and slender and aloof beside them, to eye the battle.

He thought of that—in a blinding flash he saw it—then he saw The Solitaire's face looming out of the darkness of the kitchen doorway.

"Saxon! Fill your hand!" shouted The Solitaire, and his own gun gleamed in a broken upward section of a crescent.

There was a strange falling sensation in Saxon—not of dropping to the floor, but of pitching straight forward at the open doorway. And there was no fear. It was as though the pain he had endured were a wind that had blown him clean of all terror. His gun had come out with a single lightning twitch. He had time to think of many things. He had time to remember how he had been in his hotel room, practicing with his gun at the gleaming edge of a mirror. And the flash of the rising gun of The Solitaire was just such a mark.

The gun of Saxon was barely clear of his clothes before he fired.

The gun of The Solitaire thrust out into the lamplight and swayed to this side and that. It exploded, but the bullet merely ripped up the floor at Saxon's feet.

His own answering shot, he knew, drove straight through the middle of that shadowy bulk.

Then The Solitaire walked out of the doorway into the light, moving with small steps, the gun hanging down in his loose hand, dripping off the ends of his fingers, as it were. But there was something frightful about this disarmed advance, and the frightfulness was in the face of the outlaw. For he had the blank look of an idiot.

214

He was in his shirtsleeves. The shirt was blue; a big splotch of crimson was springing out in the middle of his breast.

"Finlay! Watch Finlay!" screamed the girl.

Saxon jerked about in time to see the long left arm of the lawyer sweep out from beneath his coat, carrying a blunt-nosed revolver. And Saxon used his own Colt like a saber to strike that weapon out of the hand of Daniel Finlay.

The gun went whirling and slithering along the floor. Finlay made no effort to regain it. He simply stood there as he had been at first, his face yellow stone, with the sneer carved on it, and the jeweled glitter of the eyes.

"Solitaire! Solitaire!" the girl was crying.

She had run to him. She took the gun away from him and threw it on the floor.

"Solitaire, what's the matter? Don't look like that! Ah—my—God!"

Those last three words came out in three screams.

"He's going to die," said Saxon to Finlay. "Get out of here and—well, wait for me in your house!"

Finlay walked out of the room and Saxon stepped to the girl. He tried to help, as she was guiding The Solitaire into a chair. She struck him in the face, raging, with her solid little fist.

"You've killed him!" she screamed. "You damned fool—see what you've done—you've killed him! You've killed The Solitaire! Oh, God, God—and I gave you your break—and you've killed him!"

The Solitaire lay back in his chair, all loose as pulp. Every bone in his body seemed to be broken. There was no life in his eyes. He had that same fool, blank look of a half-wit.

"What's the matter, Molly?" he said. Blood bubbles came up to his lips and broke into a tiny spray. "What's the matter?" he said. "What time is it?"

She snatched out a handkerchief and wiped his mouth. She grabbed him by the back hair of the head with both her hands.

"Solitaire!" she said, rapidly, savagely. "You're dying. Don't blabber like a fool. You've got to die like a man. You hear me? Solitaire! You're dying!"

"What's the matter?" said The Solitaire. "Something hit me—I'm kind of numb—"

His voice was so thick that it was hard to understand the words. The blood bubbles kept rising in crowds and bursting. The girl kept her grasp on his hair and now she shook him wickedly.

"Solitaire! You're leaving me. You're going away from me. You're dying, and I'll never see you again. Solitaire! Don't you understand? Kiss me, darling, darling!"

"Hello, Molly," said The Solitaire, "what in hell's the racket about? Leave go of my hair—"

"Solitaire, I tipped him off—I gave him his play—and the fool murdered you! I didn't know. I thought fair play. Oh, God, God, God, wake up and say good-by to me!"

But The Solitaire would not say good-by. The blood bubbles no longer broke on his lips. His eyes looked beyond the girl; a loose smile had formed on his face.

And suddenly, understanding, she groaned, and grasped his head to her breast in both her arms, and kissed the horrible crimson welter of his mouth.

CHAPTER XLII

BIG JOHN SAXON went with short steps back through the town. He tried to keep everything out of his mind, and by fixing his eyes on the objects of the night—shattered rays of lamplight, thin beams from the stars—he was able to be in the present moment, only.

When he got to the house of Finlay, he went softly up the front steps and pulled the door open without rapping. Finlay sat in the corner behind his desk. He had some packages of currency before him. He was calm, deliberate, at ease.

"How are you, John?" he said. "That was a clean bit of work that you did, back there. Very quick and clean!"

For a moment, Saxon had a sick feeling that the man might be trying to talk his way into another good position.

For answer, he pushed the bulldog revolver onto the desk, the muzzle pointing toward the lawyer.

"Certainly," said Finlay, gently, almost cheerfully. "Of course, John. I understand perfectly. And I thought that, since we've done a good many things together in the past, we might do one more at the present moment. I thought I could make a little bargain with you. Here is the rest of the money I've stolen from you. Nearly fifty thousand dollars more of it. See how money comes home to roost where it belongs, like so many good chickens! And furthermore, I'll be able to leave a tidy little sum to you, John, if you'll undertake not to tell what you know about me. I've always been a black devil, John, but a good many people have been thinking that I'm white. I've been a horrible hypocrite, of course. But it was my peculiar pleasure. We all have to have our pleasures, eh? We can't live when life is too dry a bone, you know. So I want to know if, in return for everything I have in the world, you'll not talk about what you know? There won't be much good in it. It will only be harming the dead, you see? Do you think that you could do so much for me—for the sake of the friends that we used to seem to be?"

Saxon said: "There's the girl. There's Molly. She knows!"

"She'll never mention my name," said the lawyer. "I'm beneath her, you see. A great, savage soul like Molly would never even remember me, any more than she would remember dirt under her feet. Besides, she has her dead man to think about. Was it frightful—the dying, I mean?"

Saxon said, heavily: "What did you mean, in the beginning—when you gave me the gun? What would you gain by seeing me kill Bob Witherell?"

"The pleasure of power that is not seen. The pleasure of a god in moving the minds of men. Isn't that understandable? Conceivable, I should say."

"And all the rest—" muttered Saxon. "You were with The Solitaire when you seemed to be with me."

"I worked one against the other. I didn't much care, except that I wanted to see blood. Not until the money hunger got into me."

"Why, I loved you," said Saxon, gently.

217

"Other people do, almost," said Daniel Finlay. "What I'm begging is not life. Tut! I'm not afraid of dying. But I don't want to die out of the minds of all the people in Bluewater. I've always despised them. But now I see that they're my only immortality. Saxon, for the sake of mercy and the kind God, will you give me my chance?"

"Yes," said Saxon, suddenly, shortly.

He picked up the Stillman money.

"The rest—your own property—I don't want it, Finlay," he said. "But—good-by—poor Finlay. I'm not hating you, just now!"

"Aren't you?" said Daniel Finlay.

"No," said Saxon. "Good-by."

He held out his hand. It was grasped eagerly.

"After that," said Finlay, hungrily, "I know that you'll be true to your word. You'll not speak ill of me, John. God bless you, God bless you! God forgive my evil life, and bless your good one! I tried to make you a crook, a scoundrel, but the steel in you was too straight and true. Good-by, John. Good-by!"

He saw Saxon pass through the door, and as the steps descended to the street, Finlay was already writing:

"To all whom it may concern, I, Daniel Finlay, being in my right mind in full possession of my faculties, sit down to take away a life which is no longer useful to the world or pleasant to me. If I sin in breaking the sanctuary of life, I offer to the world, as my excuse, the many years of obscure pain and the friendless days of my existence. May all whom I have wronged—if any such there be—forgive me. If ever I have done good for men, may they pray for my wretched soul, lonely on earth, lonely, surely, in the life to come.

"My property, money, house, land—it is not much—I give and bequeath to a noble and glorious man, John Saxon, who was in this world the nearest of all my friends and the only one, I can attest, who really knew me.

(Signed)

DANIEL FINLAY."

218

When he had finished this document, he pushed it to the farther corner of the desk and took up, at once, the bulldog revolver which John Saxon had brought back to him from the Borden house.

He began to smile because he saw, suddenly, that his life held nothing and that for years it had been really empty. He had done nothing but gull the gullible, and now his chance of retaining a favorable place in the memory of other men depended upon the charitable kindness of one of those who had been gulled and betrayed, and who knew all about the betrayal.

But it seemed to the lawyer that he had a fighting chance of winning out, in the end. He was not altogether sure that by leaving his little estate to John Saxon he would bribe that young man. He rather doubted it. He saw, with a startled soul, what the truth was—that John Saxon would never be really moved by money.

However, the arrangements were now made, and soon the soul of Daniel Finlay would be speeding beyond land and sea.

He picked up the gun again and lifted it. His last thought was of Molly and The Solitaire. All had been so well planned—and only the fact that Molly had pointed out to Saxon the opening of the kitchen door had destroyed the scheme. He thought of The Solitaire alone, dying, and the blood bubbling on his lips.

By that red stain, among the newly come ghosts, he would be able to recognize his old companion in crime. With that fantasy in his mind, he looked down the muzzle of the gun. Some men were said to dread this moment, but not Daniel Finlay. He was still smiling as he pressed the cold, hollow rim of the barrel against his temple. He pulled the trigger. His ear heard no report. His body felt no pain. Death at one shadowy stride possessed him, and his head fell loosely back against the top of his chair.

In that position they found him, smiling, with his left hand pointing down to the gun on the floor, and his right arm lying on the desk, the puckered skin of the stump looking a little purple. He was smiling. His eyes were not quite closed. There was an air of great understanding in his face, partly disdainful, partly amused.

That was how a very good man ought to look, they

thought. When they carried him to his grave, the entire town followed. They buried The Solitaire in the morning; they buried Daniel Finlay in the afternoon. The sheriff made the speech at the grave, before the minister said the last words. The minister said: "It is almost as though we had to pay for the worst by giving up our best!"

And the whole town prayed, or tried to pray, for poor Daniel Finlay.

CHAPTER XLIII

SAXON was not at either of those burials; he had sent on a messenger to Stillman, and the messenger carried with him Saxon's share of the loot that had been taken on that other day from The Solitaire. After that, Saxon went back to bed.

He heard, there, the report of Finlay's death. He begged Mary to go to the Borden house. There she found a little crowd already gathered. The body of The Solitaire had been found laid out in his best clothes, with his hands folded across him and peace in his face.

Five hundred dollars was found in an envelope tucked under his head, and the envelope was addressed to the sheriff.

"You weren't man enough to kill The Solitaire," said that characteristic note, "but you may be man enough to bury him. John Saxon was crazy with luck four times, or he would have been four times dead!"

The letter was not signed. But of course it came from Molly. That morning, the whole town followed the body of The Solitaire to the grave, just as it followed Finlay in the afternoon; but Molly was nowhere to be seen.

That evening, word came from Stillman, brought by the weary president of the bank, there. He not only brought thanks to Saxon, but he brought ten thousand dollars. He thanked Saxon with all his heart. This partial recouping of the losses would enable the bank to open its doors again, on top of the money that already had been regained.

Saxon gave back half of the percentage of the reward.

He merely said: "Some months ago, I was wiped out. Five thousand just about covers the money that I lost then. And that's all that I want back."

"And what about the blood you've lost, Saxon?" demanded the banker. "Doesn't that count?"

"It was bad blood," said Saxon, "and it had to come out."

He got out of the hotel and the town by night, a few days later. He had to escape like a fugitive in order to escape the fuss that the townsmen would make over him, because, only the day before, he had refused to take the estate of Daniel Finlay and, instead, had donated the whole thing to the welfare of the widows and orphans of the county.

"But why?" Mary Wilson had asked him. "Even if Finlay got his money in bad ways, you could use it in good ways, John. There wouldn't be any stain on it!"

"I don't want that kind of a dead man to put any food in my mouth," answered Saxon, and he could not be moved in his determination.

When it was found that the hero had left Bluewater in the night, there was a tremendous commotion. The sheriff and all the rest dashed here and there, making inquiries; only Mary Wilson knew where to go. She had encountered Boots and Creston, searching busily, and they asked her what she knew, but she only shook her head.

Then she got on the trail that led toward the old ranch and, sure enough, she found John Saxon under the shade of a tree, with his back against the trunk, looking over the blackened site of his house and the old sheds. The horse of The Solitaire was grazing nearby, hobbled, saddled and bridle off.

She was off her mustang and down at the side of Saxon before he could rise to prevent her.

"You knew I'd be here, eh?" he said.

"I hoped it," she answered.

He pointed to the blue nakedness of the upper mountains.

"It's a cold winter up here," he told her.

"It'll be a happy winter, though," she said, "if only —if only you don't grow restless, John."

221

"I'll never be restless again," said Saxon.

He took off his hat. His face showed pale and drawn, and years older, and the bandage around his head was now a thin strip of white. These months had left many scars, more in the spirit than in the flesh.

He pointed to a small spot of newly turned ground.

"The restlessness is buried there," he said.

"What is it, John?" she asked.

"John Saxon's gun," he said.

THE END

"THE KING OF THE WESTERN NOVEL" IS MAX BRAND

THE BIG TRAIL	(C94-333, $1.75)
BORDER GUNS	(C90-888; $1.95)
BROTHERS ON THE TRAIL	(C90-302, $1.95)
DRIFTER'S VENGEANCE	(C84-783, $1.75)
FIRE BRAIN	(C88-629, $1.50)
FLAMING IRONS	(C98-019, $1.50)
FRONTIER FEUD	(C98-002, $1.50)
GALLOPING BRONCOS	(C94-265, $1.75)
THE GAMBLER	(C94-328, $1.75)
GARDEN OF EDEN	(C94-290, $1.75)
THE GENTLE GUNMAN	(C94-291, $1.75)
GUNMAN'S GOLD	(C90-619, $1.95)
GUNS OF DORKING HOLLOW	(C94-204, $1.75)
HAPPY VALLEY	(C90-304, $1.95)
THE KING BIRD RIDES	(C90-305, $1.95)
THE LONG CHASE	(C94-266, $1.75)
LUCKY LARRIBEE	(C94-456, $1.75)
MISTRAL	(C90-316, $1.95)
MOUNTAIN RIDERS	(C90-308, $1.95)
MYSTERY RANCH	(C94-102, $1.75)
OUTLAW BREED	(C98-074, $1.50)
RIDER OF THE HIGH HILL	(C88-884, $1.50)
THE SEVENTH MAN	(C98-105, $1.50)
SILVERTIP	(C88-685, $1.50)
SILVERTIP'S CHASE	(C98-048, $1.50)
SILVERTIP'S STRIKE	(C98-096, $1.50)
SLOW JOE	(C90-311, $1.95)
SMILING CHARLIE	(C90-319, $1.95)
SPEEDY	(C94-267, $1.75)

"THE KING OF THE WESTERN NOVEL" IS MAX BRAND

STORM ON THE RANGE	*(C94-300, $1.75)*
THE STRANGER	*(C94-508, $1.75)*
TAMER OF THE WILD	*(C94-334, $1.75)*
THE TENDERFOOT	*(C90-653, $1.95)*
TIMBAL GULCH TRAIL	*(C90-312, $1.95)*
TORTURE TRAIL	*(C94-344, $1.75)*
TRAILIN'	*(C88-717, $1.50)*
TROUBLE TRAIL	*(C90-314, $1.95)*
WAR PARTY	*(C88-933, $1.50)*
WAY OF THE LAWLESS	*(C94-301, $1.75)*
THE WHITE WOLF	*(C94-605, $1.75)*